BOOK ONE
THE AKHENATEN
ADVENTURE

Children of the Lamp

BOOK ONE

THE AKHENATEN ADVENTURE

P. B. KERR

SCHOLASTIC INC.

NEW YORK TORONTO LONDON AUCKLAND SYDNEY
MEXICO CITY NEW DELHI HONG KONG BUENOS AIRES

ISBN 0-439-73346-4

12 11 10 9 8 7 6 5 4 3 2 1   4 5 6 7 8 9/0

Printed in the U.S.A.   23

First Scholastic Book Club printing, November 2004

*This book was written for, and with the
help of, William Falcon Finlay Kerr, Charles Foster
Kerr, and Naomi Rose Kerr, all of London SW19.
May you always know happiness.*

BOOK ONE
THE AKHENATEN ADVENTURE

THE HOTTEST PLACE ON EARTH

It was just after noon on a hot summer's day in Egypt. Hussein Hussaout, his twelve-year-old son, Baksheesh, and their dog, Effendi, were camped in the desert twenty miles south of Cairo. As usual, they were digging illegally for historical artifacts that they might sell in their shop. Nothing moved in the desert save a snake, a dung beetle, a small scorpion, and in the distance, a donkey pulling a wooden cart, which was laden with palm leaves, up a dirt track. Otherwise all was solitude and searing stillness, and the casual visitor would hardly have imagined that this barren edge of rock and sand was part of the largest archaeological site in Egypt and that an incalculable wealth of monuments and treasures still lay hidden beneath this arid wasteland.

Baksheesh enjoyed helping his father find things in the desert. But the work was hot, and every few minutes Baksheesh or his father would throw down his trowel and go back to the

Land Rover to drink some water and spend a few minutes cooling down in the air-conditioned interior before returning to the dig. The work was also dangerous for, in addition to the snakes and the scorpions, the area was full of hidden deep pits into which an unwary man or camel might fall. It had been a good morning's work: So far they had found several ancient Shabti figurines, a couple of pieces of broken pottery, and a small golden earring. Baksheesh was feeling very happy for it was he who had dug up the golden earring, which his father said was very valuable: Catching the rays of the hot desert sun, it had burned like a circle of fire in Hussein's grimy fingers.

"Go and get some lunch, boy," he said. "You've earned it." But he himself kept on digging in the hope of finding yet more buried artifacts.

"Yes, father." Baksheesh went to the back of the Land Rover, followed closely by Effendi, who hoped he might get something to eat. Baksheesh dropped the tailgate and was about to fetch the cooler when, suddenly, the Land Rover moved. Thinking that perhaps the hand brake was not on properly, he ran quickly to the driver's door, intending to jump inside and secure the vehicle more firmly, but as he reached for the door handle, it suddenly shifted away from his grasp. A moment or two later, Baksheesh felt a terrific shock underneath his feet, as if some subterranean giant had punched the rocky ceiling over his head and, looking down, Baksheesh saw that the ground appeared to roll under him in waves that ran the length of the valley. Losing his balance, he fell against the car, which hurt his elbow slightly, and then he cried out as a second and more severe shock followed quickly on the heels of the first.

Baksheesh scrambled to his feet again and tried to keep his footing, which became easier when he stopped looking at the ground and fixed his eyes on the wall of the escarpment instead. A quarter of a mile from where he was standing, the escarpment was a place he and his father knew well, for they had often worked there. But even as he looked there, a whole cliff face gave way and fell onto the shimmering desert floor in a great curve of dust, rock, boulders, and sand.

Baksheesh sat down abruptly, simply to avoid falling down again. He had never experienced an earthquake before, and yet he felt the terrifying motion of the earth could hardly be mistaken for anything else. By contrast, his father seemed more delighted than frightened by the earthquake and began to laugh hysterically as he tried, unsuccessfully, to regain his feet.

"At last," he cried, "at last," apparently convinced that the quake was happening to his own advantage.

Even as the shocks became more and more violent — horizontal thrusts mixed with a few vertical jolts, as if Nature intended to confound all those like Hussein Hussaout who were clever enough to pretend that they were walking on the deck of a ship in a storm — it seemed to an astonished Baksheesh that his father had gone crazy.

"Ten years," Hussein shouted loudly above the ground's thunderous roar. "Ten years I've waited for this."

To Baksheesh's amazement, his father's good humor and excitement showed no sign of abatement, not even when an explosive upheaval of rock and earth lifted the Land Rover almost six feet above his head and tipped it onto its roof.

"Father, stop!" yelled the boy, and grabbed hold of Effendi, who was yowling and trembling with fear. "You're mad. Stop it, please, or you'll be killed."

In truth, Hussein Hussaout was in no more danger while trying to stand on the shaking ground than his son and dog who were clinging to it; but the boy felt that there was almost something irreverent about his father's behavior, as if the spirits of the earth might see in the man's good humor and apparently fearless demeanor, a lack of proper respect, and destroy all three of them accordingly.

And then, just as suddenly as it had started, the underground rumblings faded away, the terrifying motion ended, the dust and sand settled, the searing stillness returned as if Nature was holding her breath to see what would happen next, and all was quiet again — all, that is, except Hussein Hussaout.

"Isn't it wonderful?" he cried and only now that the ground had finally stopped moving did he fall to his knees and, still grinning like a madman, put his hands together as if in prayer.

Baksheesh turned to look at the Land Rover, now lying

on its roof, and shook his head. "It looks like we're going to have to walk back to the road and get help," he said. "I don't see what's so wonderful about that."

"No, it's wonderful," insisted his father, and held up a piece of stone not much smaller than a CD. "Look. I saw it as soon as the earth shifted. For thousands of years, the wind and sand have been the guardians of the pharaohs' treasure. But every so often the earth shifts and what was buried may now be seen."

To Baksheesh, the piece of stone looked nothing like treasure. In truth, almost anyone else would probably have ignored the square piece of smooth, gray basaltic stone covered in chiseled grooves that Hussein held up for him to see, but Hussein had recognized it immediately for what it was: an Egyptian stele.

"It's a stone tablet upon which is written an ancient inscription in the hieroglyphic writing of the Eighteenth Dynasty," explained the boy's father. "If this stone is what I think it is, then we have found the key that will help us to unlock a mystery that has endured for thousands of years. This might very well turn out to be the greatest day of our lives. A man like me waits all his life for an opportunity such as this. That is what is so wonderful, my son. That is why I am happy."

CHAPTER 1

THE NAMING OF DOGS

M r. and Mrs. Edward Gaunt lived in New York at number 7, East 77th Street, in an old town house with seven floors. They had two children, John and Philippa, who despite being twelve-year-old twins, were the least identical twins imaginable (which was much to their own relief and satisfaction). People found it hard to believe that they could be twins at all, they were so different. John, who was older by ten minutes, was tall and thin with straight brown hair and liked to wear black. Philippa was smaller with wavy red hair and horn-rimmed glasses that made her look like the more intelligent of the two; she liked to wear pink. They both felt a little sorry for identical twins and believed that they had had a lucky escape, although it could be annoying when people remarked on how they didn't look alike, as if no one had ever noticed that before.

Inside their heads, however, it was a very different story. John and Philippa often thought very similar thoughts.

6

Sometimes in school, when the teacher asked a question, they would each put up a hand to answer at exactly the same moment. When they watched TV game shows, they would speak the answers in unison. And it was impossible to beat them at Pictionary when they played as a team.

Their father, Mr. Gaunt, was an investment banker, which is another way of saying that he was rich. Mrs. Gaunt, who was better known to New York society as Layla, was a very beautiful woman and did a great deal of charity work, for which she was in much demand, since everything she touched was successful. She gave lots of dinner parties, her conversation sparkled like a crystal chandelier, and she was glamorous, which is to say she was clever and beautiful, with a cherry on top.

It could not be denied, however, that Mr. and Mrs. Edward Gaunt made an unlikely couple — almost as unlikely as the idea that their children could be twins. Layla, dark-haired with the magnificent physique of an athlete, stood more than six feet tall in her bare feet, while her husband, Edward, was barely five feet tall in his Berluti shoes, with longish gray hair and tinted spectacles. People noticed when Layla entered a room, but they seldom noticed Edward, who fortunately preferred it that way, being the shy and retiring type and quite content to let his wife and his 77th Street home occupy the limelight.

The Gaunts' house, on the Upper East Side of New York, looked more like a temple than a home and was frequently featured in all sorts of glossy magazines. The front door was protected by an enormous arch-shaped, wrought-iron gate, and all the walls of the house were paneled with the choicest mahogany. There were lots of fine French paintings, antique English furniture, rare Persian rugs, and expensive Chinese vases. Sometimes Philippa said she thought her parents cared more about their furniture than they did about their children; but she knew this wasn't true, and she just said it for effect in the same way that her twin brother, John, was fond of telling his father that number 7 felt more like an art gallery than a house that was fit to have two twelve-year-old children living in it. Whenever John said this, which was usually when Mr. Gaunt came home with yet another stuffy old picture, Mr. Gaunt would laugh and tell his son that if number 7 had been an art gallery, it would certainly not have permitted dogs, not even the two dogs that the Gaunts kept as family pets.

Alan and Neil were two large Rottweilers and they were remarkable animals, not least because they seemed to understand everything that was said to them. Once, John, too lazy to get up and look for the TV remote control, had commanded Alan to change the channel and, to his surprise, Alan had done it. Neil was no less intelligent than Alan; both dogs could tell the difference between Fox Kids, The Disney Channel, Nickelodeon, and CNN. The two dogs often accompanied the twins on their travels around New York, and John and Philippa were probably the only two children in the city who ever felt safe enough to walk in nearby Central Park after dark. But the fact that two such intelligent dogs should have such ordinary names was a source of great irritation to John.

"Rottweilers were first bred by the ancient Romans," he complained to his parents one morning at breakfast, close to the beginning of the summer school vacation. "As guard dogs. They're about the only family pets that come with a government health warning. They have a bite pressure that is greater than any other dog with the possible exception of the three-headed one that guards Hades."

"Cerberus," murmured Mr. Gaunt and, picking up his *New York Times* newspaper, began to read about the Cairo earthquake of which there was a large and dramatic picture on the front page.

"I know that, Dad," said John. "Anyway, for that reason Rottweilers are a favorite breed of the army and the police. So it seems to me that calling them names like Alan and Neil is kind of ridiculous."

"Why?" said Mr. Gaunt. "That's what they've always been called."

"I know. But, Dad, it just seems to me that if I'd been naming two Rottweilers, I'd have called them something more suitable. Names like Nero and Tiberius, perhaps. After the two Roman emperors."

"Nero and Tiberius were not very nice people, dear," said John's mother.

"That's right," agreed his father. "Tiberius lacked all affability — *civile ingenium*. And he was a disgusting human being. Nero was just plain mad. What is more, he murdered his mother, Agrippina. And his wife, Octavia. And burned the city to the ground. *Odisse coepi, postquam parricida matris et uxoris, auriga et histrio et incendiarius extitisti.*" His father laughed, cruelly. "I ask you, what kind of an example for a dog is that?"

John bit his lip; he always found it hard to argue with his father when he started to speak in Latin. There is something about people who speak Latin — like judges and popes — that makes them very hard to argue with.

"All right, maybe not *any* Roman emperor," conceded John. "So, maybe something else. Something that sounds a bit more doggy. Like Elvis, perhaps."

"In case you hadn't noticed," said Mr. Gaunt, stiffly, "neither of our two dogs is particularly doggy, as you put it. Rottweilers are, as you say, favored by law enforcement agencies and the military. They are not a very tail-wagging, doggy breed of dog. Some families have a dog that can fetch a newspaper from the mailbox. We have dogs that can run down to the deli on a Saturday morning and fetch a bag of bagels without eating one. Even Elvis couldn't have done that, let me tell you. And how doggy is it to take yourself to the vet when you feel sick? Or feed a parking meter? You know something? I'd like to see Emperor Nero try to feed a parking meter.

"Besides," he added, folding away his newspaper, "this is all a bit late now. Those are adult dogs. All their lives we've been calling them Alan and Neil. You think they can start answering to some new names, just like that? A dog isn't like some stupid pop star or movie actor. Those people can get used to having some dumb new name. Like Pink. Dido. Or Sting. But a dog sort of becomes its name in a way no other animal ever does." Mr. Gaunt glanced at his daughter. "Don't you agree, Philippa?"

Philippa nodded her head thoughtfully. "It's true that they're not very doggy dogs. So what I think is this: If we explained to them, very carefully, that they each had a new name, we could see how they responded. A dog that's bright enough to know the difference between CNN and Fox Kids is probably bright enough to deal with having a new name."

"But I still don't see what's wrong with their names. Alan and Neil are both Celtic names. Alan means handsome; and Neil means champion. I don't see what's so wrong about two dogs whose names mean handsome and champion. Really I don't."

"I think it's an excellent idea, dear," responded Mrs. Gaunt. "By no stretch of the imagination could Alan be described as handsome. And Neil has never won anything in his life." She smiled as if the issue were now settled. "So. What will we call them? I must admit I rather like the name Elvis. Alan's the bigger of the two dogs, with much the larger appetite. He's an Elvis if ever I saw one."

Mr. Gaunt gave his wife a hard, questioning look, as if he strongly disagreed with her. "Layla," he said quietly, "this isn't funny."

"And let's try calling Neil, Winston," suggested Philippa. "After Winston Churchill. He's the fiercer of the two, and with his jowls and growls, he looks just like Winston Churchill."

"He likes cigars, too," said John. "Whenever anyone in this house smokes a cigar, Neil comes right over and starts sniffing the air, like he enjoys it."

"That's right," said Philippa. "He does, doesn't he?"

"Then the only question remains, who's going to tell them?" said John.

"It has to be you, Mother," said Philippa. "They always listen to you. Everyone does. Even Dad."

This was true; Alan and Neil always obeyed Mrs. Gaunt without hesitation.

"I still don't agree," insisted Mr. Gaunt.

"All right then, let's take a vote," said John. "All those in favor of new names for the mutts, raise your hand."

As three hands went up in the air, Mr. Gaunt gave a sigh of defeat. "Go ahead. But I bet Alan and Neil won't buy it."

"We'll see," said Mrs. Gaunt. "You know, we should have thought of it before, dear. The children are quite right." She put her fingers in her mouth and whistled an ear-piercing whistle that would have been the envy of any cowboy.

A few seconds later, the two dogs arrived in the kitchen and presented themselves in front of Mrs. Gaunt, as if awaiting instructions.

"Now listen very carefully, boys," she said. "It has been decided that you're going to have some new, doggy-style names."

Neil looked at Alan and growled quietly. Alan just yawned ostentatiously and sat down.

"Now I don't want any arguments about this," insisted

Mrs. Gaunt. "Neil? In the future, your name will be Winston. And Alan? Your name will be Elvis. Do you understand?"

The dogs remained silent, so Mrs. Gaunt repeated the question, and this time both dogs barked loudly.

"Cool," said John.

"I, for one, will continue using the old names," said Mr. Gaunt. "The dogs might get used to new names, but I'm sure I won't."

"Winston? Lie down," said Mrs. Gaunt, and the dog formerly named Neil lay down on the kitchen floor. "Elvis? Stand up." And the dog formerly named Alan, stood up.

"Awesome," said John. "Who says you can't teach an old dog new tricks?"

"Those dogs should be on TV," said Philippa.

Mr. Gaunt tossed aside his newspaper and stood up from the vast cherrywood kitchen table. "Don't even think about it," he said, and stalked out looking more than a little irritated with his family.

Later on, the twins went to school as usual, and nothing much happened, as was usual, too. John and Philippa were near the top of the class in most subjects, except math, but it was in P.E. that they really excelled, if only because they were so very, very fit — much more fit than most of the children in their school, many of whom were lazy and overweight. The reason why the twins were so fit was because they were both claustrophobic, meaning that they hated being in enclosed spaces. They especially hated elevators, which, as might be imagined, caused them something of a problem in a city like

New York, with so many tall buildings. When most people took the elevator, John and Philippa took the stairs, sometimes running up as many as fifty or sixty flights of stairs to get where they were going. This made the twins as fit as a pair of fleas. In fact, fleas would have had to have joined a gym to be as fit as John and Philippa. But even two children as fit as John and Philippa could not be as quick as an elevator, and as a result, they were notoriously late for almost everything. Which might have made their father and mother very cross but for the fact that Edward and Layla Gaunt had a much better understanding of their children than John and Philippa could ever have suspected.

CHAPTER 2

A TRIP TO THE DENTIST

Most children look forward to the end of the spring school term and the beginning of summer vacation. But for the twins, the first day of summer vacation was always associated with a certain amount of fear and loathing, for this was the day Mrs. Gaunt always chose to make an appointment for John and Philippa to see the dentist.

John and Philippa had good, strong teeth that were as white as peppermints and as even as a row of parked cars. Neither of them had ever had so much as a filling, and in truth, there was usually little for them to feel nervous about. Yet, somehow, they always had the feeling that one day Dr. Larr would find something that needed to be done and then all the gleaming steel drills, needles, picks, and probes that lay on his tabletop like so many instruments of torture would suddenly be called into painful action. The twins had seen enough movies to know that any amount of pain was possible once a dentist started to work for real instead of merely carrying out the routine examinations to which they had become accustomed.

This was, perhaps, the explanation why it was that, early on the morning of their scheduled appointment with Dr. Larr, John awoke from an extremely vivid dream in which he had been suffering from an agonizing toothache: the kind of agonizing toothache that turns a huge grown man into a whimpering meringue of self-pity or causes a fierce grizzly bear to become the best friend of a boy brave enough to take on the role of veterinary dentist; the kind of toothache that, in John's dream, had ended in the extraction of all his teeth.

Panting, covered with sweat, and quaking with fear, John fell out of his bed holding his face, relieved that such a bad toothache had been nothing more than a nightmare. But there was another more curious aspect to this dream for, while he had been sleeping, the mirror on the wall beside his bed had cracked from side to side; and not just the mirror but also the headboard above his bed so that the crack from the glass led neatly into the wood. Or perhaps the other way around, for there was even a small scorch mark and tear in the pillowcase where his head had been resting, so that it was almost as if the pain created by his dreaming mind had manifested itself in some kind of power over the surrounding matter contained in the furnishings of his room.

At least, that was John's first thought.

"What did you do?" asked Philippa surveying the damage from the doorway. "Feel a little hungry in the night and start nibbling the wall?"

"Do I look like a hamster?" said John irritably, and yet he hardly dared to tell his sister what he had thought might be the explanation for the strange-looking crack in the wall, for fear that she would laugh at him.

"No," she said. "But you sure smell like one sometimes." She went up to the mirror and moved her finger carefully along the fissure. "If I didn't know better, I'd say this looked like the result of an earthquake. Only the last one of any magnitude in New York State was a 5.1 in 1983."

"You seem to know a lot about it," said John, impressed.

"I saw a TV movie about it a couple of weeks ago," she said, and then frowned. "That's strange."

"Duh, of course it's strange," said John, but Philippa had already left the room, and for several minutes he thought no more about what she had said until she reappeared carrying a copy of the *New York Times*.

"Get a load of this," she cried, thrusting the paper into his hands.

"Yesterday's paper? So what?"

"They had an earthquake in Egypt."

"What's that got to do with the crack in my mirror?"

"Observe," said Philippa and, taking back the newspaper, she placed it against the mirror so that the front-page picture of a crack in the wall of the world-famous Egyptian Museum of Antiquities, in Cairo, lay alongside the crack in John's wall mirror. John felt his jaw drop: There was no getting away from the fact that the two zigzagging, apparently random cracks were identical.

17

"Wow," breathed John. "That is so cool."

Philippa frowned again. "You did this deliberately. To freak me out."

"I did not," insisted John. "Honest. I just woke up and it was there, I swear."

"So what happened?"

"This is going to sound stupid, but I dreamed that I had a really bad toothache. And the weird thing is that the crack seems to start where my cheek was resting on the pillow."

Instead of mocking him, Philippa inspected the pillow. "So why didn't I have the dream?" she demanded. "I mean, we often tune into each other's dreams, right?"

"I've been wondering that myself," admitted John. "And I've come to the conclusion that it's because I'm more scared of the dentist than you are."

Philippa nodded: This was true. "But it still doesn't explain the similarity between the crack on your wall and the crack on the wall of the Cairo Museum."

They were still discussing the crack in the wall when, a couple of hours later, they climbed the twenty-four flights of stairs up to Maurice Larr's dental practice on Third Avenue.

The twins found their mother, who had taken the elevator, in the waiting room where Dr. Larr was already talking to her — not about dentistry but tennis, a game about which Mrs. Gaunt and Dr. Larr were both very keen.

Dr. Larr looked over the tops of his glasses and winked at the children. "She made me eat my shorts," he said, describing the last game they had played. "Took me to the cleaners and got a discount. Your mother could have been a pro. There are women playing tennis for a living who wish they had a serve like your mother's. And beautiful with it, you know? That in itself is a rarity. How many ladies' tennis champions have you seen who looked like they belonged in the men's tournament? But not your mother. You should be proud of her."

The twins nodded politely. They were used to hearing their mother praised to the heavens for being good at this and for being good at that. Immune to something as hard to define as glamor, the twins sometimes thought that their mother seemed to have a strange, even mysterious power over people, almost as if life had given her that little bit extra, so that everything about her was just that little bit better than normal. Hairdressers complimented her beautiful, dark lustrous hair and said she should do a shampoo commercial. Dress designers complimented her perfect figure and said she should have been a model. Cosmetologists complimented her silky-smooth and taut skin and said she should launch her own cosmetics line. Writers complimented her wit and told her she should write a book. Dinner party guests complimented her cooking and said she should run a restaurant. Charities complimented her ability to raise money for good causes and said she should have been a diplomat. For John and Philippa there was nothing surprising about Dr. Larr's high opinion of their mother's tennis game.

"Stop it, Mo," laughed Mrs. Gaunt. "You're embarrassing me."

But the twins knew that she didn't mind at all. If their mother did have a weakness, it was for being flattered, and she ate it up the way greedy people eat too many cakes.

Dr. Larr looked at the children, smiled his friendliest smile, and rubbed his hands together. "Okay, which of you two kids is going to be the first in Uncle Mo's chair?"

"John," said Mrs. Gaunt, which was all that needed to be said. Mrs. Gaunt was used to being obeyed in the same way as a judge or a police officer — without question.

John took his place in the chair, while at the same time Dr. Larr pulled on a pair of latex gloves so that his hands looked as if he had dipped them in a bucket of cream. Then he stood beside John and pressed a button on the floor with the toe of his tasseled loafer so that the chair, which was more like a leather couch, rose in the air, making John feel like the subject of a magician levitating a volunteer from his audience.

"Open wide," said Dr. Larr, and switched on a light that felt warm on John's nose.

John opened his mouth.

"Just a little wider please, John, thank you." And arming himself with a mirror that looked like a tiny golf club, and a sharp but equally small shepherd's crook, Dr. Larr peered inside John's mouth, leaning close enough for John to smell the toothpaste on his breath and the Acqua di Parma after-shave — the same one John's father used — on his smooth, suntanned skin.

"Mmm-hmm," said Dr. Larr with the air of a man who

said "Mmm-hmm" a thousand times a day. And then, "Oh, my. Oh, my. What have we here?"

John's grip on the armrests of the chair tightened nervously.

"Oh, my. What's this? And another? Gee."

Raising his safety goggles and lowering his face mask, Dr. Larr turned to Mrs. Gaunt. "Remind me, Layla. How old is John?"

"He's twelve, Mo."

"I thought so. I thought so." He shook his head and grinned. "I've never before seen such a thing in a boy of John's age. Young man? You have wisdom teeth. The youngest person with wisdom teeth I've ever seen."

"Wisdom teeth?" Mrs. Gaunt sat down heavily and groaned. "That tears it."

"Wisdom teeth?" asked John, pushing himself up on his elbows. Having wisdom teeth didn't sound nearly as bad as having cavities that needed filling. "What are wisdom teeth?"

"They're called wisdom teeth because you normally only get them when you're much older. You see, it's assumed you have to be older to be wise, although sometimes you wouldn't think so the way some adults behave.

"The thing is, Layla," continued Dr. Larr. "The boy's jaw isn't yet wide enough to accommodate four new teeth. Yes, that's right, John. Just like in the Apocalypse. There are four of them. And when your jaw isn't large enough for all these new teeth, it causes problems for your other teeth. These wisdom teeth will squeeze the others together so that your pinup smile will look all crooked and misaligned. And we wouldn't want that, would we?"

"So what are you saying, sir?" asked John, although he suspected he already knew the answer to that question.

"The wisdoms have got to come out, John. You'll have to have an extraction. Four extractions to be precise. A hospital bed will be necessary. You'll have to have a general anesthetic and be put to sleep while we pull 'em out."

"What?" John paled visibly.

"Hey, hey, hey," Dr. Larr said kindly. "There's nothing to worry about, young man. I'll do it myself. You won't know anything about it. Piece of cake, I tell you. Layla? I can probably schedule this for the day after tomorrow, if that's convenient?"

"Do they have to come out now, Mo?" asked Mrs. Gaunt. "Couldn't we leave it a while? I mean, this is very inconvenient."

"In a mouth as young as John's," said Dr. Larr, "I'd recommend that it happen as soon as possible. Quite apart from the cosmetic aspect, his other teeth might become impacted. And then there's the risk of an abscess and infection."

"Sure, Mo," sighed Mrs. Gaunt. "Whatever you say. If they need to come out, they need to come out. I just wasn't ready for this so soon, you know?"

"Who could be ready for something as precocious as this? All right. You're done for now, young man. Let's take a look at your sister, Philippa. Phil, come on over here and make like an opera singer."

Philippa took the chair and opened wide. She felt certain that Dr. Larr would find nothing of interest in her mouth and was quite happy for him to think hers the least interesting teeth in the world. It seemed quite typical of John to be the youngest person with wisdom teeth that Dr. Larr had ever seen. *He was always showing off,* thought Philippa as she tried to relax and think of the movie she was going to vote for when her trip to the dentist was over: Mrs. Gaunt always took the twins to see a movie after a trip to the dentist.

"Wow. I don't believe it," said Dr. Larr. "Well, what do you know? I know you kids are twins 'n' all, but wow!"

Mrs. Gaunt let out another groan.

"What is it, Dr. Larr?" asked Philippa, but because her mouth was full with Dr. Larr's fingers and dental instruments, it sounded more like "Wha — ih — ih, ah — er — ahr?"

Dr. Larr, who understood this kind of monosyllabic language perfectly, removed his instruments and fingers and pulled away his mask to reveal an enormous grin. "I'll tell you what it is, young lady. It's dental history, that's what it is. You have wisdom teeth, too, just like your twin brother."

"Perfect, just perfect," muttered Mrs. Gaunt in a way that made John think she didn't quite mean this at all.

"Well," said Philippa, staring triumphantly at John, "since I'm ten minutes younger than John, I guess that would make me the youngest person with wisdom teeth you've ever seen, instead of zit boy." Philippa always called her brother zit boy when she wanted to annoy him.

"I guess it would, too," said Dr. Larr, grinning broadly at Mrs. Gaunt. "These kids. They're amazing."

"Yes," Mrs. Gaunt said weakly. "Amazing."

"I don't know why I should be at all surprised," he continued, taking Mrs. Gaunt's hand and patting it gently. "Really I don't. Not when they have such a remarkable mother."

Philippa felt herself frown at the unfairness of this remark. Here she was, the youngest person he'd ever seen with wisdom teeth, and Dr. Larr was trying to make out that it was all because of her mother. As if it were something she had done, like being good at tennis or having great skin.

"So what does that mean?" asked Philippa.

"Trouble," said Mrs. Gaunt. "That's what it means."

"I mean, will my wisdom teeth have to come out, too?"

"Yes, they will, Philippa. It would probably be best if we got it done at the same time as your brother. We'll have you in opposite beds, so you won't get lonely." And looking at Layla, he shook his head. "And really, Layla, it's no trouble at all."

Wearily, Mrs. Gaunt made the arrangements with Dr. Larr and then walked the children back to the house on 77th Street. "Under the circumstances," she said, "I think we'd better postpone our trip to the movie theater. I have to break the news to your father. There are things to arrange."

"You mean, like calling a funeral home," said John, hoping to pay back his sister with some anxiety for the earlier zit boy remark.

"Don't be silly, dear. Dr. Larr's right. There is absolutely

nothing to worry about." She smiled thinly as if she were trying to convince herself of this.

"I might as well tell you," said Mrs. Gaunt. "I didn't want
to say it in front of Dr. Larr. He was so excited. But early wisdom teeth are not exactly uncommon on my side of the family. The fact is, I was only a couple of years older than you are
now when I had my own wisdom teeth out. And look at me
now." She smiled a perfect toothpaste-commercial smile that
was full of sadness and concern. "I have perfect teeth."

"Yes, but the hospital," groaned John.

"Look at it this way," said his mother. "It's a rite of passage into being an adult. What growing up is all about. Doubly so in your case," she added. "I mean, your being twins."

Mrs. Gaunt sighed and lit a cigarette prompting the twins
to make some faces. They hated her smoking. It had always
seemed like the least glamorous part of Layla Gaunt, especially in New York where people get more worked up about
things like smoking than they do about guns.

"Do you have to smoke?" winced John.

"Tell you what," said Mrs. Gaunt, ignoring her children's
disapproval. "If you're brave about this, if you go to the hospital and have those wisdom teeth out without any fuss, you
can go to summer camp. How's that?"

"You mean it?"

"Of course I mean it," insisted Mrs. Gaunt. "All I ask is
that you're both brave about this. And that I get to keep your
wisdom teeth."

"Mother? You want the teeth?" said Philippa. "All eight of them? Ugh, how gross. You're welcome."

"Why do you want the teeth?" asked John.

"Call it a souvenir, if you like. I was thinking I might have them dipped in gold and then hung on a bracelet."

"Cool," said John. "Kind of like a cannibal. I can understand that."

"You're going to have such a good time," said Mrs. Gaunt. "There's this fabulous summer camp I know, in Salem, Massachusetts, where you can both . . ."

"Mom," protested Philippa. "I don't want to go to the same camp as him."

"And I sure don't want to go to some camp in Massachusetts with her," said John. "I want to learn some survival skills."

"I can assure you that Alembic House is one of the best coed residential camps in North America," said Mrs. Gaunt. "Six hundred acres of fields, hills, streams, and woodland with a two-mile waterfront. You'll both have a great time. Of course, if you don't want to go, you can spend the summer with your father and me on Long Island, just like we always do."

John looked at Philippa and shrugged. Alembic House sounded a lot better than no camp at all; and anything was better than another boring summer in the Hamptons. Philippa nodded back at her brother, intuitively.

"No, I guess Alembic House sounds fine," said Philippa.

"Yes, of course," agreed John. "When can we go?"

"It will probably take you both a few days to recover from the surgery before you feel fit enough to travel," said Mrs. Gaunt. "And obviously I will have to clear it with your father. I know he was looking forward to spending some time with you both this summer. But how about sometime next week?"

CHAPTER 3

YOU ONLY LIVE TWICE

It was the morning of the surgery and John and Philippa were at the W. C. Fields Memorial Children's Hospital — a handsome modern building in New York's Gramercy Park in front of which stood a large bronze statue by the sculptor Antony Gormley of a jolly-faced man holding a medicine bottle.

Their surgery was scheduled for nine A.M., which meant that the twins had been forbidden breakfast; and when Dr. Larr stopped by their room just before eight to introduce them to the anesthesiologist, Dr. Moody, John's hunger and nerves were — in the temporary absence of his mother who had gone to fetch herself a coffee from the Starbucks on Union Square — making him feel a little quarrelsome.

"So," he said to Dr. Moody, "what kind of knockout stuff are you proposing to use on my sister and me?"

Dr. Moody, a tall weary-looking man, who was not accustomed to discussing his choice of anesthetics with anyone, let alone a twelve-year-old kid, smiled uncomfortably. "Well, since you ask, I'll be using a drug called Ketamine, which always gives very good results."

John, who had been reading all about anesthetics on the Internet and now felt he knew as much about the subject as any boy, frowned. "But isn't that what vets give animals when they want to sedate them?"

"Kids today," grinned Dr. Larr. "You can't put anything over on them, you know?"

"I wasn't trying to put anything over on anyone," said Dr. Moody, trying hard to suppress his irritation. "Are you worried about my using Ketamine, young man?"

"No, sir, I'm not worried at all," John said evenly. "As a matter of fact I was kind of hoping it would be Ketamine."

"Oh? Why's that?"

"It's supposed to be the best for giving the patient an NDE. Or at least the main features of an NDE."

"An NDE? I don't think I've heard of that," Dr. Moody admitted through gritted teeth.

"A Near Death Experience," John said matter-of-factly. "You know. When you're having surgery and you almost die and you travel through a dark tunnel into the light and get mugged by an angel at the other end."

Dr. Moody's face darkened with anger. Dr. Larr observed this and decided to try to head it off at the pass. "John, John," he said anxiously. "Relax. Everything's going to be okay. This is going to be a piece of cake. Dr. Moody is a very fine anesthesiologist. The best in New York."

"Oh, sure," said John. "I don't doubt it for a minute. I just thought it would be kind of cool to see an angel. Even if it was a hallucination."

"One thing you can be sure of," said Dr. Moody. "No patient of mine ever came out of an anesthetic and said they'd seen an angel."

"Why do I find that easy to believe?" murmured John.

The door opened and Mrs. Gaunt came in, carrying a large Starbucks coffee cup in her perfectly manicured hand.

"And talking of angels," said Dr. Larr. "Here she is."

Philippa groaned and then looked away in disgust. "Can we get started?" she said. "I already missed breakfast. I don't want to miss lunch as well."

On the wall of the corridor outside their room was an art exhibition generated by other children from the hospital, with drawings, posters, and stories about what it's like to have surgery. But none of the stories and pictures written or painted by the other children who had been in the hospital gave her any idea of what it was really like to have an operation. She had to admit it might have been something that was hard to write about. One minute she was holding her mother's hand and feeling something cold spreading up her arm, and the next, nothing. It was as if someone had flipped a switch inside her head cutting off all her senses.

Or almost all.

From her mother's conversation with Dr. Moody, Philippa had gained the impression that the minute the anesthetic took effect she would have no sense of anything at all; but as soon as the Ketamine kicked in, she found that she was walking by a mazelike, meandering river that ran through an almost limitlessly large cavern down to a sea, which might have been a little frightening but for the fact that, most curious of all, John was there, too.

"What is this?" she asked him. "A dream, or one of those NDEs you were talking about earlier?"

John looked around. "I dunno. But this sure doesn't look very much like a tunnel, and there's no small white light or angel that I can see."

Reaching the shore of a lifeless-looking ocean, they saw, floating in the air about fifty feet above the waves, a sort of Middle-Eastern–looking royal pavilion with minarets and screens, and domed roofs with tiny diamond-shaped windows that reflected the sun.

Checking out his sister's expression, John saw that she looked uncomfortable. "Don't worry, sis," he said. "You'll be okay."

"I must be dreaming," said Philippa.

John frowned. "Why do you say that?"

"Because you're being nice to me," she explained.

"Look, we can't both be having the same dream."

"Who says we are? I'm just having a dream in which you're here insisting you're having the same dream as me, that's all."

"It makes perfect sense when you put it like that," said John. "But how do you know for sure that you're not in my dream?"

"I don't. I guess I won't know for sure until we both come out of the anesthetic."

After a moment or two, one of the windows in the dome opened and a largish-looking man with flashing eyes and floating hair leaned out and waved at them.

"Hey, Phil, you know what I was saying earlier? About how I'd like to meet an angel? That was just hot air. This is scary."

"I'm scared, too."

John took his sister's hand and, holding it tightly, which made her feel a little better, he moved her behind him, as if intending to shield her from whatever was about to happen. There were times when John seemed like the best brother in the world.

"Don't just stand there like a couple of lemons," urged the man in the window of the dome. "Come on up."

"How?" shouted John. "There are no stairs."

"Really?" The man leaned farther out of the window and stared down at the sea beneath him. "You're absolutely right. We seem to be floating in the air instead of midway on the waves. My mistake. Anyway, it'll soon be fixed."

And gradually, like an enormous spaceship landing on some forbidden planet, the royal pavilion containing the mysterious stranger began to descend from the sky until it rested solidly on the beach.

"There we are," shouted the man. "Now hurry up. We haven't got much time, you know."

Still holding hands, the twins entered the building, which was so full of mirrors that each room resembled a cave of ice.

Somewhere a woman was singing to the accompaniment of a musical instrument neither of them could identify.

"Maybe it's an angel after all," said Philippa fearfully. "This is a hallucination, right?"

"If it's not, you're in a lot of trouble."

"Me?"

"You said this was your dream not mine, remember?"

Footsteps echoed in the room ahead of them and then they saw him, tall and dark, wearing a red suit and a red shirt and tie, and smiling broadly. "Well, don't you recognize me?" said the man in a loud, booming sort of voice that carried through the cavernous red-and-gold room like a foghorn.

"I don't think angels wear red," murmured Philippa.

"You don't think it's — the Devil?" said John.

"The Devil, you say?" spluttered the man. "Whatever gave you that idea? I'm your Uncle Nimrod, of course. From London." He paused as if waiting for some sort of clamorous recognition. "We met when you were born," he said.

"You'll forgive us if we don't remember," said John.

"Really?" Uncle Nimrod sounded surprised.

"But we have heard about you," Philippa added sweetly. "Only we're just a little freaked to find you here, in our dream. While we're having an operation."

"Yes, sorry about the subterfuge," said Nimrod. "But I'm afraid that can't be helped." Uncle Nimrod held open his arms. "Well, don't I get a hug or a kiss or something?"

And since it was a dream, and since he was their uncle after all, whom they vaguely recognized from a photograph on the desk of their mother's study, they smiled bravely and hugged Nimrod politely.

"What is this place?" frowned Philippa.

"Don't you like it? It's the Brighton Royal Pavilion," said Nimrod. "From the south coast of England? I thought it would fit in with your dream. You know. The man from Porlock?"

The twins looked at him blankly.

"Coleridge? 'In Xanadu did Kubla Khan / A stately pleasure-dome decree?' No? Well, never mind. Not something they teach in American schools, obviously."

"And who's that singing?"

"That would be the Abyssinian maid, with a dulcimer," he said, and shook his head sheepishly. "Package deal. Anyway, never mind her. Like I say, there's not much time, modern anesthetics being what they are." He pointed at some elegant-looking antique furniture that was arranged around a card table. "Let's sit down and talk."

They sat down and Nimrod produced a large cup made of wood into which he dropped five dice. "We can play while we chat," he said affably.

"Play what?" asked John.

"Tesserae," said Nimrod. "Dice, boy, dice. We throw while we plot, just like the Romans. Me first." Nimrod threw the dice, made a face, and scooped them up again in his palm before John and Philippa had even registered what he had thrown.

"What are we plotting?" asked John.

"Let's see," he said, glancing at his gold watch. "Whatever you like, really." Nimrod dropped the dice into the cup and handed it to John. "Your turn."

"I wish I knew what the rules were," said John.

"There's only one rule in this game," said Nimrod, as John threw three sixes. "The important rule in any game. And that's to be lucky. Which you clearly are, my boy."

Philippa scooped up the dice. "Anything he can do," she said, dropping the dice into the cup and then dumping them onto the green baize of the card table, "I can do better." And she gave a little squeal of pleasure as she saw that she had thrown four sixes.

"Excellent," said Nimrod, picking up the dice. "Now let's see what you can do together." He handed the cup to John and then placed Philippa's hand on top of her twin brother's. "Go on then. I haven't got all day."

The twins looked at each other, shrugged, and then threw . . . five sixes.

"Just as I suspected," said Uncle Nimrod.

"How about that?" cheered John.

"Luckier together than on your own. That's good. That's very good. We can use that."

"How?" said John.

"Here," said Philippa, "let me see those dice."

"They're not loaded," said Nimrod.

"There's no such thing as luck," scoffed Philippa. "That's what Dad thinks, anyway."

"Oh, my dear, don't say that," scolded Uncle Nimrod. "The odds of throwing five sixes like that is six to the negative fifth power, or zero point zero zero zero one two eight six. I estimate that most people would have to throw the dice three thousand eight hundred and eighty-eight times to have even a fifty percent chance of getting five sixes. Which is just a fancy mathematical way of saying that you're a pair of lucky young kids."

"I haven't noticed it," said John.

"Oh, not yet, perhaps. But you will. You will. We shall have to get you playing Astaragali."

"What's that?"

"A game played with seven hexagonal dice," said Nimrod. "A game that was invented thousands of years ago to circumvent luck. I could tell you the rules if you like."

"I really can't see the point," insisted Philippa. "If this is a dream."

"Nonsense. Among the Aboriginal peoples of Australia, for example, it is recognized that dreaming is as important as real life. Quite often, it's where all the really important things happen."

"Yeah, and look what happened to them," said John.

"I'd like to know another human culture that's been as successful as the Aborigines," said Nimrod. "Everything they have has lasted for eighty thousand years. You, on the other hand, I bet you couldn't tell me what you got for Christmas two years ago." Nimrod nodded firmly as if closing the discussion, smiled, pocketed the dice, and glanced at his watch again. "Anyway, now that we've established that you are lucky, let's talk about your futures. Now listen very carefully. It so happens that I have need of your help. So here's what I want you to do. When you've recovered from your operation, on no account must you mention to your mother that you've seen me. I've been in pretty bad odor with her since you two were born, for reasons that we won't go into now. But I promise to tell you all about it when you get to London."

"London? When are we going to London?"

"As soon as you like. You do want to go to London, don't you?"

"Of course," said the twins.

"Then all you have to do is to tell your parents, politely, that you would very much like to come and stay with me. In London. On your own. That's what I'm trying to tell you." Nimrod looked at his watch again. "Oh, dear, we're running out of time. Any minute now you're going to wake up."

John laughed. "You're joking, aren't you? They'll never agree to that. No way."

"On the contrary," said Uncle Nimrod. "I think you'll find that they will go along with the idea. Unless, that is, you really want to go to this summer camp in Salem. Although, in actual fact, it's really more of a school."

"A school?" John was outraged.

"Yes," said Nimrod. "A summer school, for gifted children."

"Summer school," John repeated the words with something close to disgust.

"Then my advice would be to come to London. Just try to remember not to mention that it was me who put you up to this. That's quite important, really. Your mother and I don't see eye to eye on a number of issues."

"Such as?" said John.

"Well, for one, the proper way for two young persons to spend their summer vacation. There's the having-fun school of thought, to which I subscribe. And there's the not-having-any-fun-at-all school of thought, in Salem, and to which your mother proposes sending you this summer."

"No contest," said Philippa, and John nodded his head in agreement.

Nimrod stood up. "Right then. We're done here. You're starting to wake up."

"Wait a minute," said John.

"It's all over," said Uncle Nimrod.

"What if they do say no?" he asked.

"It's all over," announced Dr. Larr.

John sat up groggily on his hospital bed and reached instinctively for his jaw, probing the new hollows in his gums with the tip of his tongue.

"Your mouth will feel a little tender for a few days," explained Dr. Moody, the anesthesiologist. "But that's to be expected. And I'll go get you something for the pain." He smiled and then left the operating room.

"Is he gone?" asked Philippa, sitting up on her own bed.

"Yes, he's gone," said Dr. Larr, thinking Philippa's question was meant for him. "Would you like to see your wisdoms?" said Dr. Larr. "Here they are," he said, presenting her with a kidney-shaped steel dish in which lay four small wisdom teeth, covered in blood.

Philippa thought they looked like pieces from a chess game that had ended badly. "Ugh," she said. "Take them away."

"Did you see him?" John asked his twin sister. "Nimrod."

"Yes. Did you?"

"They're right here," said Dr. Larr, still thinking, not without good reason, that the twins were talking about their extracted teeth, and handing John the tray bearing his own wisdom teeth. "Take a look, John."

John looked and felt vaguely nauseated. He thought his teeth looked like something an African poacher had cut from some small but rare elephant. At the same time he knew that it wasn't just the professions of investment banking and chartered accountancy he was going to avoid; he was never going to be a dentist, either. "Yes," John told Philippa. "I saw him."

"So," said Philippa. "Was it just the Ketamine? A dream? And the twin thing?"

"Maybe."

"On the other hand, it's not something I think we should mention to Mom and Dad. At least not for a while."

CHAPTER 4

CHANGES

On the evening of their return from the hospital, by which time the faces of both twins looked as if they had stuffed their cheeks with food like a couple of greedy hamsters, they were standing on the stairs when they overheard their mother and father talking.

"Well," said their father. "They both seem okay, don't you think? I mean nothing strange has happened so far."

"You don't think so?" said Mrs. Gaunt.

"No. Not that I've noticed." Mr. Gaunt paused. "What? What? Tell me. Has something happened?"

"Nothing, dear. Well, not much, anyway. It's just that unless I'm very much mistaken, John is already changing." Mrs. Gaunt sighed. "Well, haven't you noticed? Since he came back from the hospital, the boy's pimples have disappeared."

Philippa stared closely at John's face. "Hey, zit boy, what do you know? She's right. They're gone. There's not a zit on your face."

John bounded up the stairs, heading for his mother's dressing room and the full-length mirror that stood opposite her enormous walk-in closet. For most of the last year he had been plagued with pimples — angry, red, easily remembered hills on his face that occasionally erupted quite horribly.

"You'd think someone would have said something before now," John muttered to himself. Scrutinizing his face, he stretched the skin one way and then the other, but try as he might, John could not find so much as a single pimple or blackhead on his now unblemished features. Normally, he tried to avoid looking in mirrors so as not to get depressed about being pimply, but now he saw no good reason why the rest of his family should not have noticed this apparent miracle or, in his mother's case, should have regarded the absence of pimples on John's face as a cause for concern.

Philippa appeared in the doorway of the bathroom and seemed to sense her brother's irritation with his family. "I swear," she said, "when we came back from the hospital — your face still looked like a map of the moon."

"It's incredible," said John. "Looks like those doctors were right after all. The pimples did clear up on their own."

"Yeah," said Philippa, hardly persuaded by her brother's restored faith in medical science. "Sure. If that's what you want to think, be my guest."

"What do you mean?"

"You don't think there's something strange going on here?"

"Maybe," allowed John. He was still too impressed with

his own face to be paying much attention to what his sister was saying. "I dunno." Making a loud tutting noise, he sighed irritably and added, "Believe me, if something like this had just happened to you, Phil, you'd be feeling pretty good about yourself."

"So what do you think they were just talking about?"

"I dunno. Adolescence maybe. I hear a lot of parents get pretty worked up about that when it happens. Their kids' hormones kick in and their parents start sending them to see a psychiatrist. Felix Grabel's parents sent him to see a trichologist when he started to grow a mustache."

"Felix Grabel's parents are weirder than he is," said Philippa. "But if you want weird, come with me. I'll show you something really weird."

Philippa led John up one floor to her bedroom, a place that he seldom ventured, so nauseating did he find his sister's fondness for cuddly toys, furry animals, and pictures of girlish-looking boy bands. On the wall behind the door was a Short People in Hollywood height chart (SEE HOW MUCH TALLER YOU ARE THAN YOUR FAVORITE MOVIE STARS, it proclaimed). Philippa pointed to the most recent entry, made the day before she had had her wisdom teeth extracted.

"The day before yesterday I was exactly five feet tall," she said, handing John a ruler and a pencil. "Now look." Philippa kicked off her shoes and then stood between Tom Cruise and Robert De Niro.

John placed the ruler flat on his sister's head and then marked off her height with the pencil.

"I'm pretty sure I've gotten taller," she said.

"Okay, Phil," said John. "You're done."

Philippa stepped away from the chart and they both let out a gasp of astonishment. There could be no doubt about it: Philippa had grown measurably taller. John checked the increase in her height.

"A whole inch?" he said. "That can't be right. You must have mismeasured the last time."

"No," insisted Philippa. "Mrs. Trump did it for me."

Mrs. Trump was the woman who their parents employed as the cook and housekeeper.

"Then she must have made a mistake. Nobody grows a whole inch in less than forty-eight hours."

"All right. When did you last measure your height?"

"Last week. Dad measured me. He says that as soon as I make five foot six I can have a new pair of skis. He wouldn't make a mistake. He's always accurate."

"Then let's take a look."

They went into John's room where John stood with his back to his own James Bond height chart (SEE HOW YOU MEASURE UP TO 007) between Sean Connery and Pierce Brosnan, and waited for Philippa to take the measurement.

"No doubt about it," she said. "You've grown, too. Let's see — by an inch and a half."

"I have? Whoa, I have. That is so awesome."

"It's like I keep saying," said Philippa. "There's something very weird going on here. First, we have wisdom teeth

years earlier than we're supposed to; then, while we're having surgery to remove those teeth, we have the same dream in
which our uncle shows up. Not only that but each of us experiences an extraordinary overnight growth spurt."

"Don't forget my zits."

"Not forgetting your zits."

"And the crack on my bedroom wall. And the way it
looked exactly like the crack on the wall of that Egyptian
museum."

Philippa paused for a moment and then said, "You want
to know something else that's weird? Is it me, or does the
air-conditioning seem a little high to you?"

"Ever since we got back from the hospital." John shrugged.
"Mrs. Trump. She probably turned up the air-conditioning.
When she's vacuuming the rugs she gets pretty hot."

"Let's go ask her."

The twins galloped down five flights of stairs to the basement kitchen where Mrs. Trump was emptying the dish-
washer. It was hard to believe but once, in a faraway galaxy a
long time ago, Mrs. Trump had been a beauty queen; the
children had seen the pictures and newspaper cuttings to
prove it. Time had not been kind to Mrs. Trump, however,
and now she was a rather plain, sad-looking woman with a
tooth missing on her upper jaw and two daughters living in
Europe whom she never saw.

"Mrs. Trump?" asked Philippa. "Did you turn up the
air-conditioning?"

"No, I didn't turn up the air-conditioning. Why would

I turn up the air-conditioning? I love working in an oven. Some people pay a lot of money to go to a gym and sit in a steam bath and sweat. But me? I'm lucky enough to be able to come here and get the same treatment for free." Mrs. Trump laughed at her little joke and, slamming the cutlery drawer shut and leaning forward on the kitchen countertop, she smiled, covering her mouth with her hand so that the children wouldn't notice her missing tooth, which they always did.

"We've been feeling a little chilly since we got back from the hospital," said John.

Mrs. Trump laid a cold hand on John's forehead. "You don't feel like you have a temperature," she said. "But you're probably coming down with a cold."

"Really," insisted John. "We feel fine. We were just feeling a little chilly, that's all."

"Chilly, he says," chuckled Mrs. Trump. "It's ninety degrees outside with seventy-five percent humidity." She shook her head. "All I can say is, don't blame me, blame your mother. Is it true what I've been hearing about you two?"

Philippa stiffened and eyed Mrs. Trump suspiciously. "What did you hear?"

"You're such lucky children," said Mrs. Trump. "When I was a kid I never went to summer camp. I never went anywhere at all."

"Where would you go, Mrs. Trump?" Philippa asked, humoring her a little as she relaxed again. "If you could go anywhere."

"If I had the money? I'd go to Rome and see my two daughters. They both married Italians."

"Does it cost very much to go to Rome?" asked John.

"To someone like me, it costs enough, let me tell you. But, perhaps one day I'll go, if I win the lottery."

"Someone has to win," said Philippa, who liked Mrs. Trump and felt sorry for her. "Why shouldn't it be you?"

"One day, maybe." Mrs. Trump raised her eyes and one hand to heaven. "I wish."

Philippa groaned and sat down suddenly on a kitchen chair.

"Are you all right, dear?" asked Mrs. Trump.

Philippa nodded. "I'm okay. Just for a moment there I felt kind of funny, that's all. Like I lost all my energy." She shook her head.

Mrs. Trump fetched Philippa a glass of water that she drank before remembering how much she loathed the taste of New York water.

A minute or two later, finding herself quite recovered, Philippa let out a breath and smiled. "That's strange. Now I feel fine again."

"It's like I was saying. After an operation, you shouldn't be up and around so soon. You two kids should be in bed. Would you like some more water?"

"Ugh. No thanks," said Philippa. Her eyes fell on Mrs. Trump's purse that lay open on the countertop and the packet of cigarettes she could see near the top. "But — you know, it's the strangest thing, I really can't explain this at all but suddenly I have this tremendous desire to —" Philippa hesitated to finish what she was saying, as if it were too awful to articulate, which it was. She was appalled at herself.

Mrs. Trump let out a shriek of laughter and then self-consciously covered her mouth, particularly her missing tooth, with her hand as she guessed what Philippa was suggesting.

"You children say the funniest things," she said.

"I can't explain it," said Philippa. "I mean I hate the idea of cigarettes. I think they're really bad for you. And I wish my mother wouldn't smoke. But it's just that I have this sudden attraction to the whole idea of lighting one. Please, Mrs. Trump. Could I light one of yours?"

Mrs. Trump looked at John. "Is she kidding or what?"

John shrugged and said nothing. Quietly he was hoping that Mrs. Trump might agree, because the peculiar thing was that he was experiencing the same strange feeling as his twin sister. The idea of a cigarette and — more important — the smoke it generated and the little glowing ember of heat on the end, seemed only too fascinating and filled him with none of the disgust that normally he felt when watching a cigarette smoker. He seemed to need smoke and heat, almost as if his body thought that the whole fiery rigmarole of lighting a cigarette might offer some kind of warmth in response to the chill he was continuing to feel.

"Please, Mrs. Trump," persisted Philippa. "Pretty please, with a pink ribbon around it."

"Do you want to get me fired?" Mrs. Trump laughed nervously. "Goodness me, I never heard of such a thing. Have you smoked before?"

"No," said Philippa. "I guess I just felt sort of attracted to the idea."

"Me, too," confessed John. "And I have no idea why."

"That's because you're twins," said Mrs. Trump.

John nodded. "The thing is," he said. "To tell the truth, we were just fooling around." He looked meaningfully at his sister, willing her to understand. "So you just go ahead and have one in the yard, like you always do. We thought that if we said we wanted one, you'd be so shocked you might give up yourself. Isn't that right, Phil?"

"Yes," she said, beginning to understand where her brother was going with this. For some reason she had started to think of the way Winston, the Rottweiler formerly known as Neil, would come over when their father smoked a cigar, and start sniffing the air. "It was just a bad joke. You go ahead and have one. We wouldn't want to spoil your pleasure."

Mrs. Trump nodded. The fact was that when the twins had come into the kitchen, she had been just about to go in the backyard and have a cigarette, something she had been looking forward to for hours. She picked up her packet of Salem cigarettes and went into the yard.

Their plan formed almost telepathically, the twins followed Mrs. Trump into the yard and sat next to her on some garden chairs, watching intently as she lit the cigarette and then puffed out a cloud of blue smoke.

"That's where the summer camp we're supposed to be going is," said Philippa. "In Salem."

Mrs. Trump looked surprised. "Strange place for a summer camp," she said. "I mean what with the history 'n' all."

"That's what we've been thinking," said John. "We were doing Arthur Miller's play, *The Crucible*, in school. And —" He sniffed the smoke-filled air. "And you're right: It's not the kind of place you expect to go to summer camp."

"No, indeed," said Mrs. Trump. "Still, I expect it will be very nice when you get there."

"Yes," said Philippa, breathing Mrs. Trump's smoke deeply through her flaring nostrils. "Only we've been thinking we might prefer to go to Europe."

Gradually, Mrs. Trump felt their eyes on her, like cats watching someone eat a nice piece of fish.

"It's a lovely evening," John said innocently as his sister sniffed loudly.

"Yes, isn't it?" said Philippa, as her brother did the same.

Mrs. Trump frowned. "Are you — ?" Crossly she stood up, threw the cigarette on the paving stones, and crushed it beneath her sneaker. "Honestly," she said, going back into the kitchen. "I never saw such a thing. I ought to tell your mother, that's what I ought to do. Lucky for you that I'm not the kind of person who goes telling tales on people. Even two people who deserve a good spanking."

Feeling more than a little ashamed of themselves, the twins remained sitting in the yard, staring up at the orange sky.

"Was it that obvious, what we were doing?" said John.

"I guess it must have been, otherwise she wouldn't have noticed."

"Back in the kitchen, a few minutes ago, when you sat down and groaned, what was wrong with you?"

"I don't know, John." Philippa paused as she tried to find a description that might satisfy her brother. "It was like something tugging at my mind. Something long-forgotten. All I know is that suddenly I thought how nice it would be if Mrs. Trump did win the lottery because then she could afford to go see her daughters. But as soon as I'd had the thought, I felt tired all of a sudden. The same way you feel after you've run a race." She shrugged. "I guess it only lasted for a moment. Like I was going to faint, I suppose."

"And now?"

"I feel fine."

"Hormones," said John.

"How's that?"

"I've been thinking about something you said earlier, and I believe that they might be what's happening to us."

"Maybe. I dunno." Philippa stood up, hugging herself. "Come on. Let's go back inside. I'm cold."

Their parents were still talking in the living room, and the twins sat down on the stairs like before to eavesdrop once again. Eavesdropping on the stairs is how most children find out about the important things that affect their lives. And it was quickly clear to John and Philippa that Mr. and Mrs. Gaunt were attaching a greater significance to their teeth and their trip to summer camp in Salem than somehow seemed appropriate.

"Holy mackerel. Everything was fine," said their father, "and then this had to happen."

"It's not as if you didn't know this day would come," said Mrs. Gaunt. "I've done my best to make this a normal house. Made considerable personal sacrifices as a woman. Given up what I was doing when I met you."

This was news to the twins who never thought of their mother as having done anything except be their mother.

"I know, I know, and don't think I don't appreciate it, Layla honey."

"But I've always, always been straight with you about our children, Edward."

"Sure, sure, only I never expected this to happen so soon. I mean, for Pete's sake, Layla, what father expects his children to lose their wisdom teeth before they are even teenagers? I was twenty-four when I had my wisdom teeth out. Twenty-four."

"I told you. The aging process is different on my side of the family."

"Don't I know it?" said Mr. Gaunt. "Look at you, Layla. You look fabulous. And me, I look like — I don't know. Older, anyway. Like I'm your father, or something."

"Older and distinguished," said Mrs. Gaunt. "I like that in a man."

"Oh, stop it. I'm immune to flattery. I have a shaving mirror that tells me the truth every morning. So what's going to happen now?"

"They're going to Alembic House for the summer, just like we agreed. Before things start to happen."

"Good grief, Layla, you make it sound as if it could be —"
Mr. Gaunt whispered the next word, as if he couldn't bring
himself to utter it, so that momentarily at least, the twins
were unable to hear what he said. "To have them around."

"But don't you see? That's exactly what it is. They may not
yet know it, but they're on the threshold of a kind of awaken-
ing. This is what I'm worried about. Either we send them to
Dr. Griggs or you are going to have to learn to watch what
you say. Everyone is."

"Layla, tell me you're not serious," said Mr. Gaunt.
"They're my own children for Pete's sake. Why would I have
to mind what I say?"

"Because they can't help themselves. Suppose one of
them gets cross with you. What then?"

"It just sounds so drastic what you're proposing," said
Mr. Gaunt. "This camp. Alembic House. I mean is it a nice
place? What's this guy Griggs like?"

"Edward, honey, there's really nothing to worry about, I
can assure you. This is for their own good. The whole point
of sending them off to Alembic is so that they can establish
some parameters about what they can and what they can't do.
William Griggs is very experienced in these matters. Much
more so than I am. You want them both to have happy normal lives don't you?"

"Of course I do. You know I do."

"That does it," whispered John. "I think it's time we found
out a little more about Alembic House and this Dr. Griggs
guy, don't you?"

Philippa followed her brother up to his room where, sitting down at his computer, he started to type into an Internet search engine. After less than a minute he had what he was looking for.

"Dr. William Griggs, M.D., Child Psychiatrist and Pediatrician. Specialist in the transfiguration, transformation, transmutation, and general socialization of gifted children. Owner of and Chief Consultant at Alembic House, Salem, Massachusetts, Clinic and Summer School for young savants, infant prodigies, and junior genii. What's a genii?"

"The Latin plural of genius, you dork."

"So it's just like Uncle Nimrod said in our dream. It's not a summer camp at all. It's a summer school. For geniuses."

"Genii." Philippa frowned. "The word is genii. Some genius you are."

"Wait a minute," said John. "Wait just a minute."

"What?"

"Don't you see what this proves? We couldn't possibly have known that it wasn't a real summer camp. How could we have dreamed that fact?" John shook his head. "No, that wasn't a dream at all."

Philippa nodded. "Yes, I do see what you're driving at. That it really was Nimrod who appeared to us."

"That does it," said John. "Let's just tell them. Like Nimrod said. That we want to go to London. If he's right about the school at Salem, it stands to reason he'll be right about Mom and Dad letting us go to London if we tell them."

Philippa winced. The truth was that she was a little scared

about the idea of them traveling to London on their own, only she didn't want John to know that.

"Perhaps we should sleep on it. See how things look in the morning."

John nodded. "Good idea." He pushed Philippa gently toward the door of his bedroom. "Until then I'm going to sit here and contemplate the real possibility of my being a genius. I always did want to win the Nobel Prize for something or other."

CHAPTER 5

THE SCREAM

The next day began with a loud scream.

John jackknifed out of bed and padded into Philippa's room to find her sitting up in bed, rubbing her eyes, and yawning.

"What's happening?" said Philippa. "I heard a scream, I think."

"I thought so, too," said John. He looked in the mirror, just to check that during the night his pimples had not made a vengeful return; but his face was still smooth and zit-free. "That's a relief," he said. "I thought I might have dreamed it."

"What? The scream?"

"No. Losing my zits."

They went downstairs and found their father and mother whispering in the hallway.

"Perhaps it's just a coincidence," said Mr. Gaunt.

"Do you know what the odds against that kind of

coincidence are?" asked Mrs. Gaunt. "About ten million to one. No, this is just the beginning."

"Maybe you're reading far too much into this."

"Am I? I don't think so."

"Besides, how could they? They don't even know." Mr. Gaunt paused. "Do they? But then again you might be right. I guess it is kind of suspicious, this happening so soon after —" Seeing the twins, Mr. Gaunt checked himself from saying any more. "Er . . . good morning, children," he said nervously.

"We heard a scream," said Philippa. "What happened?"

Mr. Gaunt looked at his wife and smiled thinly. "Your mother will tell you everything, won't you, dear? I have to go to work. I'm late as it is. Now . . . er . . . be good, kids, and try not to . . . er . . . get into any trouble."

"What's that supposed to mean?" demanded John.

"Nothing," said Mr. Gaunt, affecting innocence. "Nothing at all. It's just an expression. Like 'take care now.' Or 'have a nice day.' No need to take offense. I wasn't scolding you."

"Well, it sure sounded like you were," said John. "I think it's a little unfair, your suggesting that we might have to try not to get into trouble. As if getting into trouble was something normal for us."

As soon as he had finished speaking, John thought he might have gone too far, speaking to his father like this. And, even as the last word was out of his mouth, John expected his father to snatch off his tinted glasses and fix him with his most armor-piercing stare. So what happened next was all the more surprising.

Mr. Gaunt apologized.

"I'm sorry, John. Sorry, Philippa. Yes, you're right. It was thoughtless of me. I couldn't ask for better behaved children than you guys." Even as he spoke he thrust his hand into his back pocket, pulled out his enormous, sandwich-sized billfold, and peeled off a couple of hundred dollar bills. "Here," he said, thrusting the money at John and Philippa. "One each. Buy yourselves something nice. For summer camp."

"Edward, there's no need for that," protested Mrs. Gaunt. "You're just being paranoid."

John, who thought being paranoid sounded like a really good thing if it resulted in each of them receiving a hundred dollars, reached out to take the money from Mr. Gaunt before his mother persuaded him to change his mind, and was shocked to see his father flinch as he brushed his hand. And the pleasure that John took in receiving a hundred dollar bill suddenly evaporated as he realized that his father seemed to be afraid of him. Catching his sister's eye, John perceived that Philippa had noticed this, too; and as their mother followed Mr. Gaunt down the steps in front of the house to the door of his waiting limousine, John gripped Philippa's arm and hissed in her ear:

"Did you see that?" he said. "Did you see him? The way he looked at us? We're never going to get a better chance than this."

"For what?"

"To do like Nimrod suggested. To tell them both that we want to go to Europe."

"I dunno."

"Do you want to spend all summer in some school for young geniuses?"

"Genii," corrected Philippa. "The plural is genii. If you really were a genius then you might remember that." Philippa nodded. "All right. Let's go for it."

The twins followed their father down to his car.

"We've been thinking," said John. "We don't want to go to this summer camp. We checked it out on the Internet. And it seems that this place in Salem is more of a school than a summer camp."

"What is more, this Griggs guy is a shrink," said Philippa, as if that made things worse.

"Yeah. He'll have us on Ritalin before you know it."

"Oh, John, that's nonsense," said Mrs. Gaunt. "Dr. Griggs is a wonderful man. Alembic House is a wonderful place, for gifted children," she added, stroking Philippa's hair. "Where you can learn how to make the very best of yourselves."

"But I don't want to be a gifted child," insisted John. "I want to be a normal child."

"So what do you want?" asked Mr. Gaunt.

John glanced at his sister, took a deep breath and said, "We want to go to Europe."

"That's right," said Philippa. "We want to go and visit Uncle Nimrod, in London."

"On our own," said John. "We want to go by ourselves."

Mr. Gaunt was frowning and shaking his head. "Absolutely —"

John felt sure that a "not" had been coming swift on the heels of "absolutely," but at the last moment, Mr. Gaunt caught his wife's eye, and both twins saw her shake her head, as if advising him against uttering a refusal.

Mr. Gaunt checked himself and, instead of answering John in the negative, he smiled. Then, to the astonishment of his two children, he nodded. "Absolutely," he said. "Absolutely. If that's what you both want. If they want to go to London on their own, then that's what they'll have to do. Don't you agree, Layla?"

"Of course," she said patiently, as if the twins had made the most reasonable suggestion in the world. "I don't see why not. You're both responsible enough to travel on your own. I'll speak to Nimrod today and tell him that you'd like to come stay with him, and find out when is convenient."

"And I'll have my secretary book your plane tickets," said Mr. Gaunt. "BA Club class okay with you?"

John felt his jaw drop. He and Philippa had never flown anything but economy. "Club class?" he said, awestruck at the prospect.

"All right, all right, First it is," said Mr. Gaunt. "No problem."

Seeing his father's face now, John felt he would not have been refused if he had told him that he wanted to join the circus.

"Club class will be fine, Dad," said Philippa. "And thanks."

"Yeah, thanks a lot, Dad," smiled John.

Mr. Gaunt smiled affably, closed the door of his limousine, and breathing more easily now that he was away from his children, ordered his driver to drive.

The twins came back up the steps to the front door, still waving at the disappearing limousine.

Their mother smiled politely. "What brought this on?" she asked. "You never mentioned Nimrod much before."

"That's hardly our fault," said Philippa. "You don't mention him much yourself." She shook her head. "I don't understand it at all. He's your brother."

"Once we were pretty close, just like you two." Mrs. Gaunt shrugged. "But we grew apart, that's all."

John and Philippa followed their mother down to the kitchen where Philippa put her arms around her mother's waist. "It's really nice of you to let us go to London on our own like this."

Mrs. Gaunt smiled bravely but it was clear to the twins that something was making her sad.

"Don't be sad," urged Philippa.

"Any mother feels a little sad when she sees her children growing up," admitted Mrs. Gaunt. "It happened sooner than I was expecting, that's all. Like the wisdom teeth. Probably because you're twins. In a few years you'll want to go to college, and then you'll be leaving home." She shrugged. "That's life, I guess."

In the kitchen, Winston and Elvis shrank away from John as he tried to give their ears a good-morning pet.

"What's wrong with you two mutts?" he asked, pursuing

the dogs around the table with his hand held out in front of him to show that he meant them no harm.

Mrs. Gaunt viewed the two Rottweilers crossly.

"First Edward, and now you two," she said. "This really is the end. Winston? Elvis? Come here."

Reluctantly, the two dogs presented themselves sheepishly in front of Mrs. Gaunt's Jimmy Choos. She extended a straight, no-nonsense forefinger at their huge muzzles.

"You're both being very silly," she said. "There's absolutely no reason for either of you to be afraid of anyone in this house, least of all the children. If there's any more bad behavior from the two of you, there will be no food and no TV for the rest of the day. Understand?"

The dogs barked in unison.

"Now go say sorry to John for being so rude."

Their heads lowered in shame, the two dogs walked toward John and then licked his hands in contrition.

"That's okay, no hard feelings," he said. In truth he was more intrigued by something his mother had said. Why had he never understood until now? Winston and Elvis actually liked watching TV. This understanding added a whole new dimension as to how they were able to change TV channels.

"Where's Mrs. Trump?" asked Philippa.

Instead of fixing the children's breakfast like she usually did, Mrs. Trump was nowhere to be seen.

"She's in the backyard, getting some air," said Mrs. Gaunt.

"Was it Mrs. Trump who screamed?" asked John.

CHILDREN OF THE LAMP

"I don't know how much exactly. But it would seem that she has won the New York Lotto."

"What?" yelled Philippa. "That's fantastic. How much?"

"Like I said, I'm not exactly sure. These things are a bit of a mystery to me, I'm afraid. But according to her, she picked six numbers and believes she might have won the jackpot."

Seeing the tabloid newspaper that Mrs. Trump was in the habit of reading lying on the countertop, John picked it up and found it already turned to the page with the Mega Millions numbers and the estimated size of the jackpot. "Wow," he said. "It says here that there was one winner of a thirty-three million dollar jackpot." John glanced around the kitchen and there, by Mrs. Trump's handbag, was her lottery ticket. He picked it up and checked the numbers. "Awesome," he breathed. "She really has got the six numbers."

"Isn't it wonderful?" said Philippa. "Now Mrs. Trump will be able to go to Rome and visit her daughters."

"Is that what she said she'd like to do?" asked Mrs. Gaunt.

"Yes. She said she wished that one day she would win the lottery because that looked like the only way she was going to be able to afford to go."

"I'm beginning to understand what happened," said Mrs. Gaunt.

"How do you mean?" asked Philippa.

"I'm beginning to understand why your father was upset this morning," Mrs. Gaunt said plausibly. Seeing her daughter frown at this, she added, "I mean he'll be sorry to see her go. Because she feels like part of the family. I mean, can you see someone with thirty-three million dollars wanting to be a housekeeper? She'll probably want her own housekeeper, now that she's a rich woman. I had no idea it was such a lot of money."

They went into the garden to find Mrs. Trump, who was fanning herself with a packet of lupin seeds. Her face was stained with tears and her jaw was trembling as she spoke. "What am I going to do?" she muttered. "It's such a lot of money. What am I going to do?"

"Do?" said John, incredulously. "Do? I think you'll have a pretty good time spending it. That's what I'd do."

"I'm not going to leave here, you know," Mrs. Trump said tearfully.

"Oh, Mrs. Trump, you'll not want to keep working, surely. Not now that you have all that money. You owe it to yourself to take things a little easier from now on."

"No, I've been sitting here, thinking about it," sniffed Mrs. Trump. "I'd miss you all terribly if I gave up this job. I don't have a lot of friends, you know. And what would I do? Go shopping all the time? That's no way for a person to live. No, if it's all right with you, Mrs. Gaunt, I'll just take two weeks vacation. Go see my daughters. Give them some of the money, I suppose. And then come back here. If that's all right with you."

"Take as long as you want, Mrs. Trump. And don't decide anything yet. That's my advice. You might feel very differently about things in a day or so. People usually do after their wishes are suddenly granted."

In the afternoon, Mrs. Gaunt persuaded Mrs. Trump to take off a few days, to recover from the shock of suddenly becoming almost as rich as her employers.

"Enjoy yourselves at summer camp," she told John and Philippa as she was leaving the house to catch the subway back to her apartment on Aqueduct Avenue in the Bronx. "I know you're just going to have a wonderful time."

"We're not going to summer camp, Mrs. Trump," said John.

"We're going to London," said Philippa triumphantly.

"That's nice," said Mrs. Trump. "Send me a postcard if you get a chance."

"We will," said Philippa, and tried not to shed a tear as she wondered if they would ever see Mrs. Trump again.

CHAPTER 6

THE DISAPPEARING BARSTOOLS

A couple of days later, Mrs. Gaunt took John and Philippa to New York's John F. Kennedy Airport to catch the nine P.M. flight to London, helped the twins check in their luggage, and then escorted them to the British Airways Departure Lounge.

"In case you do feel an attack of claustrophobia coming on," said Mrs. Gaunt, "here's something that will make you both feel better, dear." She handed Philippa a small purple bottle with a gold screw top. "Take one every four hours."

"Thanks, Mother," said Philippa, breathing a sigh of relief. She had been counting on being given a supply of Mrs. Gaunt's special travel pills; on previous journeys, the twins had always received anti-claustrophobia medicine already dissolved in a drink, or crushed in a teaspoonful of jam. Since this was the first time they had ever traveled without their parents, it was also the first time they had ever been entrusted with their own medication.

"You should get to London at around seven thirty in the morning," said Mrs. Gaunt, handing the tickets to John. "Nimrod will be there to meet you at the airport."

Mrs. Gaunt bent down to hug her children. "Good-bye, darlings," she said tearfully. "I'm going to miss you a lot. London and Nimrod might seem a little strange at first. But whatever happens, try to remember that your father and I love you very much. And that everything we've done has been for your own good." She swallowed the lump in her throat and took a handkerchief from her crocodile leather Hermès Kelly bag and dabbed at the corners of her misty-looking eyes. "Good-bye."

And then she left.

After what seemed like an age, the flight attendant came to escort the twins to the airplane, which was their cue to take the pills that their mother had given them to combat claustrophobia. John eyed the silver pill on the palm of his hand with curiosity. "I don't know whether to swallow it or polish it."

"They are kind of pretty, aren't they?" said Philippa, and swallowed hers. "Aren't you taking it?"

"I think I'll wait until we're on the plane. Just in case you drop dead."

By the time they reached the plane, John was sweating with fear as the idea of spending seven or eight hours inside a large metal tube began to prey on his mind.

"It seems so small in here," he said when they found their seats. "Like being inside a vacuum cleaner. Do you mind if I have the window seat, Phil? I'm feeling kind of shut in. Gee, it's stuffy. How do you get more air inside this thing? Does he have to close that door right now?"

"Take the pill," Philippa said coolly.

And without any further argument, John swallowed the silver pill. The effect was almost miraculous. Immediately, a warm glow started to spread from his throat and chest into his stomach and then his head and limbs. It was as if some-one had thrown a switch to make him feel more relaxed and at ease with his surroundings. John thought that someone could have corked him inside a bottle and he really wouldn't have minded at all.

Twenty minutes later, they were airborne.

Drinks were served and with the drinks came the in-flight entertainment. Both the twins had been looking for-ward to watching all the movies they would not have been allowed to watch if their parents had been traveling with them. John stayed awake all night, viewing two and a half un-suitable movies in a row without a break. But after the first movie, Philippa fell asleep.

She was woken by turbulence that shook the airplane vio-lently as if they were in a bus that was driving over a road with lots of deep potholes. The plane creaked alarmingly, like a cheap fairground ride and, outside the window, the wings shook up and down like a springboard over a swimming pool. Feeling a little nervous again at being enclosed in the aircraft's pressurized atmosphere, Philippa took another anti-claustrophobia pill, which tasted strongly of meat cooked on a barbecue, and then proceeded to eavesdrop on the couple across the aisle. Holding hands and trembling visibly, it was clear that they were not enjoying their bumpy flight to London.

"Oh, my good Lord," exclaimed the female half of the couple, a largish woman wearing a baseball hat and a brightly colored poncho. "This is terrible. Oh, my goodness. Is the plane supposed to bounce around like this? It feels like it is breaking up. Otis? If we live through this night, promise me we won't ever fly again. Except to come back home to the States."

Otis, the woman's other half, was even larger, with a body that looked like the sixth or seventh chin underneath his Rushmore-sized head. He looked at Philippa and smiled weakly as if, even in the depths of his fear, he hoped to bring comfort to someone else. This was quite enough to make Philippa feel that she liked Otis and felt more than a little sorry for him. He hiccuped a little, swallowed uncomfortably as if trying to control a desire to throw up, put one pudgy hand to his mouth, and said, "All right, little lady?"

Philippa nodded. "All right," she said.

"I admire your pluck, young miss. Yes, I do. Me, I wish I was back in Poughkeepsie. I don't mind telling you. I wish I was back home." Poughkeepsie, as everyone knows, is a small city, population 30,000, near New York and famous for the manufacture of electric lightbulbs.

Philippa smiled back at Otis in a way she hoped looked sympathetic. It was clear that the poor man was terrified.

"We're going to London," announced Otis.

Philippa resisted the temptation to remind him that everyone on the plane was going to London. "Small world," she said. "So are we."

"But right now? We both wish we were back in Poughkeepsie."

"It is kind of rough," admitted Philippa.

"Well, nice talking to you, little lady. I have a daughter myself. Growed up now. But don't be afraid to holler if you need anything. I'll see what I can do to help."

"Thanks a lot." Philippa thought Otis was probably the sweetest man she had ever met.

Soon after that she dozed off.

Philippa had no idea how long she slept but when she was awoken, rather roughly she thought, by the flight attendant, John was watching an entirely different movie about talking apes. The flight attendant was looking worried.

"Have you seen the couple across the aisle?" She indicated the two seats where the couple from Poughkeepsie had been sitting.

"You mean Otis and his wife?"

"That's right. Otis Barstool and his wife, Melody."

"Yes, I've seen them. I talked to Otis. He's nice. A bit scared of the air turbulence, but nice."

"Do you know where they are now? If they might be hiding someplace?"

"Hiding?" If Philippa sounded surprised it was because she thought that there were only a limited number of places you could hide on a Boeing 747, even for a child like her, let alone two people as large as Otis and Melody Barstool. She herself might just have managed to climb into an overhead locker, but not Otis, and certainly not Melody; and apart from the toilets and the coat closets, Philippa had no idea where to suggest that the poor flight attendant might look for the missing couple. Besides, Otis had not struck her as the kind to do anything quite so mischievous as to hide on a transatlantic flight for which he already had a ticket. "Why would they be hiding?"

The pilot appeared behind the flight attendant.

"Well, we were hoping you might be able to tell me that," said the flight attendant. "Since you seem to have been the last person to have spoken to them. You see, Philippa, they're not in their seats, and the captain has switched on the fasten your seat belts sign because we're going to be landing in London soon, and the fact is we've looked all over the aircraft and we simply can't find them anywhere. We've even looked in the luggage hold."

The pilot squatted down beside Philippa's seat, smiling kindly. "We keep a record of who gets on the plane and where they're sitting, so you see it's not like you can just get off or anything. They must be hiding somewhere. The only question is where and why. If we knew the why, we might know the where." He shrugged. "It's a very serious matter, losing passengers during a flight. Very serious. There are all sorts of regulations that are meant to prevent it from happening. If there's anything you can think of that might help us find them, anything at all, then we'd be immensely grateful."

Philippa shook her head. She was stumped for an answer. "I'm sorry, I can't think of a thing. Only that he didn't seem to like flying very much."

"You've done a head count?" asked John.

"Of course," the pilot said patiently. "Four hundred ninety people got on this plane at JFK. There are now just four hundred eighty-eight that we can account for."

"Whoops." John grinned.

The pilot and the flight attendant nodded wearily and went away looking more worried than ever.

"What do you think could have happened to them?" asked Philippa.

"I don't see how they could have parachuted out and closed the door behind them," said John. "Not unless they had a collaborator on board. But then the pilot would have known the door had been opened. We all would. So I guess there's only one other possibility."

"And that is?"

"Well, you read of people disappearing off ships. Like the *Marie Celeste*. The Bermuda Triangle, that kind of thing. Maybe this is something similar. Maybe they've been taken aboard a spacecraft."

"I'm sure glad you didn't share that thought with the pilot," said Philippa.

The twins stared across the aisle at the two empty seats,

which looked to all the world as if the two missing passengers might return at any moment.

"I expect they'll turn up," sighed Philippa. "He was a nice man. I just hope that this doesn't ruin their vacation."

"Listen," said John. "When they do show up, it'll be me who's been proven right. They'll confirm what I said, you mark my words. That aliens abducted them."

"Aliens," scoffed Philippa. "Will you stop all this aliens thing? That theory is so totally improbable that I wonder how you can even be my twin."

"Ever read *Sherlock Holmes*?"

Philippa shook her head.

"You might care to bear in mind something that he once said."

"Which is?"

"When you have eliminated the impossible, whatever remains, however improbable, must be the truth." John nodded. "They've searched the plane from top to bottom. Therefore they are not on the plane. Once you've admitted that, then it seems to me that you're stuck with the improbable whether you like it or not."

CHAPTER 7

NIMROD

oming through the arrivals gate at London's Heathrow Airport, the twins had little problem in identifying Uncle Nimrod in the crowd of people waiting to greet passengers off the British Airways flight from New York. For starters, he was wearing the same red suit, red shirt, and red tie with gold stars he had been wearing in their dream. Among the ordinary-looking people at Heathrow, he stood out like a solitary red strawberry on a plain sponge cake. Now that they were meeting him again, they saw that Nimrod was perhaps a little more frightening than they had remembered, as if he really belonged on the English stage playing some oratorical tyrant king in a play by William Shakespeare. His resonant, deep voice carried across the terminal, as he spotted his young niece and nephew, as clearly as if he had been holding a microphone instead of a cigar that was as thick as a small telescope.

"Well, light my lamp, here they are at last," he said, hardly caring who heard him, and indeed, fifty feet away, two con-

ceited girls in the bookstore on the other side of the terminal turned around, thinking that someone was talking to
them. "And my, how you've both grown. You seem taller than
when last we met."

"An inch and a half since we had our wisdom teeth out,"
explained John proudly.

"An inch and a half, eh? Well, I'm not at all surprised.
Everything is larger than life in New York, isn't it? Buildings, cars, sandwiches, people, everything. Why should you
two be any exception?" Placing the enormous cigar in his
mouth, Nimrod landed two huge, heavily gold-ringed hands
on the cart bearing the twins' luggage. "Is this all there is?
Being related to my sister I assumed you would arrive with at
least half a dozen bags each."

"That's all of them," said John.

"It is? Then let's go find Groanin with the car."

The children, following Nimrod as he pushed the cart
bearing their luggage outside, yawned like cats as they moved
into what passed for fresh air at Heathrow Airport. It was
7:30 A.M. and they shivered a little as an English summer's
morning chilled their bones.

"You said 'since last we met?'" observed Philippa. "Were
you referring to when we were babies, or the dream we had
last week — the one in which you appeared to us?"

"Did I?" smiled Nimrod.

"You were wearing that suit," said John. "And you said
you had an urgent need of our help."

"All in good time," said Nimrod. "All in good time. Sad that we've seen so little of one another these past ten years."

"Mother didn't exactly say why that was," said Philippa, probing.

"What, nothing at all?"

"No, nothing," said Philippa.

Nimrod made a face. "Oh, I say. Well, that's your mother for you, I suppose," said Nimrod. "She never was very comfortable talking about this thing of ours."

"What thing is that?" asked John.

"Let's find the car first, eh? Oh, the three of us are going to have such fabulous adventures. What an exciting summer this is going to be. I've been hoping against hope that one day this might happen. Ever since you two were born." Although it was early, Nimrod seemed quite effervescent, like a bottle of fizzy soda that had been shaken rather than stirred. "Of course, it's possible our association might turn out to have its dangerous side. But any real adventure should contain a strong element of risk and, after all, that is the only way we can test ourselves and become stronger characters. Through adversity, what? Now, where's Groanin with the car?"

Nimrod squinted as he looked up road, which was the opportunity for John and Philippa to exchange a wide-eyed, what's-all-this-about-danger? sort of look.

"The trouble is, I've come out with the wrong glasses," Nimrod murmured.

John spotted an enormous maroon-and-silver-colored

Rolls-Royce that was parked about fifty yards away and, next to it, a man who seemed to be waving furiously at them.

"Is that it there?" said John, directing Nimrod's gaze toward the Rolls-Royce.

"Ah, there he is," boomed Nimrod, starting toward the car. "And about time, too."

Nearing the Rolls-Royce, they saw that the driver — a tall, portly, corpselike man, with a gray suit and a peaked cap on his bald head — had only one arm, which the twins thought seemed to be the most interesting thing about him, for both the children had always assumed that driving any kind of car, let alone a Rolls-Royce, required two.

"This is Mr. Groanin," said Nimrod.

Mr. Groanin managed to grunt a greeting and began to pack the bags into the trunk of the huge car.

"A traffic policeman obliged me to move the vehicle, sir," explained Groanin in a voice that belonged more properly to a Lancashire undertaker. "I say, I was obliged to move the vehicle, sir. And then I had to keep driving around until I observed you all here just now. I am sorry for any inconvenience you may or, more probably, may not have suffered."

"You always have a good excuse, Groanin," said Nimrod, ushering the twins into the rear seat.

"Thank you, sir."

"As you will have observed, children," said Nimrod, "Mr. Groanin is not only insolent, he has only one arm. It is, you will think, unfortunate for Mr. Groanin, but it does not prevent him from being an excellent driver. And I can assure you, we will be quite safe with him at the wheel of this car."

"Thank you, sir. Very kind of you, I'm sure."

"Which, as you will also observe," he added, pointing at a steering wheel to which a large knob had been attached, "has been specially modified to permit a one-armed person to drive it."

When at last they were in the Rolls and driving to Nimrod's house in London, Nimrod relit his cigar and puffed out such an enormous cloud of blue smoke the twins almost wondered if there might also be a hole in the car's tailpipe. More smoke billowed from Nimrod's flaring nostrils and, suddenly aware of the interest the twins seemed to be taking in his cigar, Nimrod glanced first at it, and then at them with the air — or perhaps we should say the *smoke* — of someone who thinks he might have made a huge blunder.

"Oh, my dears, but I was forgetting," he said. "You're Americans, aren't you? My apologies to you both. It hadn't occurred to me that you might not care for my cigar."

"We don't mind the smell of cigars at all," said Philippa.

"I expect you get that from your mother. She used to be very fond of a good cigar herself."

"Mother? You're joking."

"Oh, no. She was a great one for cigars, your mother."

As Nimrod talked eloquently of subjects close to his heart, the Rolls-Royce floated smoothly through the streets of London like a magic carpet with a roof, and Philippa stared out of the tinted windows to take her first look at the city. London seemed much more spread out than New York, so that the sky was a thing on its own and not something that was shared with tall skyscrapers, and her first thought on seeing the city's buildings was a feeling of relief that she would not have to climb so many flights of stairs. She liked all the little gardens that she saw, and the many trees, and almost cheered when she saw her first red bus and her first black taxicab.

John was more interested in the car than the city. He had never been in a Rolls-Royce before and, with the red leather seats, thick carpets, and walnut tables, it reminded him of his father's study back in New York; certainly it was every bit as quiet, even when moving.

"I love your car, Uncle Nimrod," said John.

"Very handsome of you, dear boy," said Nimrod. "The quality remains even after the price and the company that gave it birth have been forgotten. I acquired this from a film director whose chromatically challenged wife, it turned out, was prompted to steal when she saw the color red. And so, sadly for him, he was obliged to sell it to me."

"Does everyone in England talk like you, Uncle Nimrod?" asked John.

"Indeed, no. The best English is spoken by the Dutch and the Germans. The English themselves speak a very mangled mashed-potato form of English, which has no obvious beginning and no obvious end, and is just a sort of thick mess that they dump on your plate and expect you to understand.

Especially up in the north of England." Nimrod now seemed to address the back of Groanin's head. "The language is especially shapeless up there."

Mr. Groanin groaned quietly, as if he recognized that the remark had been meant to provoke him.

Uncle Nimrod lived at number 7 Stanhope Terrace, off the Bayswater Road and very close to Kensington Gardens, which he pointed out from the window of the car.

"There is a statue of Peter Pan in there somewhere," he said, adding in mock grave tones. "The Boy Who Refused to Grow Up. Never trust a child who enjoys being a child. It's as peculiar as not liking meat, or chocolate, or zoos, or circuses, or theme parks, or fast cars, or Christmas, or birthdays. Do you know what we call a child who likes none of these things?"

Philippa thought for a moment. "Stupid?"

"Close, but no cigar. A baby. That is what we call a child who likes none of these things. *A baby.*" Nimrod's face wrinkled with disgust. "Milk, milk, milk, that's all they ever think about. I can't stand the creatures. I feel sick just thinking about the little bald brutes. Greedy, selfish, incontinent horrors."

"But you were a baby once, Nimrod," said Philippa, who rather liked babies. "Weren't you?"

"Don't remind me." He shuddered visibly. "The whole experience continues to haunt my every idle reverie like Banquo's unwelcome specter."

"You mean you remember being a baby?"

"I do. Every plate of mush. Every wet nappy."

"But how?"

"It is a peculiarity of our side of the family that as we grow older, we start to remember *all* the horrible details of our childhood. On the day he died, my grandfather told me he had just remembered the very moment of his own birth. In fact, I rather think it was the shock of that particular memory that killed the old boy."

"Gross," said Philippa.

"Quite so," agreed Nimrod. "Gross, to the power of one hundred forty-four."

Philippa smiled kindly at her uncle, but at the time she was wondering if Nimrod's implied dislike of children might be the real reason why she and John had never met him before in their young lives.

The Rolls-Royce pulled up outside a big, tall white house with a castellated rooftop and several towers that gave it the look of a small, recently laundered fortress. Nimrod ushered them into his magical domain.

"Welcome to my house," he said. "Enter freely of your own will and be sure to leave behind some of the happiness you bring to it."

John and Philippa, who were unused to such formality, said they would.

The house seemed much bigger on the inside and astonishingly quiet given that a busy road was only a few yards away. It was a curious mixture of styles. The oldest part of the house looked quite medieval with old wood-paneled walls, faded tapestries, ebony floorboards, and French stone fireplaces that were decorated with the carved heads of what Nimrod said were Roman gods and goddesses, while in the half-timbered tower, a large wooden salamander crawled up a wooden staircase that was surmounted by the polished oak figure of a smiling Bedouin Arab, holding an ancient brass gas lamp, illuminating the landing with a long, steady blue flame. But most of the house looked more modern, which is to say only two or three hundred years old; this part of the house was full of architectural tricks with mirrors, ceilings that looked like summer skies, bookcases that were doors and, in walls that were covered in a strange silvered, yellow wallpaper that resembled a dulled white-gold leaf, doors that were not doors at all.

In most of the rooms there were Egyptian artifacts, animal bronzes, hunting trophies, ostrich eggs, and all the chairs and sofas were upholstered in red, which seemed to be Nimrod's favorite color. Fires were lit in almost every fireplace, and grotesque sconces and huge silver candelabra, some of them with dozens of beeswax candles, made it seem like evening in the house even during the middle of the morning. Almost all of the paintings were of people in the nude, but Philippa thought that only a few of them looked attractive, and she considered that several of them ought to have lost some weight before having their pictures painted. Elsewhere, ornate humidors, full of the choicest cigars, jostled for position with fine pieces of glassware, antique cigarette lighters, and ancient Roman or Etruscan oil lamps.

A library with several hundred books was where Nimrod seemed to feel most at home, and here, occupying pride of place, was a vast ebony desk with lion's feet and a gilt chair that Nimrod insisted had been the property of the great King Solomon himself.

"Is it, like, really valuable?" asked John.

"Valuable? You mean, in terms of money?"

"Yeah. I mean King Solomon was really rich, wasn't he?"

"A common misconception," observed Nimrod.

"But didn't he have his own diamond mines?" asked Philippa.

"Yeah," agreed John. "King Solomon's Mines. Surely you've heard of those."

Nimrod opened a drawer in the desk and took out a large book that he then placed on the desktop. "Read that," he told John proudly.

"I can't. It's in some weird old writing."

"Oh, yes. So it is. I'd forgotten that neither of you has much education yet. Well, you see, King Solomon had all sorts of problems with his subjects. And he kept a sort of diary in which he would write down all the many ways in which his people irritated him. Which, because he had a sense of humor, old Solomon, he called his Big Book of Moans. You see? It could have been the result of a simple mistranslation, or someone just getting hold of the wrong end of the stick, but there never were any King Solomon's Mines. What there was, was a Book of Moans. King Solomon's Moans."

Nimrod wagged a large forefinger at the twins. "You'll

learn a great many interesting things while you're staying with me. Useful things, too, not the sort of rubbish they teach you in schools. That's the trouble with schools these days. All they care about is money and exam results. Churning out more investment bankers and certified accountants, as if the world needs any more of those. Take my advice. Education is something you'd best give yourself.

"Which reminds me," he said. "I have a present for you both." Nimrod went over to his bookshelves, selected two beautifully bound books and presented one to each twin. "This is one of the greatest books ever written. *The Arabian Nights: Tales from a Thousand and One Nights.* Tales with which the Princess Scheherazade would entertain a terrible sultan who had threatened to kill her and all his other wives if he grew bored with her stories. Read it very quickly and then tell me what you think."

"Quickly?" said John, flicking through the book. "But it's got more than a thousand pages. A thousand and one, to be exact. It might take me all year to read this book. Maybe all of next year, too."

Philippa had balanced the heavy leather book on the palm of one hand and was trying to guess its weight. She was a more avid reader than John, but even she, who had read *Oliver Twist* by Charles Dickens, was daunted by the size of the reading project that had been given to her.

"It must weigh five pounds," she said. "Fall asleep while you're reading this and you risk serious injury."

"Nevertheless, I do expect you to read it," said Nimrod. "And now let me show you to your rooms."

The twins found that they had been accommodated in the old tower, in two large septagonal rooms that were separated by their own fabulous Art Deco bathroom filled with Russian onyx-and-bronze.

"You will be very comfortable in these rooms," said Uncle Nimrod. "I can assure you. But if you decide to explore the house, remember that it is very old. Especially this part. Bear in mind that we are in England and England is not America. Our ways are not your ways, and you may perhaps find things that seem a little strange to you." He shook his head. "If anything unusual does happen, try not to be alarmed. The house is quite benign."

John and Philippa smiled bravely and tried not to look alarmed, which was difficult since what Nimrod said sounded rather alarming.

"In order that you will feel quite at home," he continued, leading them into a small sitting room with a sofa and TV set. Picking up the remote control and switching on the little TV, he added, "I have provided you with a TV where, occasionally, you might relax by yourselves. I have no use for television myself. But I believe children these days find it almost impossible to live without this thing."

"Hey, look." John pointed at the TV, for on the screen was a picture of Otis and Melody Barstool, from Poughkeepsie in New York. "Quick," he yelled at his uncle. "Turn it up. We simply have to watch this."

"Oh, I say," exclaimed Nimrod. "I had no idea that the addiction was quite so chronic."

"It must be about the couple in the next seats on the plane. They, like, disappeared during the flight."

"Did they, by Jove?" said Nimrod. He smiled a strange little smile and sat down beside the twins on the sofa. "How very fascinating. I love a good mystery."

"An extensive midair search of the plane and on the ground in London revealed no clues as to the couple's whereabouts," said the BBC newscaster. "Police were alerted in London and New York as concern grew for the safety of the couple who are in their seventies. Then, early this morning, the couple turned up safe and well in their hometown of Poughkeepsie, apparently unable to account for their own disappearance. Numerous witnesses claim to have seen the Barstools board the British Airways Boeing 747, and to have spoken to them during the flight."

"And," said Nimrod, "they were sitting next to you, you say?"

"Yes," said Philippa.

"We'd just eaten the in-flight meal," Otis Barstool was telling a reporter. "I had the steak, and Melody had the chicken. Neither of us drinks alcohol. I was just settling down to read a book, when we hit this really bad turbulence. We haven't flown very much before and I don't mind telling you, we both got real nervous."

Nimrod laughed. "Real nervous," he repeated, copying Otis Barstool's accent perfectly.

"Both of us started wishing, *praying* that we were back home. The next thing I knew, we're sitting on the sofa in our living room like we'd never been away. For a while we just sat there, trying to figure out what might have happened and eventually we came to the conclusion that we'd had some kind of mental breakdown, or even dreamed it all. But then the sheriff rang our doorbell, and I guess you all know the rest. I've heard of airlines losing your bags, but this is the first time I ever heard of an airline losing two people. As a matter of fact, British Airways didn't lose our bags. They're in London now, it just so happens."

"Do you think it's possible that your prayer was answered?" asked the reporter.

"I sincerely believe that this is the only possible explanation," admitted Melody Barstool.

"Are you planning to take any legal action against British Airways?" asked the reporter.

"We already spoke to a lawyer. But he tells us that the fact we both believe it was the power of prayer that got us off that flight could affect any claim we might make against BA. Apparently, the airline isn't legally liable when this kind of thing happens. An 'Act of God' they call it."

Nimrod leaned toward John, his eyes glittering with mock suspicion. "Tell me, young man, is your sister always so impulsive? So very artless and *ad hoc*?"

"She's weird, all right," laughed John, who had no idea what *ad hoc* meant.

"He must have said something to you, Philippa," laughed Nimrod, "for you to make the poor chap disappear like that." He laughed a big hearty laugh that echoed around the room. "I can see that I shall have to be very careful what I say to you, my dear, lest I end up like Mr. and Mrs. Barstool."

Philippa smiled as she tried to see the joke. "Laugh all you like," she said. "But they were a perfectly sweet old couple, and I am just glad they're all right."

"I blame it on the chicken," said John. "The in-flight meal. It didn't taste right to me."

"That's only because you also had the steak," declared Philippa.

"Talking of food," said Nimrod, "is either of you hungry?"

"Ravenous," confessed John.

"Good. Then I shall cook you both an enormous English breakfast. This is very like an American breakfast, with these three local variations: The fried egg has to be laid on the east side of the plate as opposed to the west, the bacon must taste like meat instead of strips of dried skin removed from the foot of an overworked rickshaw driver, and the tomatoes have to be served without an accent, or else the whole thing is called off."

After breakfast, which was as delicious as Nimrod had promised it would be, Philippa returned to the subject of the Barstools.

"How is it possible for two old people to disappear off a plane in midair like that?" she asked. "I mean there must have been some kind of mistake. That sort of thing just doesn't happen."

"Clearly it does, though," said Nimrod. "If the television news report is to be believed." He chuckled and lit a cigar.

"Yes, indeed, from now on, we shall all have to watch our wishes."

"What's that?" said Philippa.

Nimrod stood up. "I said, 'we shall have to wash our dishes.' Mr. Groanin has quite enough in the way of duties to perform around this house without the three of us adding to his burdens. And if we leave these dishes for him, he will groan about it for the rest of the day. Being a servant with one arm does not make Groanin feel equal to any of the tasks he is obliged to perform. Groanin by name and groanin' by nature, that's what I always say."

After they had all done the dishes, they returned to the library to warm themselves in front of the fire. Nimrod lit another cigar, and Philippa looked at some of the many books on the shelves and noted that among them were several dozen editions of a book on card games and other forms of gambling by a man called Hoyle, and a fifty-volume leather-bound set of something called *The Baghdad Rules*.

"What are *The Baghdad Rules*?" asked Philippa.

"They are rules of protocol," Nimrod said vaguely. "For-mulated in Baghdad, a long time ago. You know, if you've nothing better to do this afternoon, you might try to read a chapter or two of those copies of *The Arabian Nights* I gave you. Then we'll have something to talk about over dinner tonight, eh? And after you have read it, I will explain to you the facts of life. About how you came to be here."

John and Philippa were horror-struck.

"Er . . . look," said John, "we already know all that stuff about how babies get made. There's really no need."

"No, not those facts of life," scoffed Nimrod. "I'm talking about something far more interesting than how some horrible baby gets made."

"What could be more interesting than that?" teased Philippa, a remark that drew a look of sad reproach from her uncle.

"I'm talking about how you come to be here in London. About how it is that your parents did not feel equal to the task of opposing your wish to spend the summer with me instead of going to Alembic House. About how it is that I trespassed on the dream you both had when you were under the anesthetic. About who and what you are. About luck and how it works. And about the important mission that necessitates your being here now. Those facts of life."

Nimrod was about to say something else but found his words turning into a yawn. "Oh, dear," he said. "Please excuse me. I'm not used to such an early start in the morning. I think I need a nap. And I suggest that you do the same." He raised his hand as he walked toward the door of the library. "We shall see one another at dinner, when everything will be made clear to you."

CHAPTER 8

MR. RAKSHASAS

When John woke in the early part of the afternoon, he stared at the ceiling for a while. As ceilings go, it was quite an interesting one, being a painted mural depicting clouds and lightning forks, so that while he lay there, John was possessed of the feeling either that it was about to rain or that some earth-shattering event was about to happen. Half an hour passed in this way and, deciding he was now officially bored, John sat up on his bed and started to read the book his uncle had given him, which was in itself something of a surprise, since he had only intended to glance at it.

The *Tales from a Thousand and One Nights* is not a single tale, but a kaleidoscopic collection of tales told by a courageous young woman, the Princess Scheherazade, for whom the very art of storytelling is a means of survival. These are tales about kings and princesses, powerful djinn, specious miracles, clever tricksters, greedy merchants, and ingenious thieves. Some of the stories, such as those of Sinbad, Ali Baba and the Forty Thieves, and Aladdin were, of course, familiar to John. But what was most captivating about the book was the way one story appeared from within another, like a Chinese puzzle, so that after a while the book absorbed him in a way that no book ever had before, and it became quite impossible for John to stop reading until he had finished it. John had always treated with considerable skepticism reviews on any paperback that assured prospective readers that someone had been unable to put the book down, but now, to his surprise, he found that this was exactly what was happening to him. He realized how remarkable this was and, for the rest of his life, he would never forget this particular day in London when he first opened this volume of wonders.

A curious thing about the copy of *The Arabian Nights* given to him by Nimrod was its strange physical properties. For one thing, John found it was impossible to keep his place in the book by turning down the corners; once or twice he did fold a page down only to find that when he looked at it again, the corner had, somehow, straightened itself. And for another, the book seemed able to illuminate itself, for as the day passed into evening, John found he could read the book without an electric light and, experimenting, he found he could even read it in near-total darkness with a quilt over his head and without the aid of a flashlight.

Just as remarkable to John, however, who had never in his life read such a long book, and with such enormous pleasure, was the speed with which he found himself turning the book's silky-smooth pages. His eyes seemed to fly across the words and where once he might have taken as long as two or three minutes to read a single page, he now read the same in a tenth of the time, so that the book, all 1001 pages of it, was finished in less than six hours. As soon as he had turned the last page, John felt so proud of himself that he ran into Philippa's room to boast of his achievement only to discover that she, too, had read the book from cover to cover, and that she had apparently finished the book at least an hour before him.

"There's something weird going on here," he declared, suppressing his irritation with his twin sister.

Philippa, who had always been an avid reader — much more so than her brother — laughed. "You're telling me. When did you ever spend a whole afternoon with a book? No, wait, there was that time last Christmas when Dad promised you fifty bucks if you read *The Call of the Wild* by Jack London."

"I earned every cent of that fifty," said John. "It was the most boring book I ever read. Besides, you know exactly what I'm talking about."

Philippa smiled. "More than you, John," she said. "I've been waiting for you to come in so I could carry out an experiment in the presence of a witness."

"What kind of experiment?"

"This kind," she said and, picking up her copy of *The Arabian Nights*, she threw it onto the fire burning quietly in the grate.

"Hey," said John. "Are you nuts?"

"I thought as much," she said triumphantly and pointed

at the book, which remained on the hot coals but without being consumed by fire. "It's a strange book that doesn't burn, wouldn't you say?"

They waited for several minutes, watching the book as it steadfastly refused to catch fire until finally, John got the coal tongs and removed the book from the fire and placed it carefully on the hearth before touching it gingerly.

"There isn't a scorch mark on it anywhere," he said, opening the book and turning the pages. "And feel it. It's not even hot."

Philippa laid a hand on the page, which was noticeably cool to her fingertips. "I wonder what it's made of?" she said.

"Why don't we ask Nimrod?"

On the stairs going down, they were a little surprised to meet a tall, thin, creepy-looking man with a white beard, wearing a white turban and a white frock coat, who was coming up. And seeing the twins, he pressed his hands together, bowed his head as he passed them by, and then continued on his way before he opened a trick door in the silvery wall, and then closed it behind him.

John let out a nervous breath. "Who do you think that was?" he asked.

"Relax," said Philippa. "He's probably just a friend of Nimrod's. He was smiling at us, wasn't he?"

"Don't you think it's a little strange that the first person we see after reading *The Arabian Nights* is a guy who looks like something in the book? Like a genie."

"A genie? How do you figure that?" Philippa laughed. "In case you didn't notice, he didn't float out of a bottle. He walked up the stairs."

"He was wearing a turban."

"These days, not everyone who wears a turban comes with magic powers." Philippa shrugged. "Still, maybe you should have played it safe and asked him for three wishes, anyway."

"Even if he wasn't a genie," said John, "I think Nimrod's got some explaining to do."

They found Nimrod in the dining room where the table had been laid with a dozen different dishes, including a whole roast goose, a side of venison, a roast ham, a leg of mutton, vegetables, cheeses, fruit, wine, and Coca-Cola. Nimrod seemed to be expecting them, too, for the table was set for three and he was already carving the goose.

"Ah, there you are," Nimrod said smoothly. "You're just in time for a bite of dinner. Help yourselves."

He silenced their first volley of questions with the palm of his hand, and for several minutes at least, all thoughts of interrogating Nimrod about the strange book and the even stranger man on the stairs were forgotten as the twins realized how hungry they were. Quickly sitting down, John and Philippa began to heap their plates with food.

"We just saw a weird-looking man dressed in white," said Philippa, stuffing her mouth with ham. "Including a turban."

"Was he a ghost?" asked John.

"A ghost? Oh, no, not in this house. The little swine wouldn't dare. No, that was not a ghost. That was Mr.

Rakshasas. He's from India originally. And he'll be joining us presently. I expect you gave him quite a fright."

"We gave him a fright?" John frowned. "What about us? He scared the living daylights out of us."

"Mr. Rakshasas would be very upset to hear you say so, John. He's really a terribly shy sort of fellow. Wouldn't say boo to a goose." Nimrod hesitated for a moment and then stuffed a whole breast of goose into his mouth. "Not that there would be much point in saying boo to this particular goose, since it's dead. But I imagine you get the idea."

"John's exaggerating," said Philippa. "Your Mr. Rakshasas wasn't all that frightening. But," she added pointedly, "he did look kind of mysterious."

"Patience, patience," said Nimrod. "I said I'd tell you the facts of life and I will."

Mr. Groanin came into the room bearing an enormous cake on his one and only hand.

"But look here," said Nimrod. "I've gone to considerable trouble to put this spread on —"

Mr. Groanin snorted with contempt and placed the cake on the table. "Trouble, he says," he muttered. "That's a laugh."

"So I think the least you can do is apply yourselves until justice has been done to this magnificent repast. Eh, Groanin? What's that you say about trouble?"

"No trouble at all, sir. Will that be all?"

"Yes, yes." Nimrod forked a large slice of ham onto his already full plate. "Now then, you two. No more talking until we're well and truly stuffed."

Thirty minutes later, Nimrod unbuttoned his red jacket, checked the time on his gold watch, poured himself another large goblet of Burgundy, lit an enormous cigar, and then leaned back in his creaking armchair. "Oh, I say. That was a good feast. What? What?"

"Awesome," agreed John.

There was a knock at the door and Mr. Rakshasas came into the dining room and bowed gravely.

"A hundred thousand greetings to this brethren of the lamp," he said. "May you get all your wishes except one, so you'll still have something to strive for. And may the saddest day of your future be no worse than the happiest day of your past."

To John and Philippa's surprise, Mr. Rakshasas spoke with an Irish accent and seeing their eyebrows lift, Nimrod felt obliged to offer the twins a swift explanation. "For many years, Mr. Rakshasas was obliged to live alone, and learned all of his English from Irish television."

Mr. Rakshasas nodded gravely. "May the enemies of Ireland never eat bread nor drink whisky, but be afflicted with itching without the benefit of scratching."

Now that the twins saw him again, and in a brighter light, they perceived that Mr. Rakshasas was not at all frightening. He wore a long white jacket buttoned up the neck, white trousers, white slippers, and a white turban with a small white teardrop pearl that hung just above his forehead. A long shaggy beard and mustache that was as white as his turban completed the *tout ensemble* of his unusual appearance.

His brown eyes were kind and smiling, and yet Philippa sensed that these concealed some great tragedy that had once befallen Mr. Rakshasas. He sat down on the leather-covered fender by the fire, so close it seemed to both the twins that he might be set alight, and warmed his long, thin hands over the flames for several minutes before lighting a pipe.

"As usual your arrival is most timely, Mr. Rakshasas," said Nimrod. "I was just about to tell my young nephew and niece here about their gifts."

John's heart leaped in his chest like a wild salmon. A gift, and it wasn't even Christmas or his birthday. Philippa had a better idea of the kind of gift Nimrod was referring to, however, and immediately started to worry again that this meant she was destined to become some sort of bookish eccentric.

A grandfather clock that had been beating time throughout dinner like a knife tapping on a piano string stopped suddenly, creating a loud, almost palpable silence, and it seemed to prompt a realization on the part of the twins that somehow their old life had ended and a new one was about to begin.

"Now then," said Nimrod. "I think it's best if I talk and you just listen. Because there's quite a lot for you two kids to comprehend. And perhaps I'd better start from the beginning, eh, Mr. Rakshasas?"

He answered slowly between puffs on his pipe. "Aye," he said. "Perhaps the whole story is best. 'Tis a fact that a Tyrone woman will never buy a rabbit without a head for fear that it's a cat."

"Everything I am going to tell you now is true," said Nimrod. "There is much you will find astonishing, nay, unbelievable, and I ask for you to trust and to suspend your disbelief for a while, as if you were in a movie theater watching some far-fetched film fantasy." Nimrod puffed the cigar thoughtfully and a large cloud of smoke escaped from his mouth. "Now, as any wise man or magus will tell you, there are three types of higher intelligent beings in the universe. There are angels, who are made of light. There are human beings, who are made of earth — I'm sure you've all seen funerals on TV where the priest says, 'Earth to earth; ashes to ashes; and dust to dust,' et cetera, et cetera. Well, that's all a human is really. Earth, or carbon if you want to be scientific about it. Earth and water if you want to be really scientific. Anyway, for the purpose of our conversation, we're not concerned with human beings. No, we're concerned with the last of these higher intelligent beings. These are djinn. A djinn is the proper way of describing what is vulgarly known as a genie. I hope no relation of mine would ever use a word like *genie*?* That is a word for Christmas pantomimes and animated films, not for people like you and me. The word is *djinn* and djinn are made of fire. Yes, fire." Nimrod expelled some more cigar smoke as if to prove the point.

"Is this a joke?" asked Philippa.

*As Nimrod explains, the word *genie* is repugnant to the djinn; for this reason, the normal singular of djinn, which is *djinni*, is scorned (because it sounds exactly like genie) and, among the djinn themselves, the word *djinn* is used as both the singular and plural.

"I can assure you I'm perfectly serious," insisted Nimrod. "Now, there are many tribes of djinn. We could spend all night describing these, could we not Mr. Rakshasas?"

"Oh, indeed."

"But you and I and your mother and Mr. Rakshasas here are fortunate enough to be djinn of the most distinguished tribe. The Marid. We are the fewest in number, but we are also the strongest of the djinn.

"There now," chuckled Nimrod. "I've said it. The djinn is out of the bottle, so to speak. No doubt you have heard this expression before. I daresay you never gave a moment's thought as to how it might apply to your young selves. Well, I am here to assure you that it does. For you are both children of the lamp."

CHAPTER 9

DJINN

"You mean we're djinn, like in *The Arabian Nights*?" said John. "Where the guy finds a lamp or a bottle and lets the djinn out?"

Nimrod nodded.

"You've got to be kidding," said Philippa.

"It's a little hard to believe, I know," said Nimrod.

"You're telling me," said John.

"But if you think about some of the strange things that have happened to you of late, certainly since you had your wisdom teeth removed, then surely you'll have to admit the possibility of an equally strange explanation."

Nimrod studied his cigar before returning it to his mouth, whereupon he drew on it until the end glowed as red as his jacket, and then blew a huge smoke ring. For a moment the smoke ring took on the shape of the same floating pavilion the twins had seen in the dream they had both experienced during the extraction of their wisdom teeth, then it disappeared into the air.

"For example," continued Nimrod, "is it not strange that I know everything about the dream you had while you were under the anesthetic? About how we met at the Brighton Royal Pavilion. That there was a lady playing a dulcimer. That we played dice? That John threw three sixes, Philippa four, and together you threw five. If a dream it was, then how would I know all that?"

"So what was it, if it wasn't a dream?" asked John.

"Quite simply, I went to New York, left my body at the Carlyle Hotel on Madison Avenue, and traveled, in my astral body — which is to say, the ethereal counterpart or shadow of my physical body — to the hospital where you were having your teeth out, and entered your bodies."

"Wow."

"During the time you were under the anesthetic, I took possession of your minds. Planting some of the experiences you remember so vividly. And suggesting that you only had to tell your parents you were coming to London for it to happen."

"And why was that, exactly?" asked Philippa. "That they agreed so readily?"

"Human beings and djinn age at different rates," explained Nimrod. "Being a djinn doesn't start to amount to anything until your wisdom teeth appear and are removed. In human beings, wisdom teeth — or dragon teeth as djinn prefer to call them — serve no real purpose. But with us djinn, they are there for a good reason. They're a sign that your powers are ready to use. As soon as your dragon teeth are pulled, your true life as a djinn can begin." Nimrod's next smoke ring took on the shape of the New York skyline. "Once you had your dragon teeth removed, your parents did not dare to resist you."

"Djinn wisdom begins here," said Mr. Rakshasas.

But Philippa was still shaking her head.

Uncle Nimrod looked at Mr. Rakshasas and shook his head, somewhat exasperated. "This is more difficult than I had thought," he said. "Wait, I thought of something." He snapped his fingers at John and Philippa. "Do you ever get claustrophobic?"

They looked at each other and then nodded.

"Aha," he said, and blew a smoke ring shaped like an oil lamp. "That comes from so many of us finding ourselves trapped inside lamps and bottles by clever men, of which, these days, fortunately, there are fewer than there used to be. That is why we have charcoal pills, to keep ourselves warm inside and stop us from getting all panicky when we find ourselves closed in somewhere. When a djinn is warm, a djinn is calm and relaxed. Is that not so, Mr. Rakshasas?"

"The cat is his own best advisor, right enough," observed Mr. Rakshasas.

"Those were the pills that Mother gave us, right?" said John, who was much readier to be convinced that he was a djinn than his twin sister.

"I expect so. Like I said, the djinn are made of fire, so you'll find that all sources of heat will help to keep you calm."

Philippa glanced uncomfortably at Mr. Rakshasas sitting at the hearth, smoking his pipe, and reflected that it was easy enough to think of him as something made of fire; if he'd been any closer to the flames, he would have been toast.

"Just about the first thing a djinn does after he or she has been released from a lamp or a bottle is, with the help of the oxygen in Earth's atmosphere, to turn into smoke," continued Nimrod. "Open fires, barbecues, candles, charcoal pills, even the odd cigarette, they all help."

"But isn't smoking bad for you?" objected John.

"It's terribly bad for human beings, yes. But not at all bad for djinn. You'll find that human beings try to do a lot of things we can do, usually with disastrous consequences. It's taken a long time, but finally we're managing to get the message across that smoking is bad for them."

"Assuming this is all on the level," said John, glancing uncertainly at his sister, "and I'm not saying I think it is, does being a djinn mean I can give people three wishes, and stuff like that?"

"Well, yes, eventually. But what you have to understand first, young man, and most important of all, is that the djinn are the guardians of all the luck in the universe — the keepers and custodians of the imagined tendency of what is popularly known as chance. The fortuitous happening of events favorable or unfavorable to the interests of human beings. In short, chance, as a cause or bestower of success or failure, exists as a physical force in the universe, which may be controlled exclusively by the djinn. You will be able to grant three wishes when you have understood how and why. But until then, until your djinn power grows a little stronger, it's something that only your subconscious mind will be able to do."

"You mean, like if we dream it?" asked Philippa.

"Exactly so," said Nimrod.

"That might explain Mr. and Mrs. Barstool on the plane," said Philippa. "I suppose."

"Now you're getting it," agreed Nimrod. "One of them must have used the word *wish*, and you must have felt that you liked him."

His next smoke ring looked like a Boeing 747.

"He said he wished he was back home," she said. "I felt sorry for him."

"There you are. A classic case of what we djinn call subliminal wish fulfilment. You probably went to sleep thinking how nice it would be if poor Mr. Barstool got what he wanted."

"That's true." Philippa pursed her lips and looked thoughtful. "In our dream, assuming for a moment that it really was you, did the reason you had us throw dice have something to do with luck?"

"Yes. I wanted to test your current capacity for influencing chance. And it so happens that together, yours is excellent. Together, it's as good as any adult djinn's. Which is most useful to our current purpose. Let me explain. . ."

"This sumbilical . . . thingy," John said to Nimrod, interrupting.

"Subliminal wish fulfilment," repeated Nimrod.

"That would explain what happened to Mrs. Trump, our housekeeper," he said. "Just before we came here, Mrs. Trump won thirty-three million dollars in the New York Mega Millions Lottery."

"I do remember thinking how nice it would be if she won enough money to visit her daughters in Europe," admitted Philippa.

"Well, no harm done, eh?" said Nimrod. "These things happen. But you know, when people use the word *wish*, they aren't the ones who have to be careful. We djinn have to be careful, too. It's not always a good thing when people get what they wish. As Mr. and Mrs. Barstool have discovered. We might feel that we want to help them, but sometimes — usually, if I'm being honest — it's best that they get the thing themselves. Through their own hard work. That way, they tend to appreciate it more when they get it, whatever the 'it' might be. Equally, there are many occasions when they just don't think their wish through. When they don't consider the full implications of actually having their dearest wish come true."

"There's many a time a man's mouth broke his own nose," offered Mr. Rakshasas.

"Like in some of those stories in *The Arabian Nights*," said John.

"That's it."

"If what you say is true," said Philippa, "that we are djinn. Then there's an easy way to prove all this."

"What would you suggest?" asked Nimrod.

Philippa shrugged. "I don't know. I mean, you're the expert here. What about making something appear or disappear?"

"And what would that prove?" asked Nimrod.

"Sure, a trick isn't a trick until it's done three times," said Mr. Rakshasas.

"It might prove that you are a djinn," said Philippa.

"Would it? And if I did make something appear, then how would you know it hadn't been there all along?"

Philippa looked carefully around the room.

"Such as?" she asked.

"A rhinoceros, perhaps," suggested Nimrod blowing out a smoke ring shaped like a rhinoceros.

"Cool trick," said John, in huge admiration.

"That's just smoke," objected Philippa. "There's not a real rhinoceros in here."

"But how can you be sure of that?" asked Nimrod.

"I'm sure," said Philippa, and nodded firmly as the smoke rhinoceros finally faded into nothing.

"But what if it was a very small rhinoceros?"

"Why then, it wouldn't be a real rhinoceros," said Philippa.

"Good answer," said Nimrod. "But as it happens, there is a rhinoceros in the room. And I can prove it."

He pointed to the other end of the room where a rhinoceros was now standing. Twelve feet long and five feet tall at the shoulder, the rhino snorted loudly through its huge nostrils and then shifted on its thick, padded feet, so that the floorboards in Nimrod's dining room creaked under the animal's two-ton weight.

"Holy mackerel," said Philippa taking a step back and, hearing her voice and sensing movement, the rhino rotated its large ears, twitched its prehensile upper lip, and then jerked its twenty-eight-inch-long horn aggressively in the air.

Nimrod grinned at his niece. "Satisfied?"

"Yes," she whispered, petrified. "Get rid of it."

"Get rid of what?"

"The rhino of course."

"What rhino?"

She looked again and saw that the rhino was gone. The sharp, animal smell that had accompanied the creature was gone, too.

"Magic," breathed John, who was terribly impressed by Nimrod's display of power.

"Magic? Good Lord, no, my boy. A djinn doesn't do magic. That stuff is for kids and simpleminded adults. A djinn works his will. That is the proper way to refer to what we do. We work our will. It is, to put the case slightly differently, mind over matter. That is all. Never call it magic. There is no magic involved. Light my lamp, next you'll be asking me if I have a rabbit and a top hat. But you see what I mean about proof. One minute it's there and the next, it isn't."

"What about Dad?" asked Philippa. "Is he a djinn, too?"

"No, your father is human," said Nimrod. "Djinn power comes only through the mother. Lots of djinn marry humans, however. Female djinn who marry humans will produce djinn children. But male djinn who marry humans will only produce human children."

"And does Dad know about this?" asked Philippa.

"Of course. Although he didn't know about it when he married your mother. She had fallen in love with him at a distance, so to speak, and resolved to find out what kind of person he was. So she played a trick on him. Not a bad trick. Just a clever little subterfuge to see if he had a kind heart. She dressed herself in rags and, pretending to be homeless, she asked your father for some change for a cup of coffee. Your father was very kindhearted, and he could see that there was something special about your mother. So he fixed her up with a home and a job. Eventually, they married and that's when Layla told him that she was a djinn. But all the great wealth he has accumulated, he has made through his own endeavors."

"How romantic," said Philippa.

"Up to a point," agreed Nimrod. "Your mother did perform him one important service as a djinn without which he wouldn't be where he is today. Two men, who were very jealous of Edward's success planned to kill him and steal his money. Layla found out about it and would have killed them both, but Edward pleaded with her to spare their lives. You see, those two men were his brothers, Alan and Neil."

"You don't mean —?" John felt his jaw drop as Nimrod exhaled not one but two smoke rings, which, momentarily at least, resembled the Gaunt family's two beloved pets.

"Layla turned them both into dogs."

"That explains a lot," said Philippa.

"Doesn't it just?" agreed John, wishing now that he had not persuaded everyone to change the names of the dogs: No wonder their names sounded so human, and no wonder his poor father had been so against changing their names to Winston and Elvis.

"Your father was so shocked at your mother's angry display of djinn power that he persuaded her to promise him never to use that power again. More important, when you two were born, Edward made Layla promise to bring you both up not as djinn, but as normal human beings. A promise that she has kept until now. And which, I regret to say, is the reason she and I have remained strangers to each other for these last ten or eleven years. Whatever your mother and father intended, they meant it to happen for the best reasons. But I always believed that the knowledge of who and what you are should not be kept from you."

Nimrod shrugged. "This was none of my business until she decided to send you to the school in Salem. You see, it takes a certain kind of concentration and focus to be a djinn. And Dr. Griggs's school offers an environment where young djinn such as yourselves can become indistinguishable from any other gifted children."

"You mean there are other parents like ours?" said John. "Who want to stop their kids from being djinn?"

"A few," said Nimrod. "In the society we live in today, conforming to what is considered normal is everything. Griggs preys on the human fear of being different."

"But how does he stop you from having power?" asked John who was already experiencing a sense of outrage that there existed a place where they might have managed to stop him from being something that looked like as much fun as a djinn.

"His Alembic technique is very simple," explained Nimrod. "He gives you so much schoolwork that your mind becomes quite diverted from the exercise, unconscious or otherwise, of your djinn powers. Worst of all, he persuades his pupils never to believe in anything that cannot be proved according to what are commonly regarded as the laws of science. This is disaster for a djinn, for to believe only in what is conventionally possible affects a young djinn mind so irrevocably that forever after it is impossible to exercise djinn power. To be able to use that power, self-belief is everything. So, when news reached me that your mother planned to send you to Griggs — I have long suspected that she would — I resolved to act."

"To be sure, it is a shame to try to make a goat's beard out of a fine stallion's tail," said Mr. Rakshasas.

"But," objected Philippa, "if a djinn cannot use its power until after the wisdom teeth have been extracted, wouldn't it just have been simpler for our mother not to have let us have the surgery? To have left the teeth in our mouths?"

"As soon as the teeth are present in your mouths," said Nimrod, "they may manifest their power in some way. In Philippa's case, by the granting of subconscious wishes." Nimrod looked at John. "Doubtless there was some way in which you, John, felt their hidden power, too."

"The crack in my bedroom wall," said John. "It came right through the headboard on my bed and seemed to originate in the pillow underneath my own cheek."

"There we are then." Nimrod raised his hands in the air as if he had proved his point. "What is more, the longer you postpone an extraction, the more dramatic, the more violent the eventual manifestation of djinn power," said Nimrod. "Your mother quite reasonably gambled that it was best to act now, while your djinn power is still immature."

Philippa thought for a moment. "Mom and Dad," she said. "They did what they did for the best of motives, right?"

"They only want the best for you," confirmed Nimrod. "As they see it, being a human being gives you a better chance of leading an ordinary, normal sort of life than comes from being a djinn."

"I'm not sure I want an ordinary normal sort of life," said Philippa. "At least not all the time. But I don't want to leave home, either. Not yet, anyway."

"Me neither," said John. "Couldn't we learn about the djinn and then go back home to New York?"

"I was going to suggest the same thing myself." Nimrod smiled and embraced both John and Philippa. "Besides, there is urgent work for us to do. Good Lord, yes! We must get cracking."

"Talking of cracking," said Philippa. "I have a question. I was wondering why the crack on John's bedroom wall should have been identical to one we saw in the newspaper."

Philippa explained how the crack on John's bedroom wall had been identical to one she had seen in a photograph of the wall of the Cairo Museum following the recent Egyptian earthquake.

Nimrod looked shocked.

"Why didn't you tell me this before?" he said.

John and Philippa shrugged. "We thought it was no more than an interesting coincidence," said John.

"Coincidence?" Nimrod laughed. "That's just a scientist's word for chance."

"The desk diary of coincidence contains too many appointments to keep itself, to be sure," nodded Mr. Rakshasas.

Nimrod shook his head. "No, this was a message intended for you. The only question is from whom."

"Who or what?" said Mr. Rakshasas. "You don't need to see the earth move to know that it has spoken."

"Precisely so," said Nimrod. "We were going to have to go to Egypt, anyway. That's what I've been trying to tell you. And this only underlines the necessity of going there as soon as possible. But I had hoped to keep your existence a secret."

"From whom?" asked Philippa.

"From our enemies."

"Is this the danger that you mentioned at the airport?" she asked.

"Did I say that? Well, yes, there may be some danger. We won't be the only djinn arriving in Egypt to look for treasures. If you remember your *Arabian Nights,* there are other tribes of djinn who, unlike us, do not much care for humankind, and mean it harm."

"The Ifrit?" said John.

"The Ifrit. Yes, boy, well remembered," said Nimrod. "They are the worst djinn of the lot. An evil wicked tribe who are our mortal enemies. It may be that we shall meet them on our trip to Egypt."

"I don't like the sound of them," admitted Philippa.

"The world is full of wicked things," sighed Mr. Rakshasas. "And if you want to avoid them, you only have to live alone with the door locked and the curtains closed."

"If we leave London tomorrow afternoon and catch the five thirty flight, we can all be in Cairo by midnight," said Nimrod.

"To be sure, Egypt is the best place for training young djinn like yourselves," said Mr. Rakshasas.

"Is it?" said John. "Why?"

"Egypt is a desert country and djinn are always at their strongest in a desert country," said Nimrod. "The djinn came out of the desert, you see." He found a taper and, relighting his cigar, puffed at it for several long seconds like an excited dragon, finally blowing a smoke ring that was shaped like the Sphinx.

"I don't know why," said John, "but now that I come to think about it, it does seem that I've always wanted to go to Egypt."

"That's the djinn in you, boy," beamed Nimrod. "That's the djinn talking."

"Well, if you'll excuse me," said Mr. Rakshasas. "'Tis time I was getting back to my bottle." And bowing gravely he left the room.

"Mr. Rakshasas suffers from agoraphobia," said Nimrod.

"That's a fear of open spaces, isn't it?" asked Philippa.

"Yes. You see Mr. Rakshasas was once trapped inside a bottle by a Ghul for a very long time indeed. So long, that now he feels nervous whenever he is outside of his bottle for too long. I mean, just think how nervous you would feel about all these people if you'd been shut away for a long time. The world gets noisier all the time."

"Poor Mr. Rakshasas," said Philippa.

"I think it will be very good for his mental health to have young djinn like you around to talk to, and ask him questions," said Nimrod. "You'll find he's a very interesting sort of djinn. Which is hardly surprising given that he's devoted so many years to the study of who and what djinn are. Books were just about the only thing that kept him going during his long incarceration. That and Irish television."

"But how can you study or watch TV if you're in a bottle?" asked John.

"Even though you're in a bottle, you still have the willpower to furnish it pretty much however you want. Radio, TV, newspapers, books, food and wine, sofas, chairs, beds, depending on the size of the lamp or the bottle. You see, a djinn entering a bottle requires that he or she step outside of three-dimensional space. Thus it's much larger inside there than you might think. It's just that you can't leave the receptacle until someone lets you out. And you can't have anyone in to visit. It's a bit like solitary confinement in a really luxurious jail. It's the solitude that gets you most. Otherwise it's really quite bearable."

"Have you ever been trapped inside a bottle?" asked John. "Against your will."

"Oh, yes. Several times. It's something of an occupational hazard for a djinn. The longest I was ever out of circulation was about six months. An accident, really. Couldn't be helped. I found myself stopped up inside an antique decanter. I'd been browsing in a lovely old antiques glass shop in Wimbledon Village, just outside London. The owner was in the back, wrapping something up, and so I thought I'd quickly pop inside one bottle just to see if it was suitable. But while I was in there, it couldn't have been for more than thirty seconds, the man who owned the shop put the glass stopper back in. It wasn't his fault. I mean, he didn't know that I was in there. There was nothing I could do until someone else bought the decanter. It was jolly expensive, so I had to sit it out until the decanter found a new home."

"What happened?"

"Mr. Groanin happened, that's what."

"You mean, he bought the bottle?"

"Actually, no. Groanin will hate me for telling you this but the fact is, he stole it. The bottle in which I was trapped."

"And you still granted him three wishes?" Philippa sounded surprised. "For stealing something?"

"I had to. There's an unwritten code among good djinn

that you should always grant three wishes to someone who frees you. But never four. A fourth wish will undo the previous three. *The Baghdad Rules.*"

"Why is that?"

"Oh, you'd best ask Mr. Rakshasas," said Nimrod. "He knows much more about *The Baghdad Rules* than I do. He's made a lifetime study of them, and believe me it would take a lifetime to know them all."

"So what did Mr. Groanin wish for?" asked John.

"Normally, it's not considered good form to say." Nimrod puffed his cigar for a moment. "But as you will have gathered from your reading of *The Arabian Nights,* it's not uncommon to grant humans three wishes and for them to waste the wishes on something useless. They'll say, 'I wish I wasn't so thirsty,' and then, when you go fetch them a glass of water, they look all hurt and cheated. Well, that's what happened with Groanin. When I first met him, ten years ago, he had only one arm, just like now. He lost the other in the British Museum. But that's another story. Anyway, instead of wishing straightaway for a new arm, which is what any sensible person would have done, he frittered away his first two wishes on something really useless. The plain fact of the matter is that now he doesn't know whether to wish for a new arm, or something else, like lots of money. And until he can make up his mind and think of his third wish, he can't afford to let me out of his sight, and I'm obliged to keep him with me. So I employ him as my servant. This is why he mumbles, too. So that I can't hear him. He's terrified he might use the word *wish* by accident, you see. And that I might grant him a third useless wish. If either of you ever hears him use the word *wish,* I'd be jolly grateful if you'd tell me, because I don't mind admitting I would like to settle this thing once and for all, so he can get on with his life, and I can employ a servant with whom I can have a decent conversation."

"Poor Mr. Groanin," said Philippa.

"Clever people wish for something intangible like talent or wisdom," said Nimrod. "A few people used to wish they were good writers. Today, however, most people go for the cash or being a movie star. Very boring. But what can you do? A wish is a wish."

CHAPTER 10

CAIRO

Arriving in Cairo late that night, they were met by Creemy, Nimrod's enormously tall Egyptian servant, whose height was increased by the presence of a red fez upon his head and who hardly seemed in need of the thick walking stick he held in one of his huge hands. Creemy clearly liked children much better than Mr. Groanin, for he never stopped smiling at them and offering the twins some of the King Fahd's Extra-Strong Mints he was particularly fond of crunching with his equally strong, extra-white teeth; and together they waited a long time for their luggage at the carousel in the baggage reclaim hall.

"Why didn't Mr. Rakshasas come with us?" asked John.

"Oh, but he is with us," said Nimrod.

"With us? Where?" John looked around and frowned. "I don't see him."

"That's because he's in a lamp inside your bag. I put him in there because my own bags were full. That's how djinn get around — in each other's luggage — when they want to save on the airfare or, as in the case of Mr. Rakshasas, they suffer from agoraphobia."

Finally, the carousel started moving and minutes later, seeing his bag, John reached to grab the handle only to find himself pushed roughly aside by Creemy who then proceeded to beat at the bag with his walking stick, which caused near panic among the other tourists waiting to collect their bags, and prompted a policeman to draw his gun.

"Hey!" yelled John. "What's the big idea?" And it was another moment or two before Creemy bent down and picked up the body of a greenish golden-brown snake, now dead, that had wrapped itself around the identically colored handle of John's leather bag.

The policeman holstered his gun and clapped Creemy on his back, as John inspected the dead snake closely. It was four or five feet long and, from the reaction of the excited crowd that quickly gathered to look and congratulate John on his narrow escape, obviously venomous.

"*Naja haje*," said Creemy.

"Good grief," said Nimrod. "If you had picked up that bag you would surely have been bitten and killed. That's an Egyptian cobra, John. The most deadly snake in Egypt."

John gulped, suddenly appreciating his narrow escape. "Thanks, Mr. Creemy," he said.

Creemy smiled, shook John's outstretched hand, and then began to collect the other suitcases off the carousel, which was easy with most of the other people arriving from London now proving a little reluctant to pick up their bags just in case there was a snake attached to another suitcase handle.

"This whole country is alive with pests," muttered Groanin. "And I don't just mean the snakes and the bugs. If you touch anything hereabouts, wash your hands with antiseptic soap, that's my advice."

"I don't think that was an accident," said Nimrod as they went outside and waited for Creemy to fetch the car. "Egyptian cobras are shy creatures, at least until they're provoked. A luggage carousel is not somewhere I would ever expect to find one."

"Are you saying that someone deliberately put it there?" said John, smiling nervously. "Intending for me to be killed?"

"If you remember, that's the bag containing Mr. Rakshasas's lamp," explained Nimrod. "His presence must have been detected when the bag was being transferred from the plane. So, it's my fault. But look here, if that makes you feel at all uncomfortable, we'll go straight to the American Airlines ticketing desk and get you booked on the next available flight to New York."

John thought for a moment. "No," he said bravely. "You said this might be dangerous, after all. Besides, I haven't seen the pyramids."

But the evening's dangers were still not over; ten minutes after leaving the airport, in an old white Cadillac Eldorado, Creemy announced that they were being followed.

"Black Mercedes, boss," he said, glancing in the rearview mirror.

Instinctively the twins glanced back and sure enough, a large black Mercedes was driving along the highway about thirty or forty yards behind them, and at exactly the same speed.

"Can you lose them?"

Creemy grinned. "This is Cairo, boss. You watch."

A few miles farther on, Creemy hit the gas, turned off the highway, and drove down one side street, then another, until they were in an area that was full of old shops and crowds of people. "This old bazaar, boss," said Creemy, driving down a narrow alley and then through an ancient-looking passageway. "Many old streets. Even traffic police get lost here. But old Creemy, he knows Cairo like the back of his hand. No problem."

The car sped around one corner, throwing the twins onto Nimrod's lap, and then another; and pedestrians scattered on a moonlit square as the Cadillac raced through a series of red lights. Nimrod glanced back through the rear window and saw the black Mercedes remained on their tail.

"They're still with us," he told Creemy.

"I see him." Creemy grinned and, racing up a hill, he turned sharply into a hotel parking lot. Pulling into a space between two buses, he quickly turned off the lights and the engine. A moment or two later, the Mercedes raced past, and they all breathed a sigh of relief.

"Good work, Creemy," said Nimrod.

"Was it the Ifrit?" asked Philippa.

But Nimrod did not answer her. "Take us home, Creemy," he said, and relit his cigar.

In a part of Cairo known as Garden City, Nimrod's house was more of a palace than a house, with beautifully kept green lawns, lush palm trees, and great white walls. Inside the cool interior, the marble floors were covered with Persian rugs, and everywhere there were more Egyptian antiquities so the house felt even more like a museum than their father's house in New York. But the most unusual thing about the house was what Nimrod called the Tuchemeter Room wherein a large, round clocklike instrument hung on a wall facing an ornate-looking chair, which, when he wasn't driving the Cadillac or cooking in the kitchen, was occupied by Creemy, or sometimes Nimrod himself. Closer inspection revealed that the clock, which was made of gold and was about six feet in diameter and had one hand, was not a clock at all; three words were painted in large letters on the tuchemeter's silver face: GOOD, BAD, and HOMEOSTASIS. The single hand, shaped like a muscular arm with a human index finger extended, was pointing very slightly to the left of the word HOMEOSTASIS so that it was entering the segment labeled BAD.

"It's a tuchemeter," explained Nimrod proudly as he showed them around the room. "This measures the luck in the world, all of it, good or bad. It's an exact replica of a larger one in Berlin owned by the Blue Djinn of Babylon, which records the official amount of luck around the globe, the so-called BML — Berlin Meridian Luck. I have a smaller one back at my house in London."

"Can you really measure all the luck in the world?" asked John.

"As easily as you might measure weather with a barometer," said Nimrod. "The laws of physics in the universe rule out the possibility of things just happening. Nothing is a matter of pure chance. When the universe was created, man was given dominion over the earth, and the angels over the heavens, and the djinn over the interaction between the two, which some men have called fate. Fate often seems like a matter of pure chance. But it isn't, of course. It's luck and it's controlled by the djinn. Good luck is influenced by the three good tribes of the djinn. And bad luck by the evil tribes. There exists a perpetual struggle between the two. A very fine balance, which we call the 'homeostasis.'

"This tuchemeter, of which Creemy is the unofficial guardian, enables me to see if the evil tribes, of which the worst are the Ifrit, are generating enough bad luck to require our intervention."

"Like giving someone three wishes?" asked John, who was eager to do just that.

"Exactly so," said Nimrod. For a moment he looked concerned. "Ever since the earthquake, the hand has been pointing to the left of the homeostasis, which concerns me greatly and leads me to suspect that the Ifrit are up to something. Very probably it was them who tried to follow us from the airport and who put the snake on the handle of John's bag." He glanced at his watch and shook his head. "But time is getting on, and I wanted to show you something of the city before bed. Although perhaps it might be better if we chose a less conspicuous means of transport."

Nimrod had Creemy summon a horse-drawn carriage called a ghari and, although it was now very late, the three of them went for a drive through the still-busy, bustling heart of Cairo. Even though it was past one o'clock in the morning, many of the shops were open, selling things the twins had never seen before, and there was little or no sign of any obvious earthquake damage.

"It's cooler to go shopping at this time," explained Nimrod.

Philippa had never seen so many people or, indeed, quite so many cars and said as much to Nimrod.

"Twenty million people live in Cairo," explained Nimrod. "It's a very poor place, but somehow they all manage to walk around with a smile on their faces."

"Just like Creemy," said John.

"His real name is Karim," said Nimrod. "But I've always thought that Creemy seemed more suitable. He never stops smiling. Just like a cat that's had the cream."

Nimrod lit a cigar and waved it at the surrounding streets. "So," he said. "What do you think of Cairo?" It was clear from his tone that Nimrod thought very highly of the city. "Do you like it?"

"Yes," said Philippa, her nose wrinkling a little as the carriage passed through a very crowded bazaar. For a moment, they were almost swamped by people climbing in and trying to sell them something until they heard Nimrod's telling them in his flawless Arabic to push off, and the driver cracked his whip to pick up some speed and make a getaway. "Only it smells a little funny," she added.

"Everyone says that when they first come here. Open sewage. You'll soon get used to it."

"I didn't mean that. Well, perhaps just a bit. Some parts smell worse than others. What I really mean is that it smells peculiar. As if it's very old. Like people have been living here for a very long time. There's a smell you get in a crowded part of downtown New York, on a really hot day. Well, this city smells like that, only times a hundred."

John nodded. "Yes, that's what I think. But I also have this weird feeling that I've been here before. That somehow I'm at home."

"Yes, you're right," admitted Philippa. "But it's more than that, I think. Ever since we arrived here I've had the sense that we were being watched."

"Excellent," said Nimrod. "Of course, in one sense you are at home, John. And Philippa? There are more djinn in Cairo than almost anywhere, with the possible exception of Istanbul. You can probably feel them."

"Does this mean we're Arabs?" asked John.

"Good Lord, no," said Nimrod. "Arabs are a race of humans. We are djinn. The djinn are quite different from any human race. Mr. Rakshasas will tell you all about these tribes, tomorrow, if you wish."

"Right now, I just wish that the driver of this carriage would stop using his whip on that poor horse," said Philippa, flinching as the Egyptian cracked his whip in the air.

Nimrod chuckled. "Your wish is my command, young mistress," he said and, closing his eyes, he muttered something under his breath. The next second the horse broke into a gallop, pulling the ghari along at such a speed that they began to overtake cars and buses. The driver yelled something in Arabic but the horse refused to pull up, its hooves clattering loudly on the greasy road. "Time we were getting home, anyway," said Nimrod coolly. "It's much later than I anticipated."

"This is not what I meant," shouted Philippa, grabbing on to the side of the ghari as they careered around a corner.

"What do you mean?" laughed Nimrod. "The driver's stopped using the whip, hasn't he?"

"That's only because he doesn't dare use it in case the horse goes any faster," said Philippa. As the ghari bounced over a large hole in the road, she screamed with fright.

"Exhilarating, isn't it?" said Nimrod. "Nothing like a horse-and-carriage ride in Cairo on a warm summer's evening."

They reached the outskirts of Garden City and a minute or so later, the horse stopped, unbidden, right outside Nimrod's house. The three djinn got down from the carriage. So did the driver who was looking alarmed not only at the speed of the horse, but also that it should have found its own way back without any help from him. Nimrod clapped the horse enthusiastically on the shoulder to show the man that he was not cross and gave him an extra-large tip, just in case he had been inclined to punish the horse later on.

"We could have been killed," said Philippa scolding him when they were back in the house.

"Oh, I don't think we were ever in any real danger." Nimrod smiled. "But perhaps now you see what I mean about wishes. They can be unpredictable. You never know how things are going to turn out. You wanted the driver to stop using his whip, and so he did. You just didn't like the reason *why* he stopped using his whip. It's an important lesson for any young djinn to learn. When you play around with the future, there is a random, unexpected, even unpleasant aspect to what you're doing. The trouble is we live in a very complicated world. Small variations in initial conditions can already result in dynamic transformations in the concluding event. And large variations, of the kind brought about by a djinn granting a wish, can result in enormously dynamic transformations in the concluding event."

"Er . . . yes," said John, glancing nervously at Philippa in the hope that she wouldn't appear to understand any of this better than he did. Catching his eye, she shrugged back at him.

Nimrod ushered them into the drawing room where Creemy had prepared some hot drinks for their return. "The djinn have a proverb, which goes: 'A wish is a dish, that's a lot like a fish — once it has been eaten it's harder to throw back.'" Nimrod paused. "Perhaps it does lose something in the translation from the original Arabic. But all it means is that anyone should be careful what he or she wishes for in case the wish comes true, but in a way he or she could never have foreseen."

John yawned loudly.

"Well, I think you get the general idea."

"Yes," said Philippa. "I think so."

John made a face in his sister's direction. It was typical of her to pretend that she understood something even when she didn't.

"That's enough excitement for one evening," said Nimrod. "Don't you agree? I think it's time we were all going to bed."

And so, with their legs still feeling a little like jelly after their carriage ride, the twins retired to their rooms, which were as large and handsomely appointed as anything they had pictured in *The Arabian Nights* of the Princess Scheherazade and, upon going to bed, they went immediately to sleep.

CHAPTER 11

ALMOST IN THE SHAPE OF A CAMEL

Late the next morning, Creemy announced that Nimrod had a visitor. It was Mrs. Coeur de Lapin, the wife of the French Ambassador to Egypt, who lived in the house next door. Mrs. Coeur de Lapin was a tall, very elegant-looking woman with flawless skin and the profile of an empress, which is to say her long thin nose was so often in the air that she seemed almost to look down on people as she spoke. This was just her manner, and she was not at all unfriendly, for a Frenchwoman. She greeted Nimrod like a long-lost cousin, gushing over him for several minutes like Niagara Falls and it was several more minutes before, eventually, she came to the point.

"I heard the sound of children in the garden," she said in her mellifluous voice. "And I thought that I must come visit you right away. In case there was anything that I could do to make your stay in Cairo more enjoyable."

Mrs. Coeur de Lapin wore a long, thin purple dress, a green scarf around her swanlike neck, and around a haystack of blond hair, a black-and-greenish-gold headband that gave her a distinctly Bohemian air, as if she might have been a fortune-teller or a palm reader instead of the ambassador's wife.

"That is very kind of you Mrs. Coeur de Lapin," said Nimrod, who was clearly very taken with her. At least Philippa thought so; the way Nimrod fiddled nervously with his tie as he spoke to Mrs. Coeur de Lapin — almost as if he had been playing with a clarinet — was the same thing that other men did when they spoke to her mother.

"It's so nice to have children in the neighborhood," she said, smiling warmly at the twins. "My own children are all grown up and living in France, so my house feels very quiet without them. Perhaps you might come next door sometime. We have such a beautiful garden. While I am here in Cairo, I am just like the English. I live for my garden."

"Well, it's very kind of you," said Nimrod, "but we are going to be very busy while we're here in Cairo."

"We could have a picnic," said Mrs. Coeur de Lapin, ignoring Nimrod's objections. "Tomorrow, perhaps. Would you like that, children?"

"Yes," said John, who liked picnics very much. "Very much."

"Then that is settled," declared the Frenchwoman.

"Very kind of you," said Nimrod, now playing a spirited solo on his tie. "I'm sure."

"No," she pouted, stroking John's hair. "I am being selfish. I love children." Mrs. Coeur de Lapin gave a little sigh. "For many years they were my whole life. Such handsome children, too. Nimrod, you did not tell me that you were uncle to such a good-looking boy and girl. They remind me of my own children."

After Mrs. Coeur de Lapin had gone, Philippa asked Nimrod why he had seemed unwilling to accept her hospitality.

"We're not here on a holiday, you know," said Nimrod. "There is much to be done. Much you don't yet know about. We must commence your training. But before I can do that, there is your initiation to take care of. Your Tammuz."

"An initiation?" said John. "I'm not sure I like the sound of that."

"Thousands of years ago," explained Nimrod, "one of our ancestors was a king, also named Nimrod, most famous for building the Tower of Babel. He was quite a chap, this Nimrod, and lived to a good old age. Very soon after his death, and before she could mourn Nimrod, his queen, Semiramis, gave birth to a son whom she named Tammuz. As soon as she was well enough, Semiramis went into the desert to fast for forty days and forty nights to mourn her husband. During which time it came to her in a revelation that Tammuz was actually Nimrod reborn.

"Today, all young djinn of our tribe observe the rite of Tammuz, which commemorates this rebirth and marks their passage into adulthood. No one can be a djinn and use djinn power before he or she has fasted in the desert. For from the desert you came and until you feel the heat of the desert burn into your bones, you cannot understand the djinn flame that burns inside of you."

"Wait a minute," said Philippa. "Are you saying we have to spend forty days and forty nights alone in the desert?"

"It's not forty days," Nimrod said awkwardly. "Nothing like. In fact, it's hardly any time at all."

"How long?" John asked suspiciously.

"One night," said Nimrod. "Dusk until dawn."

"On our own?" exclaimed Philippa.

"In the dark? With no food and water?"

"You do want to become djinn, don't you?" said Nimrod. "With the power to grant three wishes. And things like that? Or do you want to be ordinary?"

"Of course, we want to be djinn," said John.

"Really there's nothing to it," said Nimrod. "There's rather a nice bit of desert I know near the pyramids where you'll be quite comfortable."

"When?" asked Philippa.

"The sooner the better, eh? I was thinking tonight might be best."

John and Philippa said nothing for a moment.

"Why don't we take a trip out there now, in daylight, so that you can take a look at this place and get used to the idea? See the pyramids, too."

Nimrod had Creemy drive them out to Giza, which is a

village near the pyramids. Along the way, the car made several brief stops at antiques shops and small museums where they would get out of the car, and Nimrod would make inquiries about the earthquake and what might have been uncovered, as if he were searching for something in particular.

John and Philippa wondered what it might be.

Finally, the car stopped on a quiet, dusty-looking street, and Nimrod led the twins through the door of an anonymous-looking little perfume shop that stood between a stable and a fruit-and-vegetable market. To the twins, it seemed a curious place to sell perfume. Just as curious was why Nimrod should have wanted to go inside the shop, at least until they saw a glass case containing several antique glass bottles and ancient Roman oil lamps. A man wearing a long white shirt bowed very gravely to his three visitors and then kissed Nimrod's hand respectfully.

For a moment, the two men spoke in French and then Arabic before Nimrod turned to the children.

"This is Huamai," he said. "Huamai, this is my niece, Philippa, and my nephew, John."

Huamai bowed to the children. "You do me great honor," he said. "To bring the young ones here like this."

Nimrod patted Huamai on the shoulder. "Not at all, old friend. Tell me, Huamai, is your son, Toeragh, here? I should like to rent the three white camels."

"Please to wait in here," said Huamai. He showed Nimrod and the twins into a small, glass-walled room, and pointed to a set of scatter cushions on the floor where they might sit for a while. "I will tell him immediately." Then he bowed once again and left them alone.

"Huamai is a great perfumer," explained Nimrod. "One of the greatest. After our camel ride, we will come back here and try a few, and then perhaps you will understand how it was that Delilah was able to enslave Samson, Sheba to bewitch King Solomon, and Cleopatra to charm Mark Antony."

"Not me," said John. "You won't catch me wearing perfume. That stuff is for girls."

Nimrod smiled quietly. "We shall see." He stood up as Huamai put his head around the door of the room and bowed again. "Come on. Our camels are ready."

The children followed Nimrod through the sweet-smelling shop to a small yard at the back where, hitched to a post, knelt three white camels and, sitting on them, laden with cameras, bottles of water, and guidebooks, three American tourists for whose descriptions the word *large* hardly seemed large enough; each of them looked like a pile of enormous bagels heaped one on top of the other.

"A camel provides the best method of going around the pyramids," said Nimrod. "For one thing, it's quite a walk. And, for another, it's the only way not to be endlessly pestered by all the locals trying to sell you something you don't want."

A young smiling man with a mustache and a camel whip ran toward Nimrod and bowed.

"This is Toeragh," said Nimrod and began to speak to the

young man in Arabic. After a minute or two of negotiation, Nimrod handed Toeragh some greasy-looking banknotes called piastres, and then turned to the children.

"It's all fixed. These three camels are ours for as long as we require them."

Even as he spoke, the three camels stood up, braying loudly, their riders squealing with a combination of alarm and delight.

"But surely these camels are taken," protested John. "Look." He pointed at the tourists who were already taking pictures of one another. "They've got riders."

"No, no, no," said Nimrod. "You misunderstand. We're not going to *ride* the camels. There's not much fun in that. Jolly uncomfortable if you ask me, with that great hump in the middle of them. No, we're going to *be* the camels. Now that's a much more interesting proposition, don't you think?"

"What?" exclaimed Philippa. "But I don't want to be a camel. They're so gross." Her disgust at the idea of being a camel increased rapidly as one of the camels started to pee on the ground.

"Nonsense," said Nimrod. "These are very beautiful camels. The best in Cairo. What is more, the camel is a very important animal to our tribe of djinn. The Marid have been turning themselves into camels for thousands of years. Besides, this sort of experience is going to be useful to you when you're djinn."

"But how?" said John, who was no keener on the idea of

being a camel than his sister. "How is it going to be useful to us? We live in New York. A cat, or a dog, or even a horse, I could understand. But not a camel."

"Especially one that's peeing," said Philippa, holding her nose. "When is it going to stop?"

"I haven't got time for arguments," said Nimrod. "They'll be off in a minute. Look here, I've been a camel, your mother's been a camel, and your grandmother was a camel. And it's only for a couple of hours."

Philippa was already walking back to the perfumer's shop. "No way, José," she said as Nimrod raised his hands in the air. "I'm not going to be some lousy camel."

"Me, neither," said John, only his words came out as an enormous camel-sized burp, for he already had the hump.

Philippa burped back at him, for she, too, was now a camel.

Don't talk, just think, Nimrod seemed to be saying in her head. *If you try to talk in the usual way, it'll just come out as a belch.*

John burped loudly, several times, as did Philippa who was horrified. To her knowledge she had never burped before.

This is so gross, she thought unhappily.

That's better, thought Nimrod.

I can hear your thoughts, observed Philippa.

Of course. Did you think camels can speak?

Toeragh tugged on Nimrod's bridle, and he began to walk. John and Philippa, attached to Nimrod's saddle by a length of rope, had little choice but to follow. They walked awhile and, turning a corner, saw the pyramids for the first time.

There, declared Nimrod. *What do you think of that?*

Wow, thought Philippa. For a while she forgot about the man on her back and stopped listening to his chatter. It wasn't very long before she had given herself up to the whole experience of enjoying the pyramids, albeit as a camel; indeed, within half an hour of setting out from Huamai's perfume shop, being a camel began to seem like the most natural thing in the world. She was enjoying herself, although she hardly felt like admitting as much to Nimrod.

Being Philippa's twin, John of course was thinking exactly the same thoughts as his sister. There were, he reflected, some distinct advantages to walking around the pyramids in the shape of a camel. Even with the woman on his back, who clearly knew nothing about camels, so incompetently did she occupy her saddle, it was very little effort to walk around the site. What was more, he felt incredibly strong, as if he could easily have carried two tourists, perhaps for thirty or forty miles. There was no doubt about it in John's mind: In Egypt at least, being a camel had its good points.

Couldn't we spend an initiation night in the desert as camels? he thought.

Sadly, no, answered Nimrod. *It has to be in your normal human shapes. But I'm very glad you've taken so well to the whole experience of being animals. Just as well, since taking the shape of some kind of animal is crucial in the development of your own djinn power. You can become almost any animal you choose, although, with the exception of the camel, for only a limited period of time. A camel is a creature that we Marid can occupy indefinitely.*

They had ridden a mile or so farther south, beyond the smallest of the Giza pyramids, to an arc of isolated desert called Abu Sir, where Nimrod explained that two pyramids still lay buried under the sand. *This is the bit of desert I was telling you about,* explained Nimrod. *Where I'm going to bring you tonight. For your initiation ordeal.*

John belched loudly, as if to indicate his lack of enthusiasm for the whole enterprise.

"Why did we come here?" asked one of the tourists. "There's nothing to see. Let's go back."

"How do you make this stupid animal go faster?" complained her husband, untying the rope attached to the other two camels, and kicking Philippa on the side.

Philippa broke into a fast trot, which the tourist seemed to enjoy, and then a gallop, which he did not. Burping loudly with excitement, Philippa raced back toward Giza, chased by Toeragh on foot, and the other two camels until, clearly fearing for his life, the man leaped from Philippa's saddle and fell, without harm, into a sand dune. Philippa slowed her gallop to a trot, and then turned to spit on the ground near her fallen rider.

That will teach him to kick me, she thought happily.

Back at the perfume shop, when the tourists had left, Nimrod transformed himself and the twins back into their human shapes and right away John noticed something unpleasant about himself.

"Ugh," he said. "I smell revolting."

"We all stink," said Nimrod. "That's the thing about animal transformation. The smell and sometimes the taste can linger a little after one takes on human shape again. It's one of the reasons why Huamai runs the perfume shop together with the camel hire. So that djinn like us who have an urgent need to smell good again can do so."

They went inside the shop where Huamai was waiting to sell them a bottle of his finest scent — Air d'Onajeestringh.

"Do you still think that perfume is for girls?" chuckled Nimrod taking the bottle from Huamai's hand.

"I suppose anything is better than smelling like a camel," grumbled John dabbing some perfume behind his ears and on his chest reluctantly. "Even smelling like a girl."

"Listen to him," remarked Nimrod. "How like Groanin he sounds."

"Speaking of Mr. Groanin," said Philippa, "where is he? I don't think I saw him this morning."

"Is he feeling disgruntled about something?" asked John.

"No," said Nimrod. "But he is very far from being gruntled. Groanin hates Egypt, poor fellow. He prefers to stay in his room and watch TV or read *The Daily Telegraph* or his poetry. He can't stand the heat, can't stand the food, can't stand the flies, and can't stand the people. The chances are you'll scarcely see him at all until it's time for us to go back to London."

"It beats me why you brought him," said John.

"Because, my dear nephew, I can be without butter, but I cannot be without a butler. Who would polish the silver? Who would fold my linen? Who would bring me tea and run my bath? Above all, who would answer the front door and tell all and sundry that I am not at home to those who would sell me something I don't want to buy? Mr. Groanin is my interface with the world."

"Perhaps he could come with us tonight," Philippa said pointedly. "In case anyone tries to sell us anything."

CHAPTER 12

HOW THE DJINN CAME TO BE

That evening, just before dusk, Nimrod had Creemy drive the four of them out into the desert just south of the pyramids for the twins' initiation ordeal and, arriving at the place he had shown them earlier that same day, he and Creemy opened the trunk and took out a ground cloth, an English dictionary, two pads of paper and two pencils, a couple of sleeping bags, a box of matches, and an old bronze oil lamp with a handle that was shaped to look like a bent old man.

"Everything you need," declared Nimrod.

"But there's no food," said John.

"What kind of a fast would it be if we'd brought food?" asked Nimrod.

"Haven't you got a flashlight?" asked Philippa eyeing her surroundings and then the negligible equipment uncertainly. "It's going to be very dark soon and that lamp doesn't look as though it could illuminate a birthday cake."

Nimrod looked horrified. "You don't have a Tammuz with a flashlight," he said. "You are not burglars, but djinn, and from a very distinguished family of djinn, too. Try to remember that. The whole point of the initiation ordeal is that you spend a night in the wilderness with the flame for company. Oil lamps have a very special place for us." He tutted loudly and shook his head. "A flashlight. The very idea."

"We're not used to the dark, that's all," said John nervously. "All the light pollution in New York means that it's never really very dark there at all. Not like it gets dark here in Egypt."

"This is a Byzantine lamp of the seventh century A.D.," said Nimrod. "And I can assure you it will be quite adequate for your needs."

"But what are we going to do all night?" asked Philippa.

"Try to get some sleep," said Nimrod. "That's what people normally do at night. I do recommend you use the sleeping bags, as it gets quite cold after dark. If you get bored, then you might like to play a word game with the dictionary. Or perhaps give that antique lamp a bit of a polish. I was thinking on the way here that it's looking a bit dull."

Creemy was already back in the Cadillac and starting the engine. "We'll be back at dawn," said Nimrod, climbing into the backseat.

"But what if something happens to us?" asked John.

"No one knows you're out here except me and Creemy. What could possibly happen to you? Anyway, you're djinn.

It's other people who ought to be afraid of you." Nimrod closed the car door and then lowered the window. "By the way, if you should see some strange lights above the pyramids and a pompous-sounding voice in the sky, don't worry. That will be the *son et lumière* at the pyramids. The sound-and-light show for the tourists. From here you'll hear every word, I should think. Who knows? You might even learn something."

Nimrod tapped Creemy on the shoulder and then the car was gone in a cloud of grit and dust like a great white chariot leaving the twins alone in the now swiftly lowering darkness at Abu Sir.

John was quite sure he could hear his own heart beating. "I wish Neil and Alan were here," he said. "I mean, Winston and Elvis."

"Me, too," admitted Philippa. "I don't think I've ever been so scared as I am now."

"I suppose that's the point," said John. "This wouldn't be much of an ordeal if it were just a walk in the park."

A warm breeze seemed to tease them for a moment, caressing their faces and stirring their hair.

"I hope this is worth it," said Philippa.

"I suppose it will be, if we end up with djinn powers like Nimrod," said John.

Soon after Nimrod had gone they heard some corny music and a laser beam pierced the sky as the sound-and-light show started at the pyramids, about a mile to the north. And for a while at least they were too interested in what was happening above their heads to pay much attention to the darkness. But when at last the show ended, Philippa found herself shivering with a mixture of cold and fright.

"It gets dark very quickly, doesn't it?" she said, and swallowing uncomfortably in the moonlight, climbed into her sleeping bag in the hope that it would shield her from whatever might be lurking out in the desert. "Shouldn't we light that lamp now?"

John picked up the matchbox and then the lamp, which he weighed in his hands. "That's odd," he said. "The darned thing won't light."

"Don't fool around, John. This isn't funny."

"No, really, I'm not kidding." He handed her the lamp and the matches. "Here, you try."

Philippa took the lamp and the matches and tried to light the lamp with no more success than her brother; until, having lit one of their last five matches, she inspected the lamp more closely. "No wonder we can't light the thing," she said. "There's no thingamajig to light. This stupid lamp doesn't have a wick." Nervously, Philippa began to polish the lamp with her sleeve.

"At least there's a full moon," said John, trying to improve his sister's gloomy frame of mind. Without striking another match, he could hardly see where she was. "And will you look at that sky? So many stars. Some of them so close you could almost touch them. Look at that one. Just above the horizon. Seems as if it's just a few hundred yards away. It's like I was telling Nimrod. You never see a decent night sky in New York."

Philippa stopped rubbing the lamp and glanced up. She

was just about to agree with her brother in the hope that it might take his mind off their unfortunate predicament when the lamp in her hand gave a jolt and then seemed to take off. She cried out with fright, convinced that someone had snatched the lamp from her hands and, still inside the sleeping bag, she jumped to her feet and hopped toward her brother, feeling a little like a giant caterpillar. "John," she said. "Something happened to the lamp."

Even as she spoke, a thick, luminescent smoke came out of the empty wick of the lamp, mounting into the sky high above their heads with unnatural speed and forming a huge cloud that seemed to hover over them as if threatening somehow, in the desert, to rain on them and them alone. At the same time they became aware of the curiously strong odor of what smelled like poster paint, as if someone had tried to paint the smoke with a brush.

"I don't like this," said Philippa. "I don't like this at all."

When the smoke was all out of the ancient lamp, it reunited itself and became a solid body that formed a human silhouette twice as tall as the largest giant either of them could ever have imagined, but which gradually subsided and shrank until the normal shape of the djinn became recognizable.

"Mr. Rakshasas," said the twins, breathing a loud sigh of relief. "Thank goodness it's you."

"And a very good evening to you both," he said with his Irish accent that was so fine it sounded almost theatrical.

"You gave us quite a fright." Philippa laughed when she had recovered her breath.

"Is this part of the Tammuz?" asked John.

"That it is, young djinn," said the old one. "That it is. I wondered how long it would take you to work it out, with the rubbing of the lamp, so I did. You didn't really think your uncle would leave you out here by yourselves, did you?" He sighed. "Well, perhaps you did at that. I was sure that as soon as Nimrod gave you the old lamp you would remember the story of Aladdin, from *The Arabian Nights,* but it seems that I might have been wrong. The important thing is that you felt as if you had been abandoned in the desert, which is really all that counts for the Tammuz. That and a little instruction from yours truly. In my temporary capacity as the ceremonial head of the Marid."

"I thought Nimrod was head of our tribe," said Philippa.

"Strictly speaking, your mother is the head of the Marid," said Mr. Rakshasas. "But since she has forsworn the use of all djinn power, Nimrod has charge of the day-to-day running of Marid affairs. However, he has urgent business tonight and has entrusted me with the formal initiation of your good selves."

As before, Mr. Rakshasas was wearing a white turban and a white frock coat that matched his neat white beard. He was holding another oil lamp in his hand, only this one was actually burning and gave off a strong light that illuminated the desert for several yards around them. The twins had not set eyes on him since leaving London and gradually their fear and surprise turned to pleasure, for it was the first time they had seen a djinn appear from inside a lamp.

"What's going to happen to us now?" asked John.

"The worst of your ordeal is over," said Mr. Rakshasas. "Unless you count listening to an old fellow talk to be the worst that could happen to you. Your uncle Nimrod, a very great djinn whom I am honored to call my friend, has asked me to tell you the story of how the djinn came to be. But I must ask you to pay close attention, for there are matters of grave importance relating to this story. And to be sure, it is imperative that your understanding should be as great as your significance in the scheme of things."

Mr. Rakshasas's voice became a little sterner and a little louder as he continued to speak, so that the twins began to suspect that he might not have been as shy and retiring as Nimrod had led them to suppose.

"At the beginning of the earth, there were but two powers in the world, and only three kinds of creatures that could tell the difference between them. These were Good and Evil, and only angels, djinn, and men knew them apart.

"The djinn existed halfway between men and angels and, made of a subtle kind of fire, they had the power of putting on more or less any form that they pleased. Because of the powers they commanded over luck, some men worshipped these djinn as demigods, while other men who worshipped only one God were made very angry by this. Gradually, however, a Great Choice was forced upon angels, djinn, and men alike: to choose between Good and Evil. It was called the Great Choice. The angels who chose Evil were few in number but their names are too powerful to mention lightly.

Men were the most numerous of the earth's creatures, and while some chose Good, more than a few chose Evil. With so many of them, precise figures are lacking. Things were different in the case of the djinn, however, who, being just six tribes, and fewer than men, were easier to account for in the matter of this great choice. Three tribes — the Marid, the Jinn, and the Jann — chose Good. And three tribes — the Ifrit, the Shaitan, and the Ghul — chose Evil.

"In retrospect, it is unfortunate that the good tribes of djinn had decided war to be one of the great Evils and, consequently, they did not fight for Good as they might have done. Many battles were fought by men and djinn about this Great Choice, and the evil tribes did some terrible things, not just to other djinn but also to men. Which is why, along the way, men decided to treat all djinn as wicked. Some good djinn were slain. Others fled for a quieter, albeit less powerful life in cooler climates. This weakened their power but ensured their survival in the long run and gradually, over hundreds of years, a balance of power was achieved between Good and Evil. But in a very real sense that war is still being fought today."

"Then we're at war with the Ifrit?" said John.

"A sort of war, yes. A cold war if you like, but a war right enough," admitted Mr. Rakshasas.

"How is it that we don't hear more about this?" asked Philippa.

"Because today, most men believe that the djinn no longer exist, which suits our purposes very well. Others, who call themselves wise men, or magicians, have learned to bind a djinn to their service. Some of them even have djinn blood. For all these reasons, wise djinn have learned to be careful about how and when humans shall know their true nature."

"So what do these Ifrit look like?" asked Philippa.

"Good question, child. Yes, you must learn to know the different tribes of djinn, the different kinds of djinn, if it is a friend or a foe and, if a foe, how then it may be combated. To this end I have enlisted the help of a system of djinn cards, which I shall give to you now." So saying, Mr. Rakshasas delved into his coat pockets and took out two large packs of cards which he presented — one each — to John and Philippa.

On each card was the name of a djinn, its tribe, its preferred animal shape, and its various strengths and weaknesses.

John looked at at the pack of cards. "These are really cool," he said.

"John. Do you think you could manage to stop using that word?" said Mr. Rakshasas. "*Cool* is not a word with which any self-respecting djinn can feel at all comfortable. We djinn are made of a very subtle kind of fire. And there's nothing cool about that, I can assure you."

"What does that mean?" asked Philippa. "A subtle kind of fire? Fire is fire, isn't it?"

"To a man from Cork, perhaps," said Mr. Rakshasas. "But look, you've heard that the Eskimos have eighteen different words for snow? 'Tis a fact that we djinn have twenty-seven different words for fire, not including the dozen or so words in the English language. Most of these words relate to what we call the Primordial Fire, which is hot fire, or fire by friction. But there is also the subtle fire that burns within all djinn, good or evil. Men call this their souls, although these have little practical use, unlike the subtle flame that is contained within you two. All djinn power relates to this subtle fire. It is what gives you the power of mind over matter. This is the power that humans would dearly like to have themselves."

"But how?" demanded John. "How do we do it? What do we have to do to exercise our power? Think 'wonderful thoughts' like in *Peter Pan*?"

"All you have to do is learn to focus the firepower within you on whatever it is that you want to get done. And the best way to do that is to think of a word, one word, that you will only use in association with the exercise of your own djinn power. This is the principal reason for this night. To help you find the space and solitude to look within yourselves, to meditate and arrive at a word that will help you focus your power."

"You mean like a magic word?" said Philippa.

Mr. Rakshasas winced. "We djinn prefer to call this word a *focus word*. But it's true that this is how magic words get started among humans. They hear some careless djinn using his focus word and then, having seen the result, think it might work for them in the same way. That's how SESAME got started. There's nothing special about sesame. It's merely a widely cultivated East Indian plant, but some djinn thought it might make a good focus word and, before he knew where he was, it got picked up and used by the human who wrote *The Arabian Nights* stories."

"So all we have to do," said Philippa, "is think of an appropriate focus word and we'll be able to start doing tricks."

"Tricks?" Mr. Rakshasas made a face. "Tricks are not for djinn. When I said firepower I meant it. People can get hurt. That's why you're out here in the middle of nowhere. To learn to use that firepower responsibly."

"Yes, Mr. Rakshasas," said Philippa. "I'm sorry."

"Your focus word is like a magnifying glass. You've seen the way that such a glass can focus the power of the sun onto a very small spot in the middle of a sheet of paper so that it burns? A focus word works in the same way. What you have to do is choose a word that's hardly likely to crop up in normal conversation. That's how ABRACADABRA got started. And pretty much all the others."

"What's your focus word?" asked Philippa.

"Mine? It's SESQUIPEDALIAN. 'Tis said it was a word invented by the Roman poet Horace for a word that's very long. And Nimrod's is QWERTYUIOP. Those are the first ten letters on a typewriter keyboard. Both of those words are impossible to forget and equally almost impossible to use in normal conversation."

"Yes," agreed Philippa. "They are very good focus words. I won't be able to think of anything that's as good as them."

"There's no rush," advised Mr. Rakshasas. "And really, you ought to give it quite a bit of thought. That's the point of being out here in the desert. After all, a focus word has to last you a good long while."

"How about BILTONG?" asked Philippa. "It's a sort of dried antelope meat from South Africa. I won't ever want to go in a shop and order that. It's disgusting."

"I know what it is," said Mr. Rakshasas. "But I don't advise that you choose a word that's quite so short, either. To be sure, I've known cases of djinn who muttered their focus words in their sleep with disastrous results. But I've never heard of anyone who was asleep who ever said, for example, the word FLOCCINAUCINHILIPILIFICATION."

"I don't think I could *ever* say a word like that," said John. "Especially when I was awake."

"What does it mean, anyway?" asked Philippa.

"FLOCCINAUCINHILIPILIFICATION? It means the estimation of a thing as worthless. Which makes it more or less perfect as a good focus word because no one could ever utter a word as complicated as FLOCCINAUCINHILIPILI-FICATION in any normal conversation."

Mr. Rakshasas put his lamp on the ground and got the dictionary, the two pads of paper, and the two pencils that Creemy had left there. "If you require inspiration, then I suggest you use the dictionary for some help. Jot some ideas down before you go to sleep tonight and, in the morning, when Nimrod gets here, we'll pick the best ones and then try the words out."

Mr. Rakshasas looked around. "But I'm forgetting myself. Let's see if we can make this place a little more congenial, eh?"

"A fire would be nice," suggested Philippa.

"And a tent," said John. "And while you're at it, Mr. Rakshasas, how about a hamburger?"

"You misunderstand me," said Mr. Rakshasas. "These days, my own djinn powers are limited to transubstantiations. That's what we call it when we dematerialize to leave or enter a lamp or a bottle. Otherwise I am almost powerless, really."

"Then how are we going to make this place more congenial, like you said?" asked Philippa.

"Fortunately, we are not without resources." He pointed into the darkness in the direction of the pyramids. "About a hundred yards up the road, we'll find a large box with everything we'll need for a comfortable night. Tents. Firewood. Lamp oil. Nimrod left it there for us. We only have to go get it." And so saying, he picked up his oil lamp and blew out the flame.

"How do you expect to find it in the dark?" asked John.

"Simple," said Mr. Rakshasas. "Do you see that light near the horizon? That is a lamp on top of the box. Nimrod left it there to help us find it."

"And here I was thinking that was a star," admitted John.

Half an hour later, with a large tent erected and a fire blazing on the ground, the twins felt much more comfortable.

"So where is he?" asked Philippa. "Nimrod. You said he had urgent business tonight."

Mr. Rakshasas was silent as his face adopted a somber look, as if he were about to impart something of the gravest importance.

"The fact is that he is investigating a rumor that Iblis, the wickedest djinn of the Ifrit, which is the most evil tribe of all the djinn tribes, has been seen in Cairo. *Iblis* means the cause of despair and, believe me, he is well-named, having done many terrible things. If Iblis has left the casinos and gambling palaces of the Ifrit to be in Cairo now, it is for a purpose. We must attempt to discover what that purpose is, for you can be sure it will be nothing good. When we find out what that purpose is, we must try to stop him. At all costs."

"The Ifrit have a casino?"

"Several dozen casinos. Many of the world's gambling games were invented by the Ifrit, for the general torment of humankind," explained Mr. Rakshasas. "It saves them the trouble of exercising their own djinn powers to inflict bad luck on people. Their casinos in Macao, Monte Carlo, and Atlantic City do that for them. The Ifrit are a very lazy tribe of djinn." Mr. Rakshasas nodded gravely.

"Until then, think hard about your focus words of firepower. We may have need of your powers sooner than we think." The old, bearded djinn wrapped his arms about himself and sighed wearily. "And now I am feeling a little tired at having been outside my lamp for so long. So if you don't mind, I'll be getting along home now. If you do need me, just rub the lamp, eh? Like you did before. Good night."

"Good night, Mr. Rakshasas," said the twins.

Even as Mr. Rakshasas was speaking, smoke began to billow from his mouth and nostrils, although there was no cigar or cigarette in his hand. The smoke kept on coming, too, as if there were no end to it, until the old djinn stood enveloped in his own personal cloud and was quite invisible to the eyes of the two young djinn. Then it was as if the lamp had breathed quickly in, for the smoke was suddenly sucked in through the empty wick to reveal, when the last wisp had gone from the desert air, that Mr. Rakshasas had disappeared.

"Cool," said John.

CHAPTER 13

PICNIC AT
DISAPPEARING ROCK

The next morning, just after dawn, when only half a disk of the sun had yet appeared over the eastern horizon, like the mouth of an enormous fiery tunnel, Nimrod arrived in the white Cadillac, driven by Creemy, looking very excited. Too excited it seemed to ask the twins anything about how they had found their evening in the desert. Right away, he showed them a letter he had received by hand early that same morning.

"It's from an old friend of mine, named Hussein Hussaout," he explained. "This may be just the news I was waiting for. Hussein Hussaout is one of the most successful grave robbers in Egypt. He says it would be to my advantage if we came to his shop in the Old City. It seems that he has found something of great interest."

"You mean like a mummy?" said Philippa.

"Much more interesting than that, I hope," said Nimrod.

"Very likely it is something that the recent earthquake has uncovered, and that Hussein Hussaout has already found. Nevertheless we shall have to be careful. The Ifrit may be watching him."

Nimrod glanced at his watch.

"So the sooner we commence your training the better, in case you are obliged to defend yourselves against a djinn attack."

"An attack?" said Philippa.

"It's as well to be prepared," said Nimrod, "when the Ifrit are concerned." He lit a cigar. "Your very survival may depend on at least grasping the rudiments of the use of djinn power. I'm sorry, but that's just the way it is. Someone has already tried to kill John."

"So, no pressure then?" said Philippa with a heavy sarcasm Nimrod did not fail to recognize.

He laughed his braying sort of laugh and said, "Very good, very good." And then, "All right, John, I believe you're ten minutes older than your sister so you go first. Let's hear your suggestion."

"My focus word is going to be ABECEDARIAN," said John. "It means something to do with the alphabet. I don't think I will ever need to use a word like that when I could just say alphabet, or alphabetical."

Nimrod laughed. "You'd be surprised how many adults would disagree with you," he said. "How many of them will use a long obscure word when a short one would do just as well? But go on."

"It does sound sort of special," continued John. "As if someone might use it to make something appear or disappear. And it sort of sounds a bit like ABRACADABRA, too."

"Yes, it does," admitted Nimrod. "I think that it's an excellent word. In fact, I'm quite jealous. It sounds like a word of real power." Nimrod looked at his niece. "Philippa? What word have you chosen?"

"I wanted a word that was unique to me. A new word, that had never before existed."

"Ambitious. I like that. Let's hear it."

Philippa took a deep breath and said, "FABULON-GOSHOOMARVELISHLYWONDERPIPICAL."

"It certainly sounds special," admitted Nimrod. "I'll give you that much. But for ease of use, I'm not sure I didn't prefer BILTONG to er . . . FABULOWOTSIT . . ."

"The very fact that you've just heard it and can't remember it is surely in its favor," argued Philippa.

"Yes, there is that," conceded Nimrod. "Good thinking, Phil." He pointed to some large rocks about thirty yards from where they were standing. "Very well, see if you can both start by making one of those rocks disappear. First, try to build up some power in the word you've chosen. That means closing your eyes and concentrating very hard."

Philippa and John closed their eyes as they began to concentrate on their words, each investing his or her word with a sense of it containing all the djinn energy in their young bodies.

"Try to create in your own mind the impression that your

word must only be used very sparingly, as if it was the red button that might launch a missile, or fire some enormous gun.

"John? You go first. I want you to open your eyes now and visualize the absence of one particular rock. Picture the rock's disappearance as a situation in logical space. Fix it in your mind, as if the reality couldn't possibly be any different from what you're imagining. And then, keeping that same thought, utter your focus word as clearly as you can."

John collected his thoughts and, remembering how Nimrod exercized his own powers sometimes, brought his feet together, raised his hands in the air at about chest height, like a soccer player taking a penalty kick, and then shouted, "ABECEDARIAN!"

For ten or fifteen seconds, nothing happened, and John was about to offer his apologies and say "I told you so" to Nimrod when, incredibly, the six-foot-tall rock he had chosen vibrated quite visibly and a shard about the size of a walnut fell off.

"Wow," said John. "Did you see that? Did you?" He laughed almost hysterically. "I did it. Well, I did something, anyway."

"Not bad for a first attempt," said Nimrod. "It didn't disappear, but I think we'll agree, you certainly made an impression on it. Philippa? Try the bigger one next to John's effort. Think how your picture of the rock's absence is attached to reality," he suggested. "Remember, the rock's disappearance is a possibility that must have been in the rock from the very beginning." He paused. "When you're ready, when you have accepted that logic deals with every possibility and that all possibilities are its facts, then press the red button that is your focus word."

As she concentrated on the boulder and prepared to utter the word of power she had chosen, Philippa raised one hand like a ballet dancer and then waved the other like a traffic police officer.

"FABULONGOSHOOMARVELISHLYWONDERPIPICAL!"

Even as the last consonant left her lips, the boulder she had chosen began to wobble, and it kept on wobbling, quite violently it seemed to Philippa, for almost a whole minute before it stopped again. She clapped her hands together and squealed with delight.

"Yes," Nimrod said patiently. "You certainly speeded up its molecular structure. That much was obvious. Only it seems to me you both have to get a clearer idea of nothing in your heads. You're both confusing the idea of alteration with disappearing. A common philosophical mistake. Altering the appearance of something is very different from its not being there at all.

"Now try again. Remember, whatever is possible in logic is also permitted. A thought contains the possibility of the situation of which it is the thought. So what is thinkable is possible, too."

The twins were surprised at how much concentration was

required to focus their djinn powers, so that it quickly seemed like hard work and left them feeling out of breath, as if they had lifted some heavy object, sprinted across a field, and attempted to solve a complicated algebraic equation all at the same time. After two hours, all they had succeeded in doing was making a few large boulders become smaller boulders, at which point Nimrod let them rest for a few minutes.

"This is hard work," admitted John.

"In the beginning, yes," said Nimrod. "But it's like physical fitness. You have to learn to develop the part of your brain where your powers are focused. The part that we djinn call the Neshamah. It's the source of your djinn power. The subtle fire that burns inside you. A little like the flame in an oil lamp."

Nimrod rubbed his hands. "All right, let's try making something appear. It's getting near lunchtime, so how about a picnic? Here, I'll show you the sort of thing I mean." And so saying, Nimrod waved his arms and created a very sizable picnic on the desert ground, complete with a tartan rug and a picnic basket containing lots of sandwiches, chicken legs, fruit, and thermos flasks of hot soup.

"There we are," he said. "All you have to do is remember that you cannot create anything contrary to the laws of logic. The truth is that none of us could say what an illogical world would be like. And since that is the case, the very fact that you can think of making something from the energy that is within you is enough to admit the possibility. As soon as you have convinced yourself of the possibility of creating a picnic out of yourselves, the picnic becomes easier to bring into being. Do you see?"

It took a while longer but gradually, as the twins began to realize that all objects contain the possibility of all situations, they started to get the hang of djinn power. Finally, after another ninety minutes of head-ringing thought and examination-level concentration, there were three very different, but apparently edible picnics lying on the ground.

Nimrod approached Philippa's picnic first and picked up a cucumber sandwich. "The proof of the pudding, so to speak," he said, and tasted the sandwich circumspectly. Almost immediately he spat it out again.

"This tastes quite disgusting," he said, and turned his attention to tasting one of the hot dogs from John's picnic. "And this doesn't taste of anything at all." Nimrod allowed a mouthful of hot dog to fall off his tongue onto the sand like a ball of clay. "Ugh. Like rubber." He took out his red handkerchief and wiped his tongue. "Both of you made the same elementary mistake. You were so concerned with how the picnic might look that you forgot to imagine how it might taste. Now do it again, only this time try to visualize yourselves having to eat the picnic. The most delicious picnic that ever was. Remember, there's nothing worse than a picnic that looks good but which you can't actually eat."

After another hour and several more unsuccessful attempts, the three of them finally sat down to enjoy the picnics that the twins had made with their djinn powers. The twins ate while Nimrod talked.

"Now this is much more like it," he said, tasting their respective picnics. "John, this popcorn tastes . . . er . . . just like popcorn. I can't imagine why anyone would want to take popcorn on a picnic, but there's no accounting for taste. To me, it has always tasted more than a little like foam packing. And Philippa, I can't remember ever having tasted a pretzel stick that tasted more like a pretzel stick." He shook his head. "Really, I must have a word with your mother. I can't believe the kind of picnics you must have had."

"I can't believe I'm eating food that I made out of nothing," admitted John and opened a third bag of potato chips.

"That is precisely what was wrong with your first attempts," said Nimrod, helping himself to some of Philippa's cheesecake. "The thing is, you're not making anything from nothing. Certainly not this cheesecake. You make things from the energy source that's within you. The subtle fire. Remember? And the elements that surround you, of course."

"How does it work?" asked John, forking a slice of cold ham and some pickles onto his plate. "Djinn power? I mean, there must be a scientific explanation for it."

"Er . . . some djinn who were scientists have tried to understand how djinn power works, yes. We think it has something to do with our ability to affect the protons in the molecules possessed by objects. Making something appear or disappear requires us to add or remove protons and thereby change one element into another. When we make something disappear like that rock, we are subtracting protons from the various atoms that make the rock. So you see there's nothing magical about it. This is science. Physics. It's impossible to make something from nothing, especially a good picnic. Now if you'd said you'd made it from thin air, you'd have been nearer the mark, John."

Nimrod yawned. "Anyway, I think that's enough practice for today. It's best not to think about the science too much, in case it affects your ability to use your power. It's a little like riding a bike in that respect: easier done than explained. Next time, we'll try you out on making a camel appear or disappear. Something alive. That's much more difficult than a picnic. Creating something alive can make a bit of a mess. Which is why we do these things in the desert where no one really minds if you make a creature that's inside out."

A moment later, Nimrod let out a terrible groan. "Oh, no," he said, looking at his watch.

"What is it?" the twins asked him anxiously.

"I just remembered why I thought of having a picnic," he said. "Because Mrs. Coeur de Lapin invited us to a picnic at her house, at lunchtime. In exactly thirty minutes from now."

"I'm stuffed," said John. "I couldn't eat another thing."

"Me, too," agreed Philippa. "If I ever eat another thing, I'll burst."

"You don't understand," said Nimrod. "We can't not go. For one thing she's my neighbor. And for another, she's French. They take food more seriously than any other people on this planet. She'll have gone to enormous trouble for this picnic. You mark my words. If we don't go, there might be a major diplomatic incident between our respective countries."

"But we can't go and then not eat anything," said John. "That would be as rude as not turning up at all."

"Couldn't you make her disappear?" said Philippa. "Just for a while? At least until after lunch."

"I can't do that," said Nimrod. "She's the wife of the French Ambassador. People would assume she'd been kidnapped or worse. No, no, no. That won't do at all." Nimrod stood up and wagged his finger thoughtfully, "But you could be on the right lines. We could make the picnic disappear in such a way that she might think we had eaten it."

"You pick up a sandwich," agreed John, "bring it close to your mouth, smile at Mrs. Coeur de Lapin and then, when she's not looking, you make it disappear. Yes, that might work."

"It has to work," said Nimrod.

Back in Garden City, Nimrod and the twins quickly changed into some nicer clothes and then went next door to the Residence, which was even bigger than Nimrod's house and surrounded by a high wall, so that the place looked and felt more like a fortress. Nimrod presented their passports at the Gatehouse to an unfriendly French official who regarded their British and American documents with apparent loathing.

When at last, reluctantly, the official had admitted Nimrod and the twins to the grounds of the Embassy, another no less surly official led them across a beautiful, green, well-watered lawn, past a piece of modern sculpture and a flagpole where a French tricolor hung like a limp rag in the early afternoon heat, to a small summerhouse and a lovely picnic spread out on the lawn, like a scene from a painting. Nimrod and Mrs. Coeur de Lapin kissed the air beside each other's ears and, for a moment or two, they spoke in French, which seemed to be another language in which Nimrod was totally fluent.

While these two were talking, Philippa took the opportunity to study Mrs. Coeur de Lapin more closely, for she was at an age to be interested in the appearance of older women, and decided that although the Frenchwoman was undeniably beautiful, her clothes were a little eccentric — especially the black-and-gold headband that she was wearing again. Mrs. Coeur de Lapin reminded Philippa most of how people had dressed during the 1960s, when flowers and long hair and painting your face strange colors had — if the television was to be believed — been the prevailing fashion.

Meanwhile, Nimrod looked at all the food on the Louis Vuitton rug with a great show of enthusiasm. "I say, look at this, children," he said, rubbing his hands together. "Did you ever see a more attractive-looking picnic? Marvelous. *Foie gras*, lobster, caviar, truffles, plover's eggs. And such cheeses. Brie, Roquefort. I can smell them from here. Dear Mrs. Coeur de Lapin, you certainly know what young people like to eat, don't you?"

Mrs. Coeur de Lapin smiled warmly and pushed her thin fingers through John's thick brown hair. "There is no substitute for good food, eh?" She invited everyone to sit down on the rug.

"There certainly is not," agreed Nimrod. "Well, these two will soon make this lot disappear like, poof!" He snapped his fingers. "Won't you, children?"

"We'll certainly do our best," said John, sitting down with a great show of appetite.

Philippa sat down beside her brother and helped herself to a large slice of *foie gras* that sat on a cracker like a piece of pink marble. She had no idea what it was and would have been appalled if anyone had told her; but she recognized the caviar and the lobster easily enough and was thinking herself very fortunate that she wouldn't actually have to eat any of this stuff, since she hated nearly everything that had been provided for them to eat. But smiling at Mrs. Coeur de Lapin, she said, "Delicious," adding, as soon as the French-woman's eyes were averted, "FABULONGOSHOOMAR-VELISHLYWONDERPIPICAL!"

The *foie gras* and the cracker she was holding in her fingertips disappeared immediately.

"What was that you said, *ma chérie*?" asked Mrs. Coeur de Lapin.

"Nothing," said Philippa, helping herself to a piece of cold lobster.

"QWERTYUIOP," muttered Nimrod, and a plover's egg disappeared from his hand.

John had loaded a plate with a whole selection of food-stuffs and, as soon as he thought he was ready, he pointed to the flower beds. "What lovely flowers, Mrs. Coeur de Lapin," he said politely. "Are they a local variety?"

"They are blue Nile lilies," she said, looking at the flowers, and adding that her gardener, Fatih, was the best in all of Cairo.

"ABECEDARIAN," whispered John, consigning the entire contents of his plate to nothingness.

"Don't eat so quickly, John," said Nimrod nervously. "There's a good chap. You'll give yourself indigestion."

"Sorry, Uncle," said John. "But I am feeling rather hungry."

"Me, too," said Philippa, licking her lips melodramatically. "Did you make all this yourself, Mrs. Coeur de Lapin?"

"No, my dear," she laughed. "I have most of it imported from France. And then prepared by our two chefs."

"You have two chefs, Mrs. Coeur de Lapin?" John smiled.

"Yes, we have Monsieur Impoli from Paris and Monsieur Malélevé from Vezelay."

Nimrod emptied the lobster claw he was holding with the blink of an eye. "Ah, *la belle France*," he said. "How I miss it. So clever of you to bring all these delicacies here to Egypt. It must be terribly expensive."

"Oh, *non*." She shrugged. "The French taxpayer. He pays."

The lunch went on in this way for almost forty-five minutes until nearly all the food had been made to disappear, or eaten by Mrs. Coeur de Lapin. Only then did Nimrod shake his head when Mrs. Coeur de Lapin asked him if he would like some more Brie.

"No, thank you," he said, glancing meaningfully at the twins. "I couldn't eat another thing. That was quite magnificent. Wasn't it, children?"

"Yes," said John, throwing down his napkin in the same way Nimrod had done. "The food was magic."

Nimrod winced but felt obliged to let that one pass.

"Such healthy appetites," remarked their hostess when the time came for them to leave. "Does your uncle not feed you at home?"

"Whenever we want," said Philippa. "We only have to snap our fingers and say the magic word and the food is there."

"Then you must come again and soon," said Mrs. Coeur de Lapin. "It's such a pleasure to meet young Americans who seem to enjoy proper food so much."

"Thank goodness that is over," said Philippa as they walked back up the street to Nimrod's house. "You don't suppose she noticed anything strange, do you?"

"I think perhaps you could have been a little more subtle," scolded Nimrod. "At one point, John, it looked as if you must have consumed a whole plateful of food in one bite. She's probably seen horses with smaller appetites than she now thinks you two have."

"I was only trying to do the food justice, like you said," explained John.

"Poor woman," said Philippa. "To go to all that trouble and then we don't eat a thing. It seems such a waste of good food."

"Poor woman, indeed," said Nimrod thoughtfully, and then yawned.

"Did you notice her eyes?" said Philippa. "It was weird. When she looked at you, it was like you weren't there."

John shrugged. "She's French. They all look at Americans like you're not there."

"Not just Americans," said Nimrod. "They think that way about pretty much anyone who's not French, really. Yes, it's what they call civilization." He yawned again. "Light my lamp, look at me yawning. After all that food, I should like to take a nap. Unfortunately, there is no time. We must hurry over to the Old City to visit Hussein Hussaout."

CHAPTER 14

THE BOY WITH THE BLUE FEET

The oldest part of Cairo lay south of Garden City and here, off a quiet, cobbled lane flanked by high-walled houses, medieval churches, and well-kept cemeteries, in a long narrow alley, was a large shop where all sorts of cheap souvenirs could be bought.

"Hussein knows that I'm a djinn, of course," said Nimrod as they approached the shop. "But for the moment at least, we'll keep the fact that the two of you are djinn a secret from him. When you're a djinn it doesn't do to let too many people know what you are. Besides, if Hussein thinks you're just a couple of ordinary kids, it might afford you the opportunity to befriend his son, Baksheesh. The boy speaks good English, and he may let something slip that his father would not. So keep your eyes and ears open."

John stared in the window of the shop. "This is just junk, isn't it? Stuff for tourists."

"He keeps the genuine stuff in a room upstairs," said Nimrod. "One of you might like to have a snoop around while the other distracts Baksheesh."

They found Hussein Hussaout near the front of the shop, wearing a white suit and sitting among piles of pillows rich with Bedouin embroidery, behind a coffee table laden with pistachios, Arabic sweets, lemonade, and glasses. Nervously, he handled a set of eleventh-century prayer beads made of jet, as he sat smoking something that smelled strongly of strawberries in a water pipe that was as big as a bassoon, and drinking hot sweet coffee from a little silver pot. He was a handsome, white-haired man with a darker mustache and a gap between his teeth that lent him a slightly shifty air.

Seeing Nimrod, he smiled, touched his forehead with the tips of his fingers, and bowed his head slightly. "So you came," he said. "I was beginning to wonder if you would." Then he stood up and kissed Nimrod on the cheek.

Nimrod turned toward the twins. "These are my young friends, John and Philippa. Relations of mine from America. They are staying with me for a couple of weeks."

Hussein Hussaout smiled his gap-toothed smile and bowed to the children. "You are welcome," he said, his eyes narrowing suspiciously. "But is Egypt not too hot for you?"

Sensing that this was a question that might have been designed to discover if the twins were djinn, like their uncle, Philippa nodded wearily, for only a djinn would have found Cairo's summer heat bearable, and only a human would have complained about it. "Yes. Very hot," she said, fanning herself with a map of the Old City.

"Much too hot," added John, realizing what was going on. "If it gets any hotter, I'll bake."

"Well, we can't have that," said Hussaout, pouring them each a glass of lemonade. "Here, something cool to drink."

The twins, both of whom would have preferred some of the delicious-smelling coffee, each took a glass of lemonade and thanked him.

"Few people are as tolerant of the heat as Nimrod. But then he is English, and as the song says, 'Only mad dogs and Englishmen go out in the midday sun.'"

"You got that right," said Philippa, trying to maintain the deception that she and her brother were just two ordinary American kids. "It's strange the way he never gets hot."

"Yes, he is a bit strange," smiled Hussein Hussaout. "A genuine English eccentric."

Nimrod sat down on a golden throne that was a copy of the one from the tomb of Tutankhamen in the Cairo Museum, and faced Hussein Hussaout.

"How is your son, Baksheesh?" asked Nimrod, glancing around the shop.

"He is very well, thank you."

"Is he at school? I don't see him."

"Yes, at school."

Nimrod nodded. "So then. To business. I got your note."

Hussein Hussaout glanced at the twins. "It is all right? To talk about such things in front of the children?"

"What they cannot understand cannot hurt them," said Nimrod.

"Then it would be best not to hear it at all," said Hussein Hussaout.

"As you wish, my friend." Nimrod looked at the twins and winking, nodded toward the back of the shop. "Children. Why don't you go find yourself a nice souvenir?"

"Yes, Uncle," said the twins obediently and went in the back to look at some toy sarcophagi. Inside each little sarcophagus was a perfect facsimile of a bandage-wrapped mummy. But the twins were more interested in what was being said and, bending their minds to affect their ears, they found to their surprise that they could hear almost every word that passed between Nimrod and the Egyptian curio dealer. At the same time, they kept a close eye on Hussein Hussaout, waiting for an opportunity to meander through a back door that led into a courtyard and snoop around, as Nimrod had suggested.

"So," said Nimrod, "in your letter, you said you had found something."

"That's what I do." Hussein Hussaout grinned.

"Something was turned up by the earthquake, perhaps?"

"It is an ill wind that blows nobody any good," said Hussein Hussaout. "Especially in Egypt. All sorts of things turn up in this country after an earthquake. You, for instance. And Iblis. Both of you looking for the same thing."

"You've seen Iblis? Here in Cairo?"

"Yes. The day before yesterday. At the Cairo Museum," explained Hussaout. "As you know, I often go there first thing in the morning to look at the ancient treasures and be inspired. Those old stones are full of vibrations. So it was a day like any other. Or so it had seemed until I looked around and saw that I was observed by Iblis. And not just Iblis, but several Ifrit of his descent. Maymunah, her father Al Dimiryat, and Dahnash. Our meeting was hardly a coincidence, or at least so they told me. It was not the museum they had come to see, but me. So we went upstairs to the museum café for a chat. All very polite, you understand."

"And how is Iblis?" asked Nimrod.

"He has a beard now."

"Is that so?"

"Yes, just a small blond one on the chin and with a thin mustache. Like an Arab. Otherwise, the same always. Smooth. Businesslike. Impeccable manners. Expensive Savile Row tailoring. Handmade shoes. Very English, like yourself, Nimrod." Hussein Hussaout grinned and touched the gap between his front teeth with the fingernail on his little finger. "You and he have much in common, my friend."

"For example?"

"He told me he was interested in acquiring some Egyptian artifacts that might have been found since the earthquake. Genuine artifacts. Specifically those of the Eighteenth Dynasty. And money was no object. Well, it never is with you people. I could name any price if the artifacts were of good quality."

"There is no other dynasty that is of interest to the djinn," said Nimrod. "As, of course, you know."

"Iblis said he had heard a rumor to the effect that I was in possession of some information regarding the lost tomb of Akhenaten."

"Had he? Are you?"

The curio dealer puffed at his hubbly-bubbly pipe and smiled. "Alas, I told him, it was, as he had said, only a rumor. After all, if such a thing was true, that information would be worth a fortune."

"It might also get you killed," said Nimrod.

"If Iblis knew that I had summoned you, he would be most annoyed with me, true. In which case you will understand my caution in discussing such a matter with you now."

"Supposing such information did exist," Nimrod said carefully. "What might it look like?"

"A map."

Nimrod laughed. "A map? In this country? Everyone has treasure maps to sell. And they are all useless. Shifting sands make a thing such as you describe meaningless, as well you know. You might just as easily give me a map of the moon."

"There are maps, and there are maps," said Hussaout. "This is not a map on ancient papyrus. Nor a map on an oilskin taken from the hand of a dead explorer."

"You're wasting my time," said Nimrod. "Unless —" Nimrod paused. "Unless you found the key to the Netjer Tablet. A stone stele that might enable you to decipher what was written there."

"Who knows if such things exist?" Hussaout smiled. "And, to speak frankly, a man who found such a thing, knowing what it might mean, would do well to destroy it immediately. That is my opinion." Hussein Hussaout raised his hand to silence the words of protest that the djinn was about to utter. "On the other hand, a man who had understood the Tablet might draw a map himself. More specifically, a map of Medinet el-Fayyum and the surrounding area. A map that has a new meaning since the earthquake." Hussaout tapped his forehead. "He might draw such a map with the help of a piece of paper and a pencil, and a great deal of money, of course. Such a map as this might easily be every bit as good or as useless as some old map on papyrus."

"But is this true?" said Nimrod. "You've seen the key to the Netjer Tablet? You actually know where the tomb of Akhenaten is?"

"It is a very real possibility," admitted Hussein Hussaout.

"If you said as much to the Ifrit, I'm surprised that they let you live," said Nimrod. "Especially Iblis. He is a most impatient djinn."

"They are more business-minded than perhaps you imagine, Nimrod. They are quite willing to buy what once they would have taken by force."

On the other side of the shop, John put down the mummified cat he was holding and, seeing that Hussein Hussaout and his uncle were now deep in conversation, too deep even to notice that they were not alone, he nudged his sister and pointed at the open back door. "Come on," he said. "Let's snoop around. See what we can find out."

John and Philippa found themselves in a huge dusty yard filled with larger stone Egyptian artifacts, many of which looked, to their eyes at least, like the real thing. In one corner stood another open door with a rather smelly restroom that several flies seemed to find very attractive, and in another corner, a third door through which could be seen a rickety old staircase leading to the floor above.

"In here, I think," said John, heading for the staircase. "Nimrod said there was a special room upstairs where all the good stuff was kept."

After the bright sunshine in the yard, the staircase was very dark and gloomy and, Philippa thought, a little bit scary — especially the way it creaked underfoot like in a horror film as they climbed up. With so many ancient Egyptian objects around, she half expected to find an unwrapped mummy waiting for them at the top of the stairs.

"I don't like this," she admitted as they reached the landing and turned the corner into a dark and dusty corridor that was lined with framed photographs of old excavations and explorers.

"Take it easy," said John. "We'll just give the place the once-over and then go downstairs again."

It was then that they heard a low moaning sound coming from an open doorway at the end of the corridor. Philippa felt her blood turn to ice. "What was that?" she hissed and grabbed her brother's arm.

"I'm not sure," said John, who was feeling rather scared,

and had to remind himself that he was a djinn, albeit a very young djinn, and that if the stories in *The Arabian Nights* were anything near the truth, he was going to have to get used to seeing some pretty frightening things — the sorts of things that might terrify any ordinary boy.

"Stay here if you like," he whispered.

"On my own?" said Philippa, glancing around at the long, dim corridor. She was feeling so scared she had to keep her focus word at the front of her mind in order to find the courage to put one foot in front of the other. "No, thanks. I'm coming with you."

But for a long moment she turned her face to the wall, pressing it against the cool, slightly damp plaster.

"Are you all right?" Taking her hand, John squeezed it affectionately. "Come on. We ought to take a look. Or Nimrod will be disappointed in us."

"I think," gulped Philippa, "he'll be more disappointed if we're torn apart by some monster."

Even as she spoke, another moan emanated from the room at the end of the corridor, a low, inhuman moan that could have come from a tomb or an open sarcophagus. By now, they were close enough to hear not just the moans but also a rasping, breathing noise that sounded like some vicious animal or a person experiencing great pain or great fear.

Philippa thought that the sound was not as loud as the beating of her heart and, filled with a sense of dread and wondering from where John had found his courage, she hardly dared to follow him as he stepped through the open doorway and into the room from where the moans were coming. There was a long silence before John spoke.

"It's all right, Philippa," he said. "There's nothing to be scared of."

She put her head around the door and saw that lying on a big brass bed was a half-naked boy about the same age as herself. He appeared to be unconscious although, covered with sweat, he moved around feverishly on the bed, muttering deliriously. His skin was pale and he was quite blue around the lips and feet, one of which bore two dark red puncture marks, as if he had been stabbed twice on the heel with a sharp needle.

John took a closer look at the boy's blue foot. "If I knew what I was talking about I'd say that this boy has been bitten by something," he said. "Perhaps a vampire bat."

"Vampire bats are from South America not Egypt," said Philippa.

"A snake, then. Like the one that almost bit me." John swallowed as he reflected upon the unpleasant fate he had narrowly avoided.

"Do you think Mr. Hussaout knows about this?"

"Has to." John pointed at the bedside table and a framed photograph of the boy in bed beside a Land Rover with Hussein Hussaout. "I'd say this was Hussein Hussaout's son, Baksheesh." The two were clearly very happy and, if the photograph was anything to go by, Hussaout didn't look like the kind of father who would have neglected his son.

"Didn't he say that Baksheesh had gone to school?" said

Philippa. She sat down on his bedside and placed her hand on the boy's forehead. "He's burning up. I think he should be in the hospital."

Feeling her touch, the boy seemed to relax a little, and then his eyes flickered open. "Not go to hospital," he whispered. "Please."

"Why not?" asked Philippa.

"You must go," croaked the boy. "Very dangerous for you here."

Philippa stood up abruptly. "You don't suppose he's infectious do you, John?" Hearing no reply, she looked around. "John?"

John was staring down into an open box by the window. "Look at this," he said quietly.

Philippa looked and saw that in the box lay the body of a dead dog. "Maybe we should get Nimrod," she said.

"Nimrod?" said Baksheesh, becoming more agitated. "No, he must not come here. He is in great danger. You must tell him to leave."

"From whom?" asked John. "The Ifrit?"

"Tell him to go, before it is too late," said Baksheesh and then lapsed back into unconsciousness.

"Come on," said Philippa. "Let's get out of here."

They went back downstairs and across the yard, to the curio shop where Nimrod and Hussein Hussaout were still deep in conversation.

"It's not that I don't want to help you," said Hussaout. "I do. Of course I do. You think I want to make a deal with the

181

Ifrit?" He bit his thumb angrily. "That is what I think of them. But look around, my friend. Everything is for sale. I'm a businessman. I don't have your special skills. Your infinite resources. I have to make a living." He grinned. "You understand, Nimrod. It's nothing personal. It's just business."

"How much?" said Nimrod flatly.

"It's not about money. Not from you, old friend. At least, not directly. I can get money from anyone. That's not what I want."

"What then?"

"From a djinn? What else but three wishes?"

"You could get that from the Ifrit," said Nimrod.

"But could I trust them to keep their word? They might give me three wishes and then, as soon as they had what they wanted, they would come back and turn me into a flea, just out of spite. Their reputation goes before them, Nimrod. As does yours. I can trust you to keep your word. But even if they get what they want, there's no gratitude from the Ifrit."

Nimrod thought for a moment. "Just three wishes."

"Three wishes."

"*The Baghdad Rules*? A list of wishes up front."

"If you wish."

"I don't know," said Nimrod.

Hussein Hussaout tossed his prayer beads around his hairy wrist and grinned. "Come on. You know you're going to say yes. And really what does it cost you? A day or two of life at the other end?" Hussaout shrugged. "With the sort of life span you enjoy, you can afford that."

Nimrod glanced anxiously at the twins, biting his nails for a moment. "What will you wish for?" he asked.

"*The Baghdad Rules,* like you said. It won't be anything that will be on your conscience. No, it will be the usual stuff. Plenty of money, make me more attractive to women, improve my health." Hussaout coughed eloquently. "I've got this nasty cough, see. Smoking too much, probably. Frankly, I could do with a new set of lungs. Come on. What do you say? Do we have a deal?"

"All right," said Nimrod.

"Good. You won't regret it, I promise."

"And three wishes only after you deliver."

"Then the sooner we leave the better. How about tonight?"

"Very well," agreed Nimrod. "How shall we get there?"

"Come back here at around six o'clock. You can drive us there in your beautiful old Cadillac. The journey will take perhaps an hour. But come alone."

Nimrod stood up. "Very well then. Until six o'clock."

The two men shook hands and then Nimrod and the twins took their leave of Hussein Hussaout and his curio shop.

As soon as they were outside in the alley, the twins started to tell Nimrod about Baksheesh and the dead dog, but Nimrod hushed them and told them to wait until they were in the car and safely out of earshot. "In these old streets," he said, looking around suspiciously, "you never know who might be listening. Walls have ears. Especially when those walls might contain the living spirit of the Ifrit."

"Is that possible?" asked Philippa, hurrying to keep up

with her uncle as he strode ahead. "For a djinn to take on the shape of a wall?"

"Oh, yes. It is more common to take on the shape of a tree, but a rock or a wall is possible, although not very comfortable. And only for very experienced djinn who can control the tremendous sense of claustrophobia."

They found the Cadillac.

"Now then," said Nimrod as they climbed inside and Creemy closed the car's big heavy door. "What's all this about Baksheesh?"

The twins told Nimrod about what they had seen in the room above the shop. He listened patiently without interrupting them and when they were finished, he sighed and shook his head.

"I wonder why he told me the boy had gone to school," he said. "It's not like Hussein Hussaout at all. And all that talk about business. I hardly recognized him. Baksheesh was feverish, you say?"

"Yes," said Philippa. "Very."

"He loves that boy more than his own life," said Nimrod. "He wouldn't allow anything to happen to him."

"Maybe he's already sold out to the Ifrit."

Nimrod looked at John and frowned. "How did you know about that?"

"We could hear you," said John. He shrugged. "At least we could when we concentrated."

"Yes, I wondered if you could," said Nimrod. "Then you'll know what he said about making a deal with the Ifrit. He couldn't ever trust them to make a deal and keep their word. The Ifrit can't help being treacherous, he knows that."

"What are you going to do?"

"I'll ask him about Baksheesh when I see him tonight."

"You can't be serious about going," protested Philippa. "It might be a trap."

"True, but I have no choice. This is much too important. I simply can't pass up a chance to find Akhenaten's tomb."

"Who is Akhenaten?" asked John.

Nimrod sat forward on his seat and told Creemy not to stop in Garden City but to drive on, to the northern end of Maidan Tahrir and the Cairo Museum. "I'll introduce you," he said. "It's time you met the most feared and hated human in all of djinn history."

CHAPTER 15

AKHENATEN

Cairo has more than a dozen museums of which the Antiquities Museum, also known as the Cairo Museum, is the largest, the pinkest, and the most popular. It is a huge, hot, dirty, smelly, chaotic place with broken windows, a leaking roof, poor lighting, antiquated display cabinets, and uncaring explanations of the building's priceless exhibits. It is also one of the world's greatest museums. As they entered the front door and made their way through the numerous security guards into the rotunda, Nimrod told the twins that before he introduced them to Akhenaten, he had an important confession to make.

"It's something I should have told you immediately," he said, "about exercizing your powers as djinn. Something you may have heard Hussein Hussaout mention in relation to my granting him three wishes. I wanted to tell you why we don't use djinn power more often than we do. Why I choose to fly on an airplane, for example, instead of a carpet. Why I usually choose to have someone prepare my food, instead of willing it to appear in front of me. In short, why I do so many things the human way, instead of the djinn way."

"I have been kind of wondering that myself," admitted John.

"As you've probably gathered," said Nimrod, "a djinn can live for a long time. Much longer than human beings. As long as five hundred years. Much longer than that if it's inside a jar or a bottle, where you enter a virtual state of suspended animation. But each time you use your djinn power, you use a little bit of your life force. That's why you find using your power tiring. Because something goes out of you that can never be restored."

"That's right," said Philippa. "I remember now. When I made Mrs. Trump's wish come true, I did feel something leave me. It made me feel quite faint for a second."

"Which is precisely why," said Nimrod, "the power needs to be used sparingly. Every time you grant an important wish or make something appear or disappear, the fire that burns within you, the djinn fire, dims a little, and some of your allotted time span on this earth is lost. And the older a djinn gets, the more life force it costs him to grant a wish."

"How much time is lost?" asked the practically minded John.

"No one knows for sure," admitted Nimrod. "But as a rough rule of thumb, and for a djinn of my age, a wish will cost me a day of life. That doesn't sound much at your age. But when you're as old as Mr. Rakshasas, one day can seem very precious. That is why he rarely ever uses his powers these days, except to make a transubstantiation, which, fortunately, is something that uses very little djinn power. I wasn't going to tell you for a little while, so you could have some fun without thinking of the consequences. But since you heard what Hussaout said, I have little choice. At least now you'll understand why the djinn don't go around granting everyone three wishes. Quite apart from the obvious chaos it would cause in society at large, it would also shorten our lives quite considerably."

"How much longer might a djinn live inside a bottle or a lamp?" asked Philippa.

"It's a good question," said Nimrod. "And it's also one of the reasons why we're here now, in this museum. For a long time, nobody knew how long it was possible for a bottled djinn to live. But since 1974 we've had a better idea. You've heard of the Terracotta Army, in the ancient city of Xi'an, in central China? It was unearthed by peasants in 1974, after twenty-two hundred years in the ground. Among the Terracotta soldiers was a pot containing several djinn."

"You mean that after twenty-two hundred years they were still alive?" said Philippa.

"Yes. Since then it's become clear to us that in our bottled state of suspended animation, we might live almost indefinitely. Which is where Akhenaten starts to become important."

Nimrod led them upstairs past the malodorous museum restrooms, to the far end of the building, and perhaps the strangest-looking statue in the whole structure. The figure standing in front of them had a long face, narrow almond-shaped eyes, thick lips, a dropping jaw, a long swanlike neck, sloping shoulders, a large pot belly, and the most enormous thighs the twins had ever seen.

"John. Philippa. I'd like to introduce you to Akhenaten," said Nimrod, pointing at the great black figure standing before them.

"I've never seen anyone who looked quite so ugly," said Philippa, staring hard at the statue in front of her.

"He is rather grotesque, isn't he?" admitted Nimrod. "Akhenaten. Also called Amenhotep the Fourth, King of Egypt of the Eighteenth Dynasty, who reigned over Egypt, three thousand five hundred years ago."

John touched the large granite statue, one of four in the Amarna Gallery at the Cairo Museum, and nodded affably. "How do you do, Your Majesty?" he said.

"He was given the name Amenhotep at birth," explained Nimrod. "But he changed it when he got rid of all of the old Egyptian gods — Isis, Anubis, Seti, Thoth — in favor of one god, Aten, and caused a religious revolution. This was very unpopular with the priests, who were the richest and most powerful people in Egypt. Even today, Akhenaten is called the 'Heretic Pharaoh,' which means someone who everyone regards as having committed a terrible crime against his religion. Because of Akhenaten's devotion to the new religion, it's said he neglected his people, and the defense of the country. Hostile forces took advantage of Egypt's military weakness caused by the king's indifference to the army and invaded the country. Akhenaten was forced to flee his palace, and died soon afterward. That's what history tells us, anyway. But the truth is somewhat different.

"You see, Akhenaten was more than just a pharaoh and a king. He was also a great magician. His mother was a witch whose father was a djinn, and who had learned how to bind a djinn to her service. She taught these arts to her son, who used the knowledge to make himself more powerful than any djinn. It is not known how Akhenaten was able to bind so many djinn to his service, but it's certain that it was the power of these djinn whom Akhenaten commanded that became the source of his power. Historians assume that Akhenaten introduced the practice of sun worship to Egypt. But the so-called Sun God was not a god at all; rather, the collective force of Akhenaten's seventy djinn slaves, which he named the Aten, after the disk of the sun of the same name. This disk of the sun, the Aten, became the symbol of the new religion.

"Other djinn were appalled by this blasphemy and helped the Egyptian people overthrow Akhenaten and put an end to this djinn worship. And so it was that with many of his followers and these seventy djinn that he had bound to his service, Akhenaten fled the capital city of Amarna, which he had built as the center of his new religion. He disappeared into the desert and neither he nor the seventy djinn priests who served him were ever seen again. He must have died in the desert but his tomb has never been found."

"So why would you and Iblis and the Ifrit want to find his lost tomb?" asked Philippa.

"For the treasure, of course," said John. "There is a treasure, isn't there, Uncle Nimrod?"

"A treasure? Yes, I should think so. But that's not what I want. It's not what the Ifrit want. They have plenty of money from their casinos."

"What then?"

"As I told you earlier, in the world of the djinn there exists a balance of power between Good and Evil."

"The tuchemeter," said John. "And the homeostasis."

"Exactly so. The homeostatic balance was last upset in 1974, when several djinn emerged from vases found with the Terracotta Army in Xi'an. For a while it looked as if those ancient djinn might side with the Ifrit, the Shaitan, and the Ghul against the djinn tribes who are on the side of Good. But in practice, things turned out differently, and the Chinese djinn, who were six in number, turned out to be good and bad in equal measure. But if Iblis and his Ifrit friends are ever able to find the lost djinn of Akhenaten, things might turn out very differently from what happened in Xi'an. That balance of power might be upset. And seventy is more than enough to do it."

"If you ask me," said John, "there already seems to be a lot of bad luck in the world. I can't imagine things being any worse than they are now."

"The consequences of all those seventy djinn weighing in on the side of bad luck are almost too terrible to contemplate," said Nimrod. "People mislaying things, losing money, forgetting things, missing trains and planes, people being hurt. Yes, many so-called accidents are caused by bad luck inflicted on human beings by malicious djinn." Nimrod shook his head and shuddered. "I have spent my life devising systems for beating casinos, influencing governments to outlaw get-rich-quick schemes, combating the forces of bad luck in every way I can, but always it comes back to using my own power to bring good luck to someone. Yes, sometimes even granting three wishes. But with much more bad luck around, good djinn like myself, and eventually you, would have to work much harder to make up for it. And at a tremendous cost. Eventually, we would use up all our power and die after which the human race itself would face extinction. That is what might happen, John."

"But why should these lost djinn be any different from the Chinese djinn?" asked Philippa. "With half of them turning out to be good and half of them evil."

"It's not as simple as that," said Nimrod. "You see no one was looking for the Chinese djinn. Their existence was unknown. Their discovery was a complete accident. But in 1974, after the discovery of the Terracotta Army and those six djinn, it was realized that the lost djinn of Akhenaten, which we have always known about, might command a balance of power if ever they were found. And so, for thirty years the Ifrit and Marid have both been searching for them. Whoever finds them will have the power to command them. That's the way of the djinn. The seventy djinn will be bound to the service of whoever finds them first."

"But how would Hussein Hussaout know where the tomb is to be found?" asked John. "Perhaps he's lying."

"If he says he knows, then he knows," said Nimrod. "He may run a curio shop selling cheap souvenirs, but Hussein Hussaout, his father, and his father before him, have been the greatest finders of tombs in the history of Egypt. I doubt there is anyone in the country who is more experienced in this kind of work than Hussein Hussaout.

"Besides, he has had one great advantage, not possessed by any other archaeologist. Perhaps you've heard of the Rosetta stone. It is a large piece of rock with writing in three languages that enabled an Englishman named Thomas Young to decipher the meaning of Egyptian hieroglyphics. A similar stone, the Netjer Tablet — from a Kemetic or ancient Egyptian word that means 'divine power' — was rumored to have been found by Hussein Hussaout's father in the 1950s. The Netjer Tablet was supposed to contain some important clues as to the whereabouts of several royal tombs, including that of Akhenaten and Rameses the Second. Only it was in a code that could not be deciphered without a smaller stone tablet, called a stele. It's my belief that Hussein must have found this stone stele after the earthquake."

"So when are we going back to the shop?" asked John.

Nimrod shook his head. "Oh, no. Not this time. I'm going on my own. This could be dangerous. Tonight you can stay at home and study those djinn cards that Mr. Rakshasas gave you."

They were walking away to go and look at the rest of the Cairo Museum's antiquities, including the mummies and the treasure of Tutankhamen, when John noticed something on the wall behind Akhenaten's statue.

"It's the crack," he said. "The one that was caused by the earthquake. Remember, Phil? The one you saw in the newspaper. The crack that's identical to the one on my bedroom wall."

"So it is," said Philippa.

"I wonder," said John. "Is it just a coincidence that it should appear on the wall here, next to the statue of Akhenaten?"

"Didn't I tell you?" said Nimrod. "Coincidence is just a scientist's word for chance. No, this is no accident. As I said back in London, this is a message. But from whom?"

After seeing Akhenaten's statue, Nimrod and the twins went home and lay warming themselves in the late afternoon sun like a trio of golden lizards. Then, at 5:30, Nimrod went out in the Cadillac Eldorado alone, but not before telling the twins that Creemy had cooked them his Special Special and to make sure that they offered some to Mr. Groanin before he took them out somewhere.

"Be careful," Philippa told her uncle.

"I will."

"It could be a trap," added John.

"I know."

Creemy's Special Special turned out to be a curried stew full of chilies, which, being extremely hot to eat, was something John and Philippa discovered they enjoyed a lot, much to Creemy's delight. They had just started eating when Mr. Groanin, wearing a beige tropical suit, carrying a straw Panama hat, and looking much thinner than the last time they had seen him, emerged from his room at the back of the house and informed the twins that he was ready to escort them out.

"Not before you taste this," said John. "It's one of Creemy's Specials, and it's delicious."

"I must admit, it does smell rather good," said Mr. Groanin. "Ordinarily I avoid the food in this beastly country. The standards of hygiene are not very good. It's only too easy to get what they call, with considerable understatement, Gyppy tummy." Mr. Groanin laughed bitterly. "Let me tell you, Gyppy doesn't begin to cover it. Borgia tummy more like, Crippen tummy, or some other notorious poisoner. Or maybe William Wallace tummy after that Scots rebel who was famously disemboweled by Edward Longshanks. But not Gyppy. Gyppy is much too cozy a word to describe the full gripping, gut-gnawing horror of an upset stomach in this godforsaken place."

John wolfed down a large forkful of Creemy's Special with noisy relish. "But how do you stay alive if you don't eat anything?" he asked.

"I have a fridge in my room," said Mr. Groanin. "It's full of bottled mineral water and jars of baby food that I've brought from London. I eat that."

"You eat baby food?" said John, almost choking with astonishment. "Stewed apples and pears, creamed rice and apricots, and that kind of thing?"

"It's all sterilized, you see," said Mr. Groanin. "In little sealed jars. In this filthy country, it's the only food I've found to be one hundred percent reliable in the tummy department." Groanin looked at the food on John's plate and licked his lips hungrily. "Mind you, that does look and smell rather good."

"Have some," said John.

"I don't know if I could," said Groanin. He sat down at the mahogany table, drew the big serving dish containing the Creemy Special Special toward him, and allowed the aroma to drift up his nose.

"Not a bad cook, that Creemy, I'll give him that," he said grudgingly. "If you like foreign muck." Groanin positioned his long nose over the serving dish and inhaled deeply. "By heck, that smell fair clears the head, that does. A man could eat that and never suffer from catarrh again."

"Is it having one arm that makes you more concerned about things like hygiene?" asked John.

"Perhaps."

"Do you mind me asking," said John, "but how did you lose it? The arm, I mean."

"It's an interesting story, right enough," said Groanin, who was now regarding the curry hungrily. "I was working as a librarian in the old Reading Room of the British Museum Library, and I hated them that came there to read the books. A right stuck-up bunch of nuisances. There was one reader in particular whom we all hated. A tiger tamer named Thug Vickery. Thug Vickery, an Anglo-Indian from Dulwich, had been writing what he had hoped would be the definitive book about tigers, but one hot summer day, obstructed in his work by us librarians at the British Museum, or so he believed, he decided to take terrible revenge on us all. Choosing a time of day near to closing when many of the other readers had already gone home, Thug brought a pair of hungry white tigers into the huge Reading Room, and let them go. Several of the other librarians were killed and eaten, and I myself was fortunate to merely lose an arm."

"What happened to the tigers?" asked John.

"They were shot and killed by the RSPCA. Soon after that I lost me job, and turned to thieving, which is how I met your uncle. That's my story." He picked up his fork. "I don't suppose a mouthful would kill me," said Groanin as he spooned a great dollop of the Creamy Special Special onto an empty dinner plate. "I can't survive on broccoli and carrots with cheese indefinitely. I've lost ten pounds since we arrived in this country. I'm wasting away with starvation and worry, so I am."

"But it is kind of hot," advised John. "You'd better be careful."

Mr. Groanin laughed. "Listen sonny, I was eating hot curries before you were born. Vindaloo, Madras, if there's one thing having been born in the north of England equips you for, son, it's eating hot curry. So don't you worry about me, lad. You just mind your own constitution and leave me to take care of mine." Groanin snorted with derision. "Cheeky young pup," he muttered and forked a generous load of the Creamy Special Special into his big mouth.

For a moment everything appeared to be fine. Groanin smiled sarcastically at John and a second fork-load was heading toward his mouth, when it happened. Groanin's face began to turn a very definite shade of pink, then red, and finally a deep purple.

"Bloody hellfire," he hiccuped, dropping his fork. "Quick. Don't just sit there. Water. Water."

Philippa picked up the water jug and was about to pour him a glass when he snatched the jug away and emptied the contents down his throat.

"I think that just makes it worse, doesn't it?" observed John.

"Hellfire," repeated Mr. Groanin. "More." He hiccuped again.

"Curry?"

"Water! Water! For goodness' sake give me water!"

Philippa picked up the jug and was on the verge of going into the kitchen to fetch some more mineral water when Mr. Groanin snatched the flowers out of the vase in the center of the table and drank the greenish water they had been sitting in. But the water in the vase seemed to afford him little or no relief.

"Do something," he said, somewhat indistinctly. "My tongue. It feels like a hot coal from the fire. Call a doctor! Call an ambulance!"

"What number should I dial?" asked Philippa, as she grabbed the phone.

"Search me," said John. For a brief moment he considered using his djinn power to help Mr. Groanin and then rejected the idea for fear that Nimrod's one-armed butler might end up without a tongue.

Philippa, thinking along very similar lines, feared to make the heat in Mr. Groanin's mouth disappear in case she froze his mouth solid.

And, in the event, it was Creemy who finally came to Groanin's assistance.

Stopping Groanin from finishing the water in the vase of flowers on the sideboard, he said, "Water very bad, please." Then he handed Groanin the sugar bowl. "Eat," he said. "Eat. Eat." And seeing Groanin still apparently unable to help himself, Creemy spooned up a dessert spoonful of sugar and forced it into the other man's mouth. "Sugar help burning hot mouth plenty good," he said.

Groanin ate the spoonful of sugar, and then, as it seemed to afford him some relief, another, and after about ten minutes the fire inside his mouth had been sufficiently dampened down for him to speak again.

"By heck, that was a hot curry. What was in it, molten lava? I thought my time had come. I don't know how you can eat that stuff, really I don't." He picked the shirt away from his body. "Look at me. I'm lathered with sweat, so I am." He picked up a place mat and started to fan himself furiously. "Whose recipe was that? Lucifer's? The Spanish Inquisition's?" He expelled a loud mouthful of air. "Is that your idea of a joke, young man? I say, is that your idea of a joke?"

"No, sir," said John. "If you remember, I did try to warn you that it might be a little hot."

"You did that," agreed Groanin. "I can't deny it. Only that stuff should come with a government health warning, or something."

John decided not to mention that it had been Nimrod who had put the thought in his head to offer some of the Creemy Special Special to the butler. It was clear that the poor man had been in genuine pain and distress, and it seemed unlikely that he would be able to see the funny side of what had happened for quite a while yet.

When Groanin had recovered, he took the twins to the sound-and-light show at the pyramids (which they were too polite to tell him they had already seen, albeit at a distance) almost without a complaint, and did not mention the incident of the Creemy Special Special again.

CHAPTER 16

THE THIRD WISH

The next morning there was no sign of Uncle Nimrod at the breakfast table.

"Maybe he had a late night," said Philippa hopefully.

"Let's look in his room," said John.

But neither of the twins really expected to find their uncle still in bed.

Nimrod's bedroom occupied the larger part of the first floor. Outside the double door stood two human-sized standing figures of Anubis, the jackal-headed god of the dead. Inside, things were a little more conducive for work rather than for sleep, as Nimrod also used the huge room as an office. A computer stood on a large walnut table. Next to a chair made from antlers was a tall set of shelves on top of which was a large bell-shaped glass bottle containing a huge blue lobster and upon which hung a crudely written sign that read DO NOT EAT. Next to the bed was a large Egyptian-looking gilt chest, covered in hieroglyphs, that was home to an infinite variety of medicine bottles. Elsewhere, the room gave the impression of an uncle who collected possessions or threw nothing away, it was difficult to tell which. There were piles of briefcases, laptop computers, CDs still in their plastic wrappers, Astaragali sets, boxfuls of spectacles, watches, gold fountain pens, cigarette lighters, cigar cases, medicines, notebooks, and a walk-in closet with shelves full of hats, shoes, shirts, dozens of tie racks, and as many as a hundred suits of various hues and fabrics. Several ziggurats of books surrounded a vast French Empire bed made up with the finest Irish linen sheets, which had not been slept in.

"The garage," said Philippa. "Maybe the car is there."

Nimrod's garage, at the back of the house, was no less cluttered than his bedroom. There was an ancient-looking Vincent motorcycle, a British Olympic team bobsled (which seemed doubly incongruous in Egypt), at least a dozen Persian carpets piled one on top of the other like so many pancakes, several cricket bags full of equipment, a running machine, and a stone sarcophagus made of granite. There was, however, no sign of the white Cadillac Eldorado, and finally, the twins were forced to admit in their heads what they already knew in their hearts — that their uncle had not returned from the previous night's trip.

"I've got a bad feeling about this," said Philippa.

"Me, too," admitted John. "What are we going to do?"

"We have to tell Creemy and Mr. Groanin. And then go look for him, of course."

The twins found Mr. Groanin in his room, reading a copy

of the previous day's *Daily Telegraph* and eating a jar of baby food for breakfast. "Oatmeal with blackberry and apple," he said, seeing the twins. "Delicious."

"I don't know how you can eat that stuff," said John, glancing around the room, which was papered with faded pictures of Shakespeare, Shelley, and Lord Byron.

"This from the lad with the asbestos insides," Groanin said, and scooped a teaspoonful of the gelatinous goop into his mouth. "What can I do for you?"

"It's Uncle Nimrod," said Philippa. "He's not here. He didn't come home last night. His bed's not been slept in, and the car's not there."

Mr. Groanin groaned quietly. "Well, what do you want me to do about it?" He scraped the last of the baby food from the jar and then licked the spoon greedily. "I expect he'll turn up. Besides, he can look after himself. Speaks half a dozen languages, including Arabic. Money in his pocket. Knows the country like the back of his hand. To say nothing of being possessed of supernatural powers. He's not exactly helpless, is he? Me, on the other hand, I don't speak one word of Arabic. I haven't a penny of the local money. I couldn't even find my way to the airport, much as I'd like to, mind. And, in case you hadn't noticed, I have just the one arm. So, I don't really see what I can do."

"You've got to help us find him," insisted Philippa. "He said that what he was doing last night might be dangerous. That's why he insisted on us staying at home."

"Very sensible of him," said Groanin. "In which case, what

makes you think he'd appreciate you looking for him now? You ask me, you'd be better off doing what you were told and waiting here until he pokes his muzzle around the door."

The twins explained about Hussein Hussaout and the lost djinn of Akhenaten, and how the two men had driven off to somewhere in the desert to look for Akhenaten's tomb.

"This sounds like djinn business," said Groanin, wiping his hands on a tea towel on which was printed a picture of Madonna. "We'd best find Mr. Rakshasas. See what he has got to say for himself."

They went down to the drawing room to find the antique brass lamp that housed the old djinn. It was on the table where Nimrod had left it. John picked it up and rubbed it impatiently. *Just like Aladdin,* he thought. As before, blue smoke billowed from the lamp's empty wick, and when it cleared, Mr. Rakshasas was seated on one of the library chairs. He listened patiently to what the twins told him and then nodded gravely.

"I fear you may be right," he said. "That something must have happened to our dear friend, for it is certain he would have made contact by now, to assure you that all was well. But first things first. Let us see if we can contact him."

"How? Using djinn power?" asked John.

"No," said Mr. Rakshasas, picking up the telephone. "I shall try to call his cell phone." He dialed a number and then waited awhile before replacing the receiver. "His phone appears to be switched off." Mr. Rakshasas frowned. "Either that or he is not able to receive a signal. But it may be that he has been bound to a talisman or been made the slave of someone who wishes Nimrod to do his bidding."

"There's nothing like looking on the bright side," said Groanin sarcastically. "On the other hand, someone might just have put the stopper in his bottle. Like the time Nimrod went into an antiques shop in Wimbledon, and popped inside a decanter to take a look around. He'd have been there forever if it hadn't been for me."

"Yes, that is also a possibility," said Mr. Rakshasas. "But that can only happen when a djinn has turned himself into smoke in order to enter a bottle or a lamp. Imprisoning a djinn while he is in his normal-sized body requires that you bind him. To do that, you would need to know his djinn name and have something from the djinn's own body. Such as a fingernail. Or a lock of hair."

"It sounds to me that the best place we can start our search," said Mr. Groanin, "is this shop belonging to Whoosy Whatsit."

"Hussein Hussaout," said John.

"Hussein Hussaout is a good man, and a loyal friend of the Marid," said Mr. Rakshasas. "But it may be that he has become a creature of the Ifrit and is in their control. This is the only way he would have betrayed your uncle. In which case, you had better be very careful. This could be dangerous."

"Aren't you coming with us?" demanded Mr. Groanin.

"I shall not be able to accompany you in person," said Mr. Rakshasas. "But take my lamp with you. It may be that I can offer you some advice. Besides, if Hussaout is in the control of the Ifrit, it is best that we do not yet reveal our hand. For it was my understanding that your uncle intended not to inform Hussaout of your being djinn? If Hussein Hussaout is the slave of Iblis, then it will be safer if he and the Ifrit believe you are only humans. They will not feel threatened by you."

"How are we going to get there?" asked John.

"Creemy can drive us," said Mr. Groanin.

"Aren't you forgetting something? There's no car. Nimrod took it last night," said John.

"We'll have to hire one," said Groanin.

"No," said John. "That would take too long. We'll have to create one ourselves. Using djinn power. What do you say, Mr. Rakshasas?"

"I can be of only limited assistance in this respect, John. Alas, I am very old, and my powers are as worn out as a Galway woman's bath towel. But, perhaps, if you and your sister were to hold hands with me, I could help to focus your own youthful energy. You wish to create a motorcar, yes?"

"Yes," said John.

"Then we must all attempt to visualize the same one."

"I was afraid you'd say that," admitted Philippa. "I hardly know the difference between a Jeep and a Jaguar."

"What is a Jeep?" asked Mr. Rakshasas.

"No problem," said John and, running upstairs, he got the car magazine that he had bought at London's Heathrow Airport and brought it back down to the drawing room.

"There you go," he said, pointing to the aerodynamic-looking red car on the cover. "The Ferrari 575 M Maranello. Zero to sixty-two miles per hour in four point two five seconds, and a top speed of two oh two. Now that's a car that's hard to forget. It's even got four seats."

Groanin took the magazine from John's hands and turned the pages. "Couldn't you find us something a little less fancy, perhaps?" he grumbled. "What we want is something more practical. Some kind of sport-utility vehicle. A proper four by four. A Range Rover. That Ferrari thing looks like it belongs on a racetrack, not on a desert road out of Cairo."

"As a matter of fact, a lot of Arab oil sheikhs buy this car," said John.

Philippa stared at the car on the cover carefully. The parents of one of her friends at school had a Range Rover, and she really liked it, but not as much as this Ferrari. "I like it," she said. "It's pretty. I kind of prefer red to black. Dad always chooses a black car. A red one would be nice."

They got Creemy and went into the garage where Mr. Rakshasas took their hands and closed his eyes and invited them to think of his mind as a kind of amplifier that would help them to increase the power of their own thoughts.

"Mr. Groanin?" he said. "If you would be so kind, perhaps you could provide us with a countdown from ten? John. Philippa. When you hear Mr. Groanin say 'zero' that will be your cue to utter your focus words. Understood?"

"Understood," said the twins.

"When you're ready, Mr. Groanin."

"Ten, nine, eight, seven, six, five, four, three, two, one, zero!"

"FABULONGOSHOO —"

"ABECEDARIAN!"

"— MARVELISHLYWONDERPIPICAL!"

For several seconds, the air rippled inside the garage like a mirage over hot desert sand. There was a very noticeable rise in temperature, too, followed by a small chiming noise, like the sound of a spoon hitting a wine glass. Mr. Groanin blinked and there was still nothing, but when he blinked again a gleaming pink Ferrari was standing in the garage.

"Pink?" yelled John. "It's the wrong color. How did we get a pink one? And the wheels? What happened to the wheels?"

It was true, the wheels were wrong, too. Instead of the sleek low-profile aluminum-alloy wheels with prancing horses that are normally found on a Ferrari, this one had larger all-terrain wheels of the kind that are seen on a Range Rover.

"It's my fault." Philippa winced. "I'm afraid I started to think of a pink car at the last moment."

"And what about the wheels?" moaned John.

"Well, I got a little confused," she said. "When Mr. Groanin mentioned a Range Rover, I started to think of Holly Reichmann's parents' car."

"It looks quite drivable," said Groanin, opening the door

and lifting the leather seat so that the twins could climb into the two small seats in the rear. "You ask me, it's quite an improvement."

"Come on then," said John. "Let's get going."

This was Mr. Rakshasas's cue to return to his lamp, which Philippa picked up and held close to her chest.

Creemy pressed a button on the wall to open the electric garage door, while Groanin got into the car after the twins and closed the passenger door. "Me, I prefer a Rolls-Royce. This is a bit cramped for my liking."

Creemy muttered something in Arabic and, pointing to the ignition switch, shook his head.

"Is there no oil in that boy's lamp?" muttered Groanin, twisting around in his seat to look at John. "You forgot the keys, you dope."

"Sorry," said John and, closing his eyes, concentrated hard for a moment.

"ABECEDARIAN!"

A second or two later, Creemy nodded and switched on the engine, which sounded much less powerful than John had imagined. Creemy steered the peculiar-looking Ferrari out of the garage and onto the road that led south out of Garden City, toward the old part of Cairo and the curio shop.

Cairo's dusty traffic had rarely ever seen a car as peculiar as the pink Ferrari, and people leaned off buses precariously, or came out of shops to look at it. Groanin groaned loudly as Creemy was forced to swerve to avoid a donkey pulling a cartload of maize as the donkey driver stood up and pointed at the pink Ferrari. John noticed that the man was laughing.

"This is very embarrassing," said John, sinking lower in his seat.

Creemy found a bit of open road and put his foot down. The car accelerated, putting the rest of the traffic behind them slowly. A little disappointed with his first Ferrari, John felt glad when, eventually, they reached the Old City and Creemy stopped the car.

"Remember what Mr. Rakshasas said," said Groanin. "No matter what this chap says, I think it's best that we give him the impression that we still trust him. There's an old saying we have in Lancashire: 'Have your friends under your care. But have your enemies right under your nose.' "

And leaving the lamp containing Mr. Rakshasas in the car with Creemy, Mr. Groanin and the twins went along the little cobbled lane to Hussein Hussaout's curio shop.

It was fortunate that Mr. Groanin had advised a show of trust because the first thing they saw upon entering the curio shop was Hussein Hussaout's son, Baksheesh, wearing a bandage on his foot but otherwise looking much recovered. Hussaout himself, seated on the same pile of cushions, wearing the same white suit, and smoking the same hubbly-bubbly pipe, looked tired and worried but, seeing the twins and Mr. Groanin, he did his best to look welcoming.

"Hello," he said. "What brings you here?" Almost as an afterthought, he added innocently, "And where's Nimrod?"

"We were hoping you might tell us that," said Mr. Groanin. "I am Mr. Nimrod's butler, sir. I'm afraid we haven't seen him since he left home to come here last night."

"But he never arrived," said Hussaout, rising to his feet, and looking concerned now. "I assumed that something more important must have detained him, and that he would return today."

Philippa rather doubted this story. "If he didn't come here, then where do you think he might have gone?" she asked Hussaout politely.

The Egyptian shrugged.

"Please, Mr. Hussaout," said John. "Will you help us find him?"

Hussein Hussaout glanced nervously at his son who, fortunately, showed no sign of remembering the twins having been in his bedroom the day before. "Of course," he said. "Look, why don't you go home and wait for my call. I'll make some inquiries. Search a few of his favorite haunts. The main thing is not to worry yourselves too much. Like I say, Cairo is a big city. People go missing all the time. But they usually turn up again. If I think that there's cause to be concerned, I'll telephone the police myself. How does that sound?"

"It's very kind of you, I'm sure," said Mr. Groanin. "And most reassuring to know that Nimrod has such a good friend as yourself, Mr. Hussaout. Isn't it, children?"

"Yes," said the twins, feeling hardly reassured at all, and now quite convinced that Hussein Hussaout was lying to them.

There was something about the speedy recovery of his son, Baksheesh, that seemed linked to Nimrod's disappearance. The boy himself regarded the twins nervously, his eyes flicking from one twin to the other, like a guilty-looking robot.

"One more thing," said John, as they were on the point of walking out of the shop. It was something he had seen clever lawyers do in trials on TV: allow the witness to believe that there were no more questions to be asked and then throw a last one at them, in the hope of catching them off guard. "This place you were going to, in the desert. You don't suppose he went there on his own, do you?"

Hussein Hussaout tried to look thoughtful for a moment. "No," he said. "I don't think so. I only gave him the most general idea of where the place was."

"And where was it that you told him that was?"

"Medinet el-Fayyum," said Hussaout. He shook his head firmly. "But you won't find him there. I'm sure of it. Why would he go there without me? It doesn't make sense. Only I know where he is." Hussein Hussaout corrected himself quickly. "I mean only I know where *it* is. This place near Medinet el-Fayyum. Where I was going to take him. There would be no point in your trying to look for him there."

"We'll await your telephone call," said Mr. Groanin.

"Yes. Yes, please do."

When they were back in the car, Mr. Groanin made a face. "He's a slim customer, make no mistake," he said.

"If that means he's untrustworthy," said Philippa, "then I agree with you."

"Was it my imagination?" asked John. "Or did he seem nervous at the very idea of us going to this place, Medinet el-Fayyum?"

"No, I noticed that, too," said Philippa. "And did you hear what he said? 'Only I know where HE is.' Then he corrected himself, of course, and said, 'Only I know where IT is.' There's a name for making a mistake like that. When your brain says one thing and your mouth says another."

"Yes, you're right," agreed Groanin. "It's called a Freudian slip. And it suggests that there's an unconscious cause for using the wrong word in a sentence, which can sometimes be guessed at."

"I think we should do exactly what he didn't want us to do," said John.

"And what's that?" asked Philippa.

"Go to Medinet el-Fayyum, of course. Maybe someone saw his car. An old white Cadillac Eldorado is not exactly a common car in Egypt."

Mr. Groanin tapped on the outside of Mr. Rakshasas's old bronze lamp. "Did you hear that, Mr. Rakshasas?" he said loudly. "We propose to go to Medinet and look for Nimrod ourselves."

A small disembodied voice that sounded like someone shouting up from the bottom of a very deep well, answered him. "The boy's idea is better than anything I've been able to think of myself," he said.

"Right, that's settled then," said Groanin, buckling up his seat belt. "Creemy?" He pointed through the pink

Ferrari's windshield. "Medinet el-Fayyum. And don't spare the horsepower."

Two hours later, the pink Ferrari pulled up in Medinet el-Fayyum, a largish town to the west of the great River Nile. Having parked in the marketplace, the Ferrari quickly attracted a large crowd of spectators and, with the help of some photographs of Nimrod's white Cadillac Eldorado that he carried proudly in his wallet, Creemy asked the local townspeople if any of them could remember seeing the car the previous night. But it seemed that no one did and after an hour of patient questioning, the search party began to feel a little discouraged.

"Perhaps we could just drive around," said Philippa. "And see if we can spot the car somewhere ourselves."

Groanin pointed to the other side of an irrigation canal that connected the river with the town. "You see over there?" he said. "That's the Western Desert. Several thousand square miles of it." Then he pointed the other way, which looked equally empty. "And that's the Eastern Desert. There's several thousand square miles of that as well. Drive around? I don't think so."

"Mr. Groanin's right," said John. "It would be like looking for a needle in a haystack."

"How about turning ourselves into birds of prey?" suggested Philippa. "And flying around."

"I don't recommend it," said Mr. Rakshasas from inside his lamp. "For one thing, animal transformation requires a great deal of experience. And for another, neither of you has yet learned to fly."

"That's that then," said John, kicking a stone on the ground.

By now, the sun was getting lower in the sky, and it was clear they were soon going to have to return to Cairo. The twins could not conceal their disappointment, or their fears for Nimrod's safety. Finally, just as Creemy was about to start the car and head for home, a camel driver who had heard about the pink Ferrari and the search for the white Cadillac Eldorado rode up and began a conversation with Creemy that ended with him pointing down the road and giving what appeared to be some definite directions.

"Cadillac," said Creemy and, having thanked the camel driver, started the car. "Him see."

Mr. Rakshasas, translating from Arabic into English, added that the camel driver had told Creemy he had seen an American car in the village of Biahmu, a few minutes drive from the junction with the main road, near a group of rocks and some ancient ruins.

Quickly, they drove back to the main road where, finding a sign for Sennuris and Biahmu, Creemy steered the Ferrari along a rough dirt track for several miles.

"Just as well we've got the Range Rover wheels on this car," observed Groanin as the car hit yet another pothole with a loud juddering sound. "If we'd had the original wheels, we'd never have made it along this track."

Eventually, they arrived at a group of rocks near which

stood a colossal pair of stone feet, and the face of some for-gotten Pharaoh. Creemy stopped the car and they all got out.

"These must be the ruins," said John.

"No, not ruins," said Groanin quietly. "That's poetry, that is."

"Poetry?" said Philippa. She liked poetry, but she didn't quite understand what Groanin was talking about. Before she could ask him to explain, however, Groanin was already launched on the recitation of one of the most famous poems in English literature:

> *"I met a traveller from an antique land*
> *Who said: Two vast and trunkless legs of stone*
> *Stand in the desert. Near them, on the sand,*
> *Half sunk, a shattered visage lies, whose frown,*
> *And wrinkled lip, and sneer of cold command,*
> *Tell that its sculptor well those passions read,*
> *Which yet survive, stamped on these lifeless things,*
> *The hand that mocked them, and the heart that fed;*
> *And on the pedestal these words appear:*
> 'My name is Ozymandias, King of Kings:
> Look upon my works, ye Mighty, and despair!'
> *Nothing beside remains. Round the decay*
> *Of that colossal wreck, boundless and bare*
> *The lone and level sands stretch far away."*

Groanin paused as if to let the effect of the poem sink in to the heads of his two young listeners.

"What is that poem, Mr. Groanin?" asked Philippa, who thought she'd like to hear it again sometime.

"Don't tell me you've never heard 'Ozymandias' before," said Groanin. He shook his head. "Remind me to give you a copy of the *New Oxford Book of English Verse* when we get back. That was 'Ozymandias.' The first poem I ever learned at school. By Shelley. One of the greatest English poets who ever lived."

"I guess it's supposed to be ironic," said John, and leaped onto a rock for a better view of the surrounding area. Suddenly, he grinned. "How about 'nothing beside remains . . . except a white Cadillac'."

Nimrod's white Cadillac Eldorado was parked close to the rock wall on the other side of the ruins. It was undamaged and unlocked, the hood partly buried in sand, as if a great sandstorm had covered it.

"I'll check the car," said John. "Maybe he left a note." But there was nothing.

Philippa cupped her hands around her mouth and shouted Nimrod's name while John climbed back up to the vantage point afforded by the rocks to see what else he could see, but there weren't even any vultures wheeling in the sky that might have indicated a body lying on some distant sand dune.

Philippa shouted again. Then she had an idea and, closing her eyes for a moment, she uttered her focus word: "FABULONGOSHOOMARVELISHLYWONDERPIPICAL!" A large brass bullhorn, the kind once used by sailors to speak to one another on different ships, appeared on the sand.

"That's more like it," said Groanin, as Philippa now

proceeded up and down the length and breadth of the area shouting Nimrod's name through this megaphone. "There's no way he could fail to hear that," he said, covering one ear with his only hand.

"Stop," shouted John. "I thought I heard something."

Philippa lowered her bullhorn and listened carefully.

Finally, Groanin let out a breath and shook his head. "There's nothing here," he said quietly. And waving his hand at the arid landscape he added, "Nothing. You ask me he came here in one car and then went away again in another. Kidnapped most likely. Or bottled up and taken."

John was squatting down behind the Cadillac. "There is only one set of tire tracks, besides our own," he said. "It looks like he drove the car here and vanished." He walked around the front of the car and inspected the sand dune that covered the hood. "I wonder. Does this look like it got here naturally? All this sand? I don't recall it being windy today."

"Sand is sand," said Groanin. "And how it gets anywhere is a mystery to us all."

"That's no answer," said John, irritated.

But Groanin was already walking back to the pink Ferrari. "I tell you, there's nothing here," he said crossly, and getting into the car, closed the door and turned on the air-conditioning. He groaned with relief as the cooler air enveloped his body. He watched as John and Philippa spoke for several minutes to the lamp containing Mr. Rakshasas and, when they returned to the car, it seemed to Groanin that the twins were looking at him in a peculiar way. Philippa opened the car door, letting all the cold air escape.

"Mr. Groanin," she said carefully.

"Yes, what is it?" And sensing some kind of conspiracy between the twins, he frowned and added, "Whatever it is, I don't want to know. I'm hot, I'm tired, I'm thirsty, and I want to go back to my room."

"I've got an idea," Philippa said carefully. "But it does involve a sacrifice on your part."

"Sacrifice? I'm not being sacrificed to save your flippin' uncle."

"We don't want to sacrifice you, Mr. Groanin," said Philippa. "Instead we want you to use something you have in your power, something that was for your own benefit, for the benefit of someone else."

Groanin frowned. "A little less enigma, please, child," he said, "and a little more clarity. I haven't the least clue what you're going on about so far."

"A long time ago, Nimrod gave you three wishes and, so far, you've used only two wishes, yes?" She paused. "Well, isn't it obvious? You can use your third wish to find Nimrod. All you've got to do is say 'I wish I knew where Nimrod is' and we'll find him."

"You want me to use my third — ?" Long years of habit prevented Groanin from using the actual word *wish*, and instead he made a spiraling gesture with his forefinger, as if miming the action of a djinn granting a wish.

"That's right," smiled Philippa.

"But that would mean I had no thingamajigs left," objected Groanin. "It would mean that all these years I've spent trying to think of one really fantastic thingamajig had been wasted." He frowned. "Anyway, doesn't Nimrod have to be here to grant my thingamajig?"

"We've discussed it with Mr. Rakshasas," said Philippa. "If Nimrod is within five miles of here, chances are, if you shout loud enough, he'll hear your wish. But if he doesn't hear it, then he won't and we'll certainly be no worse off than we are at present."

"And you won't have a third wish at all if Nimrod's dead, will you?" said John.

"Besides," said Philippa. "We've talked it over, and we're going to give you three wishes ourselves."

Groanin laughed. "With all due respect, neither of you is yet in the same class as your Uncle Nimrod. Look what happened when you tried to create a red Ferrari. I'm not saying it's no good, it's just that, well, in the matter of thingamajigs, no one wants to settle for second best, do they?"

He paused and got out of the car, walking around as he began to weigh the matter in his mind. "Pardon me," he said, "but this needs a bit of thinking, after so many years of indecision. This is a big thing we're talking about. Something that could affect the rest of my life." This mention of the rest of his life seemed to touch something deep within Groanin, and it suddenly occurred to him how much of his life had been wasted in contemplation of the possibilities of his third wish. Was the remainder of his life to be similarly blighted? And suddenly he knew what he must do. Not just for Nimrod. But also for himself.

"I'll do it," he said. "I'll do it, I'll do it. You've no idea how miserable this third thingamajig has made me. All that time, racked with indecision about what to thingamajig for, and always worrying that I might use the thingamajig word by accident and waste the thingamajig on something useless." Mr. Groanin smiled. "Oh, my goodness. It would be consummation devoutly to be thingamajigged if I could use the thingamajig usefully and then be done with it forever. Wouldn't it just?"

"That's the spirit, Mr. Groanin," said John.

"But wait a moment," Groanin frowned. "Wait just a minute here." He wagged his finger at the twins. "You have to be extremely careful with thingamajigs. Sometimes you can use the W word and it comes out in a way that you could never have anticipated. Believe me, I know what I'm talking about here. So, suppose I do say I thingamajig I knew where Nimrod is right now? It's possible I might find myself transported to wherever he is, and then I would know, but you wouldn't be any the wiser. Do you see?"

"Maybe we ought to write the wish down beforehand," said John. "Exactly. According to what I believe Nimrod calls *The Baghdad Rules*."

"Aye, that's right. *The Baghdad Rules*." Groanin nodded. "Yes, that's the way to do it."

"Without being anywhere different from where we are at

this present moment in time," said Philippa. "I wish that we could all know *exactly* —"

"*Exactly*," repeated Groanin. "Excellent."

"*Exactly* where Nimrod is right now," said Philippa.

John looked questioningly at Mr. Groanin and Philippa and, seeing them nod their agreement, wrote down the wish. Then, tearing off the sheet of paper from his notebook, he read the wish out to Mr. Rakshasas inside the lamp.

"It's a good wish," said Mr. Rakshasas. "Very precise. No room for error. According to the spirit of Section 93 of *The Baghdad Rules*. Let us all hope that Nimrod hears it. Otherwise I am at a loss as to what we shall do next. We can hardly drive all over Egypt repeating this wish in the hope that Nimrod will hear it. In this respect, the Cadillac presents perhaps our only hope of narrowing down our search."

John handed the paper to Mr. Groanin. "Ready?" he asked.

"As ready as I'll ever be," confessed Mr. Groanin. He looked at what John had written like an actor trying to familiarize himself with a part in a play, and then nodded. "Right then. Here goes." Groanin licked his lips nervously, and then started to make his wish: "'Without being anywhere different from where we are standing at this present moment in time,'" he read carefully, "'I wish that we could all know exactly where Nimrod is right now.'"

The next moment the ground shook and, for a second or two, they all thought it was another earthquake.

"What the heck was that?" asked Groanin.

"That was your wish being granted, you blithering idiots," said Nimrod's disembodied voice. "I'm over here. Didn't you hear me shouting earlier on?"

"We can hear you," shouted Philippa. "But we can't see you."

"Of course you can't," said Nimrod's voice. "That's because I'm buried alive. In a tomb underneath the sand about two hundred yards from the car. Start walking west toward the sun and I'll tell you when you're getting warmer."

"Are you all right?" asked Philippa.

"Yes, I'm fine," said Nimrod's voice. "Only I'm still a little cross with myself for being bound so easily by Hussein Hussaout."

"How did he do that?" asked Philippa walking toward the sound of Nimrod's voice.

"Because I bite my nails," said Nimrod. "It's always been a bad habit of mine. It's one of the things a human needs to bind a djinn over. A part of his person such as a tooth, a lock of hair, or a nail clipping."

"When we were at Hussein Hussaout's shop, you were biting your nails," recalled John.

"It seems so," said Nimrod. "But somehow he also knows my secret name. With these two things, he was able to imprison me in this tomb."

"But why should Hussein Hussaout want to betray you?" asked John.

"Because he is being blackmailed by the Ifrit. While I was

223

lying stunned on the floor of the tomb, I heard him apologizing to me and asking my forgiveness. The poor fellow really had very little choice in the matter. The Ifrit poisoned his son, Baksheesh, and the dog, Effendi, and let the dog die as an example of what would happen to Baksheesh if Hussein Hussaout didn't do exactly what he was told."

"We saw Baksheesh," said John. "He's recovered a lot from when we last saw him. We went back to the shop. We pretended to believe what he told us. That you had never arrived at the curio shop. I don't think he suspects that we are djinn."

"I'm lucky to have a brilliant niece and nephew, otherwise I might have been stuck here for centuries. It was a brilliant bit of sleuthing by you both. Not to mention remembering that Mr. Groanin still had one of his three wishes intact. Which reminds me. Mr. Groanin? I'm very much in your debt."

"Never mind that for now," said Groanin as they walked across the burning desert toward the setting sun. "Are we getting warm yet?"

"Another fifty yards and you'll be here," said Nimrod's voice. "You'll see a short escarpment. Walk to the foot of that escarpment and await further instructions."

"I see it," said John.

At the foot of the escarpment they stopped, as instructed, and surveyed a landscape composed entirely of sand dunes. It seemed almost impossible that Nimrod should be somewhere close by.

"Where you're standing now," said Nimrod's voice. "I'm

right underneath your feet. You are going to have to shift the major part of the sand dune immediately in front of you. On your own. I can't help, you see. Because this tomb has been sealed with djinn power, I can't do anything to assist you."

"Can we make it disappear?" asked Philippa.

"That would take far too long," said Nimrod. "Sand is tricky stuff for novices like yourselves to make disappear. Each grain of sand tends to behave like an individual object, which makes it hard to handle with djinn power. You can't make it disappear, and you can't blow it up. So you'll have to think of a way of shifting it."

"All right, then," said John. "An earth mover. An excavator." He looked at Philippa. "Do you know what one of those looks like?"

"I'm not sure," admitted Philippa.

"I have a remote control one at home," said John. "Yellow-colored. Sits on top of my bookcase. Remember?"

"As it happens," said Groanin. "I think we passed some roadwork on the way into Medinet el-Fayyum, and I'm pretty sure there was a bulldozer there. Look, I'll stay here with Mr. Rakshasas, to make sure we don't forget the spot where Nimrod is buried. You two and Creemy go back to the main road and see if you can get the machine. Or make another. I don't know. But you'd better hurry. It'll be dark soon, and this place is already starting to give me the jitters."

CHAPTER 17

THE SCORPION

Standing alone in the desert, waiting for Creemy and the twins to come back, Groanin felt a little like some forgotten statue himself. He would have sat down on the ground but for his being afraid that he might get stung by a scorpion, which is a creature both plentiful and dangerous in that part of the world.

"So?" he asked Nimrod nervously, as something — a bat? — flitted close to his head. "What's it like down there?"

"Cold and dark," replied Nimrod. "I've been unable to make things at all comfortable for myself. The djinn power that binds me is very strong, and my powers are almost useless in here. It must have been a double binding that Hussein used. Or even a triple. I have a flashlight but the batteries are beginning to run out. My cell phone doesn't work. And I've eaten the bar of chocolate I had in my pocket. So things are really rather miserable."

"So how were you able to grant my wish?" asked Groanin. "If your powers are useless."

"*The Baghdad Rules*," said Nimrod. "Section 152. An outstanding wish takes priority over another djinn's binding. You see, when a wish is granted, the power of that wish sort of attaches itself to the bearer. In a way I didn't really need to be around for your wish to come true." Nimrod sighed. "What a pity you only had the one wish left. One good wish and I'd be out of here."

"I wouldn't care for it at all," said Groanin. He glanced around as something slithered across the ground, and saw a snake disappear into a hole. "This whole country gives me the creeps."

Forty minutes and forty seconds later, Creemy and the twins were back with an excavator — an orange colored Tata-Hitachi, with a bucket capacity of nine cubic feet and a digging depth of twenty-four feet. To Groanin's surprise, the excavator appeared to be driving itself; at least it did until John got out of the Cadillac carrying an electronic remote control unit.

"It's just like my toy excavator at home," he explained. "I'm pretty good at driving that so I decided that it might be easier to make a few modifications to the real thing." And under his expert control, the excavator was already gouging out the first bucket-load of sand and dumping it several yards away from the site they had identified earlier.

An hour's digging brought them almost outside the door,

with Creemy shifting the last of the sand with a shovel he had found in the back of the excavator. By now it was dark, with only bats flitting around in the moonlight to keep them company, and he was obliged to work by the headlights of the excavator, and a flashlight that John had found in the trunk of the Cadillac.

"This is an evil place," said Groanin. "I can feel it. Terrible."

"Don't," said Philippa. "I'm scared enough as it is."

"We're nearly there," shouted John.

Creemy stood back from the stone door and, tossing the shovel aside, shouted to John to come down the steps with the flashlight. Philippa started to follow her brother down to the stone door. John was already inspecting the gap between the door and the wall.

"Wait a minute," he said. "There's something attached to the door."

"Whatever you do, don't touch it, John," yelled Nimrod. "I was afraid of this. It's probably a djinn seal."

"What does that mean?" asked Philippa.

"It means that Iblis or one of the Ifrit must have been with Hussein Hussaout," said Nimrod. "Only they could have done this. Very likely it's made of jade or copper, which are both talismanic to the Marid; we can't touch those materials when they've been subjected to djinn power."

"I guess that explains why Mother doesn't like jade," murmured Philippa.

"It certainly does," said Nimrod, "so on no account must

either of you touch it. The seal must only be broken by Creemy or Mr. Groanin, for the power of the Ifrit would also bind you two children if you were to touch it. Perhaps even worse."

John was shaking his head. "It doesn't look at all like jade or copper to me," he reported. "There seems to be a large piece of waxlike stuff in the gap between the door and the wall. It's about the size of a football and appears to be semi-transparent. Wait a minute. There's movement. It looks like there's something copper-colored inside. Holy cow! It's a scorpion."

"A living seal," said Nimrod. "They're the most danger-ous of all. To human beings as well as to djinn. Which means that Iblis might have been here himself. That would certainly explain the power of the binding. Whatever you do, don't break the seal or else the scorpion will escape from it and try to kill you. Instead, you must light a fire underneath the seal to melt the wax and kill the scorpion."

They went back up the stone steps to look for something to burn, which was not so easy in the dark, and with trees and bushes almost nonexistent in the desert.

"We could use the carpets from the Ferrari," suggested Philippa. "If we soak them in gasoline, they should burn easily."

"They were the wrong color anyway," said John and began to tear them out.

"One more thing," said Nimrod, as they piled the gasoline-soaked carpets underneath the seal on Akhenaten's tomb door. "When the scorpion is consumed by fire you may hear the

word Iblis gave to Hussein Hussaout to make the binding.
Make sure you keep a note of it if you do. It might be a clue."

Mr. Groanin lit a match. "I love a good fire," he said, and
tossed it onto the gas-soaked carpets.

A ball of flame rose up from the ground illuminating
their dirty, shadowy faces and almost immediately, the wax ball
on the door of the tomb began to melt, sending the copper-
colored scorpion inside into a frenzy. Even through the wax
they could see the creature's sharp stinger curling over its
back and quivering like some malevolent witch's black-nailed
finger.

"I don't want to be near that thing when the wax melts,"
admitted Groanin, moving farther up the steps out of harm's
way. But, for another moment or two, the twins and Creemy
held their ground. Finally, when there was no more wax on
the door, the biggest scorpion anyone, including Creemy,
had ever seen, fell into the flames.

The twins both gulped with horror. The creature's twelve-
inch body was as thick and leathery as a small armadillo's, the
pincers like something from the tray of some fiendish tor-
turer, the eight legs spidery and alien, but worst of all was the
tail, which was more than ten inches long, and ended in a
stinger that was as big as a man's thumb. To their horror the
arachnid was alight although not consumed by fire and, with
a large blue flame extending almost a foot above its long, curling, venomous stinger, the scorpion bounced off the burning carpets and scuttled instinctively toward the twins, as if

recognizing that they were from the same djinn tribe as the prisoner it had been set to guard forever.

Creemy and John took a step backward, but John missed his footing on the uneven ground and fell down in front of the flaming scorpion. Sensing its chance to kill him, the copper scorpion scuttled toward John's bare arm, its pincers snapping loudly and its stinger raised like a hypodermic needle, a lethal dose of venom already dripping from the sacs that feed the hollow point.

"Look out," yelled Groanin. "It's going to sting you."

"No!" shouted Philippa as she stamped and then kicked at the creature. As she did so, the scorpion managed to catch at the lace of her sneaker with its dirty-looking claws, and climbed onto her foot, advancing on her bare ankle. Now that it was on her foot, she realized with disgust just how heavy it was, thinking it must have weighed at least a couple of pounds. Philippa let out an ear-piercing scream and kicked hard at the door of the tomb, sending the scorpion flying onto the ground where it rolled into a ball, flicked a large globule of venom just past her head, and finally burst into flames. Hearing what sounded like air escaping from the scorpion's leathery body, and suddenly remembering what Nimrod had said, Philippa bent down very carefully at a safe distance to hear what sounded like a word whispered from the depths of some infernal pit. Then she climbed up and out of the trench and threw up on a sand dune. After a moment or two, John picked himself up off the ground and followed her.

"You saved my life," he said. "That scorpion was about to sting me."

Philippa wiped her mouth. "You would have done the same," she said.

John nodded and squeezed her hand gratefully.

"I know I wouldn't," admitted Groanin. "I hate scorpions."

They removed the remains of the seal from the door of the tomb, pushed it open laboriously, and then entered the ancient burial chamber to find Nimrod advancing on them out of the darkness, looking slightly more somber than was usual. The twins ran to him and hugged him warmly.

"We thought we might never see you again," said Philippa.

"You very nearly didn't," admitted Nimrod. "I might have been down here for a very long time indeed." He let out a breath and, taking out his handkerchief, wiped a tear from his eye. "I owe you my life, children, I owe you my life."

Then Nimrod swallowed his emotions, stiffened his upper lip, cleared his throat, pocketed his handkerchief, and approached his butler with a wry smile.

"And you, Mr. Groanin," said Nimrod. "Even though Section 42, Subsection 12 of the *The Baghdad Rules* excludes the granting of three wishes to a human who helps to free a djinn by means of a previous grant of three wishes, I nevertheless feel constrained to invoke Section 44, relating to situations relating to the commission of acts of outstanding selflessness, and grant you three more wishes, Mr. Groanin, and at your earliest convenience."

Groanin groaned loudly. "No!" he yelled. "Please. No

more wishes. For the first time in years I am enjoying the freedom of not having any wishes at all. You djinn have no idea of how terrible it can be to live with a choice like that. How much tension it creates in a man. Shall I have this or shall I have that? Shall I become this or shall I become that? Exhausting. So no more."

"But I've said it now," said Nimrod. "And wishes granted cannot be taken away."

"Then I wish that I might have no more wishes," said Groanin. "For the plain fact of the matter is that I've realized something very important about wishes. That sometimes you're doomed not to want whatever it was that you wished for when you get it. No, not even a new arm, for the truth is that I've grown used to having just the one, and I wouldn't know what to do with another."

"Well said, Mr. Groanin," said Nimrod. "Well said." Then he looked at the twins. "By the way, did anyone catch the word that escaped from the scorpion's dead body?"

"It wasn't a word I recognized," said Philippa. Then she shrugged. "It sounded like Rabat."

"Rabat," said John. "That's the name of a city in Morocco, isn't it?"

"Rabat, eh?" murmured Nimrod.

"Mean anything to you?"

Nimrod shook his head very firmly. "No. Nothing at all."

Meanwhile, Mr. Rakshasas had rematerialized from his brass lamp and, borrowing John's flashlight, began to examine the beautiful reliefs on the walls of the tomb, which was otherwise empty. Invested with magic, the stone carvings were meant to smooth a dead Egyptian's way to the afterlife and sustain him or her, forever. Mr. Rakshasas touched them with the tips of his fingers as if reading Braille like a blind man and the twins had little choice but to follow him around the tomb or remain in the almost palpable darkness.

"There are dozens of chambers in this tomb," said Nimrod from somewhere in the shadows. "It stretches for hundreds of yards, as far back as the rocks where I left the car, where there is another entrance that was uncovered by the earthquake. The binding that Hussein Hussaout used must have covered them both with some sort of sandstorm when he left. I walked all the way here in the hope of finding another way out. But it appears to be some sort of maze and in the dark, I couldn't find my way back to the original entrance."

"Look at these hieroglyphs," said Mr. Rakshasas. "There are none of the usual references to Osiris, god of the afterlife, that would appear on the tomb of an Egyptian who believed in the usual gods. All of these reliefs pay homage only to the Aten. This is Akhenaten's tomb, all right."

"But where is the treasure?" asked John.

"A good question," murmured Nimrod.

"It may be that some of them are already dispersed through the world's museums," said Mr. Rakshasas. "From the location of the tomb and these murals I should hazard the guess that this is Tomb 42, first discovered in 1923, and lost during a great sandstorm after being quite obviously wrongly classified as the tomb of a treasury official, or some kind of administrator. And it's easy to see why. The reliefs near the entrance where we came in are quite different from the ones farther inside. As if Akhenaten sought to disguise his tomb, for fear that it would be desecrated by those who considered him a heretic. He was probably wise to be cautious."

Mr. Rakshasas pointed at a large ancient Egyptian painting that covered one whole wall of the empty tomb. It depicted a tall man with a gold scepter that was the size of a walking stick from which the sun's rays extended toward the naked bodies of several dozen men who knelt before him.

"But this," he said excitedly. "This is quite unmistakable. To anyone with knowledge of djinn history, the story in these pictures is quite clear enough. The priests kneeling before him number seventy, a most peculiar number for the Egyptians to choose, but which leads me to suppose that this is a picture, perhaps the only one in existence of the lost djinn of Akhenaten." Mr. Rakshasas looked back across his shoulder at Nimrod. "Interesting headdress, don't you think, Nimrod?"

"I was thinking the same thing," said Nimrod. "In most normal Egyptian headdresses, the whole body of the snake goddess, Wadjet, appears on the front. But the body of this snake seems to go all the way around the king's head. It's more realistic-looking, too. Almost as if it might be a real snake. The black-and-gold body is very like that of the Egyptian cobra. And note the way Wadjet seems to hold the Aten — the disk of the sun — underneath its body, almost as if —" Nimrod punched the flat of his hand. "Yes, of course. Why didn't we appreciate this before?"

"What is it?" asked Philippa.

"For thousands of years our tribe has been puzzled as to how it was that a human, albeit a human that was part djinn, could have controlled so many other djinn. The seventy. But this headdress would seem to suggest that all along Akhenaten was not his own master at all. But that he was being controlled by a djinn. Most likely one of the Ifrit who favored the appearance of snakes and scorpions."

"That would explain a great deal," agreed Mr. Rakshasas. "Such as why the Ifrit seem to know more about this than we do."

"You don't suppose they already have them, do you?" asked Nimrod. "The seventy lost djinn of Akhenaten?"

"If they did," suggested Philippa, "they would hardly have gone to this trouble to get you out of the way, surely?"

"Good point," said Nimrod. "They would already hold the balance of djinn power and very likely I'd be dead."

"I think it's clear from this mural," said Mr. Rakshasas, "that the lost djinn were once here. In some sort of receptacle, probably. A canopic jar, perhaps. With the rest of Akhenaten's treasures. But as to where they may be now, who knows? Very likely a museum."

"But which one?" said Nimrod. "Such a receptacle could be anywhere. Wrongly classified, it might take years to find."

"Then the Ifrit's guess as to where those treasures are might be only as good as ours," said Philippa.

"Possibly," agreed Nimrod. "But really there's only one man who can answer any of these questions for sure. The man who rediscovered Tomb 42. Hussein Hussaout." He glanced at his watch. "Besides, he's got some explaining to do. I think it will be useful if we pay him a visit on our way home. He'll certainly not be expecting us tonight."

They returned to the ruins and the Cadillac where Nimrod looked critically at the pink Ferrari. "What is this supposed to be?" he asked, chuckling.

"There was no time to rent a car," explained John. "So we had to use djinn power." He shook his head. "I know, I know. The wheels aren't right. And the color . . ."

"Yes, it looks like something an Arab oil sheikh might commission for his least favorite wife so that she might drive across the sand dunes and get the children from school. Still, considering that there are about twenty thousand different parts in a motorcar, I think you did rather well, really." He smiled. "The question is what are we going to do with it now? Keep it and drive it back to Cairo to endure the scorn and laughter of some very sensible people who wouldn't be seen dead in it? Or consign it to well-deserved oblivion?"

"Consign it to oblivion," chorused the twins.

"Is the right answer," he said, and waving his hands, Nimrod zapped the strange-looking Ferrari into nothingness. "Now then, what about that excavator?"

"We borrowed that," admitted John.

"I thought as much. It looks too ordinary to have been created by you two. For a start, orange is not your color, Philippa. I'm sure you would have preferred a pink one, wouldn't you? Incidentally, if you do borrow something always try to return it in better condition than the way you found it, eh? For the sake of good manners." And even as he spoke the Tata-Hitachi was acquiring a new coat of orange paint, some new treads, a new gear box, and a tank full of gas.

After they had explored Akhenaten's tomb, Creemy and Nimrod had been digging the Cadillac out of the sand, and as soon as he saw his car again, Nimrod opened the glove compartment, found a box of cigars, lit one, and immediately blew a smoke ring in the shape of his own car.

"You've no idea how much I've been looking forward to this moment," he said, puffing on the cigar with obvious relish. "Honestly, I thought I might never taste one of these again."

They all piled into the car and followed the excavator as John, still using his remote control, steered it slowly back to the main road and returned it to the building site where they had found it, before Creemy drove them north again, back to Cairo.

CHAPTER 18

THE YOUNG VISITORS

It was well after midnight by the time they reached Cairo's Old City and, as usual, the streets were still thronging with people. Nimrod and the twins left Creemy, Mr. Groanin, and the lamp containing Mr. Rakshasas in the Cadillac, and went to find Hussein Hussaout. But as soon as they entered the narrow, cobbled alleyway that led to his shop, they realized that something was very wrong. The alley was crowded with people and, outside the shop itself, several white-uniformed policemen stood on guard, preventing anyone from going inside.

"What has happened here?" Nimrod asked another man, in Arabic.

"The owner of the shop, Hussein Hussaout, has been found dead," was the reply.

"How did he die?"

"People are saying that he was robbed. But I myself have heard that he was bitten by a snake."

"When did this happen?"

"Less than one hour ago," said the man.

Nimrod took the children by the hand, led them down another, quieter alley, through an ornate portal and up a steep stairway into an old church where he sat the twins down and told them what he had learned.

"Murdered?" Philippa felt her jaw wobble. "Poor Baksheesh."

"Let us hope that he is unharmed," said Nimrod. "It's imperative that we get into that shop and find out exactly what has happened, but it may be that the Ifrit are watching this place. At the same time, I don't want us to find ourselves spending the night at the police station, answering a lot of silly questions. Which is what will happen if we present our- selves at the door and say that we knew poor Hussein Hussaout. The Cairo police are notoriously inefficient."

"Poor Hussein Hussaout?" objected John. "He tried to kill you."

"Perhaps so," admitted Nimrod. "But he was quite obvi- ously acting under some sort of duress. I intend to find out what that was. Now listen very carefully. To get inside the shop, we must become police officers ourselves."

John and Philippa exchanged a look of puzzlement. "How can we do that?" asked Philippa.

"We shall have to leave our bodies in this church," said Nimrod. "No one will disturb them if they think we are praying. Then we shall float back up the alley and occupy the bodies of three policemen, in much the same way as we occupied the bodies of those camels. Nothing to it really."

John nodded. To him, being a policeman, even an Egyptian one, sounded like a vast improvement on being a camel; Philippa, however, was feeling uncomfortable with the idea. Her camel had been a female, but a policeman was a man, and the idea of occupying a grown man's body, albeit for a few minutes, bothered her.

"Why can't we just float around?" she asked. "Why do we need to be in somebody else's body?"

"Simple," said Nimrod. "If you want someone to talk to you, it's easier. And it's the only way you can pick something up and look at it. Besides, if you're out-of-body too long, you risk drifting off into space. A body is like an anchor, you see. It keeps you firmly on the planet." He shook his head kindly. "But if you feel unhappy about it, Philippa, then stay here and watch our bodies."

Philippa glanced around the strange little church. From the ancient ceiling, which looked like an upturned boat, burning oil lamps hung on long chains, and somewhere someone was chanting a prayer. The church looked like it was a thousand years old. "Suppose someone does something to our bodies while we're away from them?" she said.

"In a church?" Nimrod knelt down on a hassock and bowed his head in an attitude of prayer. "Would you disturb someone who looked like this?"

"No," admitted Philippa. "All right. I'll do it."

"That's the spirit," said Nimrod. "And I do mean spirit. Try to remember not to say anything while we're out-of-body. It's rather alarming for mundanes when they hear voices from out of thin air."

"For who?" asked John.

"Mundanes," said Nimrod. "From the Latin *mundus*, meaning 'world'. It's what we sometimes call human beings. Anyway, do remember what I've said. Many of the world's superstitions and religions have been caused by careless or mischievous djinn speaking to mundanes while being out-of-body. So unless you want that on your conscience, I suggest that you remain silent. What else? Oh, yes. Try not to knock anything over unless you want someone to think they're being haunted by a ghost. Believe me, it's easy enough to do when you can't see your own hands or feet.

"One more thing. Although it shouldn't be a problem on a warm night like this, but bear it in mind, anyway. When you are in a state of invisibility, don't stand in a draft of cold air. Cold always affects djinn power badly and in a state of invisibility it could make you semitransparent, so that you might appear to be a ghost."

"Does that mean there are no such things as ghosts?" asked Philippa.

"There are ghosts all right. Human ghosts, anyway. Largely they're quite benign. But a human ghost can be very nasty if it becomes possessed by the spirit of a dead djinn. Or so I believe. Fortunately, I've never encountered this kind of thing myself. You see djinn don't become ghosts, as a rule. But it's not unknown for a djinn's spirit, his Neshamah, to take possession of a human ghost in the same way as we're about to take possession of a human body.

"But, like I say, all of that is something very different from the out-of-body experience we're going to have now." Nimrod smiled. "Just try to relax and enjoy it. You'll feel strange, but we'll quickly find some bodies and everything will be fine again. I promise." He nodded to each side of him. "Come on, then."

John knelt down on Nimrod's left-hand side and bowed his head. "Ready," he said.

"Ready," said Philippa, adopting the same attitude on Nimrod's right-hand side.

Nimrod took each of the twins by the hand. "Try not to let go of my hands, until we find some policemen to occupy," he said. "It makes it easier to know where we all are at any one time. But if we should find ourselves separated, then we'll all meet back at the car. Right then. I think that's everything."

"This is going to be so cool," said John.

"Oh, I do hope not," said Nimrod. "Here goes. QWER-TYUIOP."

Philippa uttered a little scream as she felt herself rising out of her own body. For a moment it was like growing taller, much taller, except that when she looked down she found herself staring at the head of a red-haired person with glasses she did not recognize, and it was several more seconds before she realized, with a jolt, that this was her own head. Why did she have her hair like that?

John felt no less disoriented than his sister and, except for the feeling of Nimrod's hand enveloping his own, he thought he might easily have panicked.

"It's quite normal for this to feel a little strange," said Nimrod, sensing their alarm. "Just take a deep breath and follow me."

"If we're not here, then where are we?" inquired John as they floated back up the dark alley toward the curio shop.

"You might say that we're occupying two different dimensions," said Nimrod. "Or, to be rather more accurate, your body is on one side of the fence, but your spirit is on the other. I could explain it in a more scientific way, but you would need a degree in physics to understand. Possibly two."

"Please," said Philippa. "No physics. I hate physics."

"Oh, don't say that," said Nimrod. "Everything a djinn does and can do is the result of physics. One day you'll understand that."

"As long as I don't have to take an exam to prove that I can understand it," said Philippa, "then that sounds fine."

They passed through the police line and walked unobserved into the brightly lit shop, which was filled with policemen, one of whom was using a piece of yellow chalk to draw an outline around the body of Hussein Hussaout, which lay on the floor between the chess sets and the Egyptian thrones. To the twins, the dead man looked very much like Baksheesh had looked when he had been ill in bed; his lips and hands were quite blue.

"The poor man," whispered Philippa.

Hearing this, one of the policemen looked around, but seeing nothing, he gave a noticeable shudder and then moved to the other side of the shop, next to two other policemen who were leaning against the wall, smoking cigarettes, and generally looking bored.

"There," whispered Nimrod. "That looks like three bodies going begging over there." Nimrod squeezed his niece's hand meaningfully and led the twins up into the air immediately above the three unwitting policemen. "Keep your toes down, and your eye fixed on your chosen policeman," he advised quietly. "It's no more difficult than putting on a wet suit. As soon as we're in, you'll find that the spirit already occupying the body will be so overwhelmed by your arrival, that they won't bother you at all. They won't even remember anything about it afterward."

As soon as they were all located in their respective bodies, Philippa looked at the two men standing next to her and said, in a voice and language she only half recognized, "Nimrod?" One of the policemen nodded back at her.

Philippa smiled. "It feels strange being a man," she said.

"Yes," said the policeman containing Nimrod, who was a sergeant. "Best not say that again, eh? Just in case one of the poor chap's colleagues hears you and gets the wrong idea about him? And do try to speak Arabic, Philippa."

"Can we?" asked John's policeman.

"Of course," said Nimrod's policeman. "You're an Egyptian, remember?"

"I can remember all sorts of strange things," admitted John. "Some of them not very pleasant."

"Come on," said Nimrod's policeman throwing his cigarette onto the floor. "This way."

They followed the police sergeant out the back door, through the yard, and up the wooden stairs to the living quarters where they found Baksheesh alone in his room, sitting on the edge of the brass bed where the twins had first seen him, weeping quietly. The sergeant knelt down in front of Baksheesh and took hold of both his hands.

"Listen very carefully to me, Baksheesh," said the sergeant. "Don't be alarmed at what I am about to say. Your father was a good man. And he was a friend of mine."

The boy frowned as he tried to recall his father ever having mentioned this police sergeant. "He was?"

"I know that he told you all about the djinn. So I know you won't be scared when I tell you that this is Nimrod speaking to you from inside this policeman's body."

For a moment the boy looked terrified, his eyes widening with fear, and the twins had the strong impression that he was about to run out of the room, screaming. But Nimrod kept hold of his hands, and in an almost hypnotic voice kept on talking to Baksheesh until he had calmed the boy.

"Are you dead?" he asked the sergeant. "Is that why you are in this body now?"

"No, I'm not dead," said the sergeant. "I'm in this body because it's possible that those who killed your father may still be watching your shop."

The boy started to cry again.

"Do you remember the boy and the girl who came to see you last night?" asked the police sergeant. "My niece and nephew. They were looking for me. Do you remember?"

"Yes," said Baksheesh, wiping his eyes on the back of his sleeve. "I remember them."

"They are djinn, too," said the sergeant. "And they are with me now. In the bodies of these other policemen. Philippa. Come here and speak to Baksheesh, in your own voice, if you can."

Philippa knelt beside the sergeant and tried to twist the unshaven policeman's face she was wearing into something like an expression of sympathy, but to her surprise she found she could still use her own girlish voice.

"Baksheesh," she said gently. "I'm very sorry about your dad."

"I'm glad your uncle is all right," said Baksheesh. "My father, he never meant you any harm."

"I know," she said, stroking his hair.

"Iblis forced him to trick you. His snake bit me on the foot and I lay between life and death while my father was obliged to do his bidding. Only when you were captured did Iblis allow his servant Palis to lick my foot to remove the poison."

"Palis?" said the sergeant. "The foot-licker? He was here, too?"

"He is a very evil djinn," said Baksheesh, looking at his bandaged foot.

The sergeant looked at Philippa and explained. "Palis

licks the sole of your foot until he can suck at your blood. His tongue is rough you see, like sandpaper. Like the water buffalo. Rough enough to remove the skin with only a few licks. After which he drinks your blood." Turning back to Baksheesh, he said, "You were lucky he only drank some of your blood, Baksheesh. Usually Palis drinks all of it."

"I do not think I am so lucky," sighed Baksheesh.

"No, of course not." Nimrod paused. "Did you see Iblis?"

"No, I only heard his voice. So softly spoken you would think he is very kind. But he always stayed in the shadows. I think he was frightened to let me see him. Always in the shadows. Always so softly spoken, like the snake that came with him. The Egyptian striped cobra. The biggest one I have ever seen."

"Tell me exactly what happened to your father," said Nimrod. The boy said nothing for a moment, and then Nimrod added, "If I am to avenge your father, I must know exactly what happened."

Baksheesh took a deep, unsteady breath and then nodded. "A scorpion died," he said. "It was in a bamboo cage. The twin of the one that Iblis left to guard over your tomb, he said. He left it here with my father and, when it died, my father went very pale and became very frightened for he knew that it meant you had escaped and that Iblis would come back here to prevent him from telling you anything. My father knew there was no time to run. Iblis moves like the wind, he said. There was only time for him to hide me inside an old sarcophagus in the yard to prevent Iblis from having his snake bite me again. So it bit only my father."

"The lost djinn of Akhenaten," said Nimrod. "Do the Ifrit have the lost djinn?"

"No." The boy smiled. "They asked my father lots of questions. I think they search for them still."

"Where are they?" asked Philippa. "Do you know?"

The boy shook his head.

"How are they contained?" asked the sergeant.

"I don't know."

"Will you be all right, Baksheesh?" asked Philippa. "Who will look after you? Can we help you at all?"

"I have an aunt in Alexandria and an uncle in Heliopolis. I expect they will take care of me now."

"Don't forget that you have an uncle in England," the sergeant said kindly. "One day, when you have finished your schooling, come see me and I will help you in whatever you want to do. I will send you my address. Do you understand?"

"Yes, thank you, sir."

Hearing voices coming up the stair, Nimrod stood up. "I fear we must be going. Good luck to you, my boy. Good-bye."

"Good-bye, sir."

"John? Philippa? We're leaving."

Philippa stood up and turned toward the door.

"No," said the sergeant. "There's no time for that. It will be quicker if we travel as heavenly bodies. Quickly. Hold my hands."

As the twins grasped the police sergeant's outstretched hands they felt themselves floating up to the ceiling again, only this time more quickly and they just had time to see the three embarrassed policemen, as they recovered their own bodies, become conscious of the fact that they were holding hands.

"Back to the church," whispered Nimrod's spirit form, leading them downstairs again.

"What are we going to do now?" asked John, as they floated out of the shop and headed back through the shadows, along the cobbled alley toward the little church.

"We must find Iblis and his Ifrit henchmen before they find the lost djinn of Akhenaten," said Nimrod. "To do that we shall have to bring him out of the shadows and into the open."

"How will we do that?" asked Philippa.

"It will not be easy. And it might be dangerous."

Having recovered their own bodies in the strange little church, they walked — a little unsteadily in the case of the twins who were not used to making a transition from body to spirit and back again — through the darkened streets to where they had left the Cadillac and, seeing them again, Creemy flashed the car's headlights to help them find their way.

"Tomorrow I have an important job for you both," Nimrod told the twins when they were at the house in Garden City again.

"Does this have anything to do with bringing Iblis into the open?" asked John.

"Yes," said Nimrod. "Let me show you what I have in mind." He escorted them up to the roof and pointed across the darkened lawns that bordered his home, to the house of the French Ambassador, which lay on the other side of his garden wall. The ambassador's house was floodlit, with security guards moving about on the grounds, and a light was burning in a square, Italian-shaped tower.

"Do you see that tower?" he asked. "That is the French Ambassador's library. As well as being a keen student of Egyptology, he is also something of an amateur astronomer and the library contains not just a large number of books but also a powerful telescope. Using it, someone might see almost everything that was happening on this side of the house and garden. Tomorrow I propose to ask Mrs. Coeur de Lapin if the two of you might spend the day looking at the books in her library."

"What?" John groaned. "Do we have to?" he complained. "She's always touching my hair and telling me how handsome I am. And I don't see how reading some old books is going to trap Iblis."

"We're not exactly children, you know," said Philippa. "Except for us, you'd still be stuck in that tomb."

"For which I am, of course, immensely grateful," said Nimrod. "But if you will allow me to finish?"

The twins nodded back at him.

"Using the telescope in Mrs. Coeur de Lapin's library, you will be able to keep this house under surveillance."

"Why?" asked John.

"Because, my dear impatient nephew, I am going to lay a trap for Iblis, and I require that you two should spring it."

"Wow!" said John.

"What kind of trap?" asked Philippa.

"I shall let it be known around certain places in Cairo where the Ifrit are sometimes seen, such as the Ibis Café at the back of the Cairo Hilton, Groppi's, of course, and Yasmin Alibhai's Belly Dancing Club, that I have found a casket containing the lost djinn of Akhenaten. With any luck, Iblis will then turn up here in the hope of stealing the casket for the Ifrit. He will find the house empty, of course, and take advantage of our absence to search the place. In one of the rooms on this side of the house, and observed by you, through Mr. Coeur de Lapin's telescope, he will find an Eighteenth Dynasty wooden casket with the name of Amenophis the Third, in which I shall have laid a special djinn trap. A way of capturing him."

"Where are you going to get a casket like that?" asked Philippa.

"I have one in my bedroom," said Nimrod. "I use it as a sort of medicine chest. Of course, Iblis is not stupid and he would undoubtedly sense if I or Mr. Rakshasas was in the immediate vicinity. Which will only encourage him to break into the house. But I don't think he will detect the two of you next door. Not yet fully grown, you don't give off the same aura as do I or Mr. Rakshasas." Nimrod shrugged. "And that is pretty much it, really. As soon as you see that Iblis has been captured inside the casket you can call me on my cell phone."

"Where will you be?" they asked Nimrod.

"Several miles from here. As soon as I know that Iblis is inside the casket I'll come straight back to the house and complete the process of imprisoning him. Creemy and Mr. Groanin will be with me, of course. There's no point in either of them running any unnecessary risks. Good servants like Groanin and Creemy are hard to come by."

Philippa's eyes narrowed suspiciously. There was something about Nimrod's plan she didn't buy. "Are you sure you're not just trying to get us safely out of the way?" she asked Nimrod. "So that you can go off and do something more dangerous somewhere else?"

"As you are well aware," said Nimrod, "Mrs. Coeur de Lapin has taken to you both in a big way, and whereas I don't think she'll mind either of you looking through her husband's telescope, I think she would be a little less accommodating and indulgent if it were me or Creemy or Mr. Groanin asking for the run of her library. No, I am not just trying to get you safely out of the way. As you will see, if you bother to think about it, this whole plan hinges on you, my dear children."

"Okay," she said. "We'll do whatever you say."

"That should make a nice change," said Nimrod.

CHAPTER 19

SNAKES AND LADDERS

The next morning they awoke to find all of the Egyptian newspapers running a story about a sensational break-in at the Cairo Museum of Antiquities the previous night. Ignoring the fabulous gold treasures of the boy-king Tutankhamen, the intruders had concentrated their efforts on other rooms in the museum, where much less valuable Eighteenth Dynasty artifacts were displayed. Even more curious to the newspapers and the police, who pronounced themselves baffled by the crime, was the discovery that none of the artifacts had actually been taken, merely removed from their display cases: a royal scepter and some Shabti figurines had been broken, and several canopic jars used for holding the entrails of embalmed Egyptian mummies, damaged while being opened.

"Do you think it was the Ifrit who did this?" asked John.

"No doubt about it," said Nimrod. "The Eighteenth

Dynasty is the right period for an Akhenaten artifact. I must say this all fits in very well with our plan."

"You don't think they found what they were looking for?" asked John.

Philippa shook her head firmly. "According to the newspaper," she said, "the thieves entered the museum at around nine o'clock. But Hussein Hussaout was killed by the snake at around midnight. They would never have bothered silencing him if they already had what they were looking for. I bet there are a lot of museums, the world over, that are going to find themselves being broken into like this, with nothing very much stolen."

"Unless we get there first," said John.

"We must get there first," said Nimrod. "We simply must. The homeostasis demands it."

After breakfast, Nimrod telephoned Mrs. Coeur de Lapin who said she would be very happy to look after the twins for the whole day. As soon as they were ready, and clear about the plan to capture Iblis, they walked around to the French Embassy, bearing a small gift, an antique scent bottle that Nimrod said had come from Huamai, the perfumer at Giza.

"How very kind of him," said Mrs. Coeur de Lapin when she saw the perfume. "That uncle of yours. He is so very charming. And, for an Englishman, so romantic, too. You are very lucky to have an uncle like him, I think. Such an interesting man."

"Yes, he's wonderful," agreed the twins.

CHILDREN OF THE LAMP

"Now then. What would you like to do, children? I am at your disposal."

"Well," said Philippa, "Nimrod has been telling us that you have a wonderful library."

"Yes, it's true."

"With a big telescope," John added with a rather bogus show of boyish enthusiasm that drew him a sharp look from his sister.

"The thing is, Mrs. Coeur de Lapin," said Philippa. "I'd like to read up about a lot of these archaeological sites, so that I can appreciate them better when I see them."

"And I'm interested in bird watching," said John. "I was hoping to use the telescope to see some of the birds in our garden."

"Are you sure?" said Mrs. Coeur de Lapin. "We could take that boat trip, if you like. Or maybe we could go to the swimming pool at the Nile Hilton. It's a very nice pool, the best in Cairo, I think. And they do a very nice lunch there. Or, perhaps a trip to the pyramids at Saqqâra."

"No, really," said John. "The library would be fine. To be honest we've had a little too much sun over the last few days, and we've been looking forward to staying inside, in the air-conditioning."

Philippa nodded, thinking that when he felt like it, her brother could be a convincing liar.

"Very well, as you wish." Mrs. Coeur de Lapin smiled and escorted them up to her library.

The library wasn't anything like they had imagined. It was

very clean and functional, with lots of bad abstract paintings, a beige carpet, furniture that had once been so modern it now looked old-fashioned, and many dozens of yards of brushed metal shelves that were home to several hundred books. Glass cases were arranged all around the room to display the Coeur de Lapins' collection of small Egyptian artifacts, while in the window, next to a table with a computer and some elegant glass decanters, stood a large telescope on an aluminum tripod.

Philippa noted the objects and then politely inspected some of the books. "You must know a lot about Egypt," she observed. "Are you an archaeologist or something?"

"Only an amateur," admitted Mrs. Coeur de Lapin. "Monsieur Coeur de Lapin is more of an expert than I am."

John pointed to the dozen or so little green figures shaped like mummies on her plain marble mantelpiece. "Are those from a tomb?"

"Yes. They are called Shabti figurines and they were designed to be a dead Egyptian's servants in the afterlife." Mrs. Coeur de Lapin picked up one of the little green figures and showed it to the twins more closely. "Myself, I love to hold these figures, because they are so old. They make me feel as if I am in touch with the past. I feel that I can almost understand what it was like to be alive in ancient Egypt. You know?"

"Could I look through your telescope now?" asked John.

Mrs. Coeur de Lapin smiled and ran her hand through John's hair. John winced. He hated people touching his hair, especially Mrs. Coeur de Lapin, who seemed to enjoy doing it so much. "Of course," she said, waving an elegant hand in its general direction. "Help yourself. Just as long as you don't expect me to explain how it works. It's my husband's."

"I know how to work it, I think," said John. He nodded his thanks and having mounted a small ladder next to the telescope, he trained the powerful lens on the open French windows of Nimrod's drawing room. The Egyptian pharaoh's chest stood in the center of the floor and, by adjusting the viewfinder, John found that he could see close enough to read the hieroglyphs that covered the gold-colored wood. It would be impossible, he reflected, for anyone to open the chest and not be easily observed by a person looking through Ambassador Coeur de Lapin's telescope. This was going to be relatively easy, assuming that Nimrod's plan worked. He wasn't exactly sure what a djinn trap amounted to. Nimrod had been a bit vague about that, but he thought that everything would become clearer if and when Iblis showed up.

"Can you see through it all right, John?" asked Mrs. Coeur de Lapin, running her hand through his hair again. "You understand how it works, yes?"

"Yes," he said uncomfortably. "Yes, I'm fine, thanks." There was, he decided, something just a little bit weird about Mrs. Coeur de Lapin that just being French didn't quite explain. Maybe it was the black-and-gold headband she always wore that John thought made her look like an Apache Indian. Or maybe it was her rather dull, almost lifeless blue eyes that seemed to look straight through him, even when she was smiling. Either way there was no getting away from the fact that Mrs. Coeur de Lapin made John feel decidedly awkward and nervous.

"John," she said. "Would you like to see my collection of scarabs?"

Philippa was thinking exactly the same thought as her twin brother: that Mrs. Coeur de Lapin was a little too much. And she was glad that it was John who was having to do most of the talking to her. While he looked at Mrs. Coeur de Lapin's collection of scarab beetles — little brightly colored jewels of jade and lapis lazuli — and periodically through the telescope, Philippa started to examine some of the books in Mrs. Coeur de Lapin's bookcase. Most of these were in English, but even the ones that were in French seemed to have something to do with Egyptology and the pharaohs. She sat down on an uncomfortably angled modern chair and picked up another book off the floor, one it seemed Ambassador or Mrs. Coeur de Lapin must have been reading, for a pair of reading glasses lay on top of the book, which was marked with a page torn from a magazine or a catalog.

To Philippa's considerable surprise, it was a book about Akhenaten, as indeed were all of the others lying on the floor beside the chair. The discovery sent a chill through Philippa's hot djinn blood, and she felt her heart miss a beat. Was it just a coincidence that Mrs. Coeur de Lapin had been reading books about Akhenaten? Or was there a more sinister reason behind her interest in Egypt's "Heretic Pharaoh"?

Philippa stared at the French Ambassador's wife in a way she hoped might not look like a stare. Now Mrs. Coeur de

Lapin was laughing at John's dreadful, nervous jokes with a giggle that sounded as if she had squeezed it out of one of the little cuddly toy animals that lay on Philippa's bed back in New York. Mrs. Coeur de Lapin was so weirdly feminine, decided Philippa. As were her silly little gestures. Her stupid long fingernails. Her heavy eyeshadow. Her ridiculous headband. Why did she always have to wear that ridiculous headband — like some kind of flapper girl from the 1920s? *And why*, thought Philippa, *why did that headband suddenly seem familiar somehow, as if she had seen it somewhere else, and recently, too?*

And was it her imagination or did the headband seem ever so slightly *alive*?

Philippa blinked and rubbed her eyes, and then tried to get a closer look at the headband without arousing Mrs. Coeur de Lapin's suspicion that she and her headband were now an object of curiosity. Nonchalantly, with her hands clasped behind her back, Philippa meandered over to the table near the telescope where the scarabs were displayed and then picked one up.

"Why did the Egyptians consider these beetles interesting enough to want to make models of them?" asked John, glancing quickly through the telescope and then back at the scarabs, and all at the same time as squeezing in a scowl at his sister.

"Why?" Mrs. Coeur de Lapin collected a fine piece in her bony hand. "I'll tell you why. There are many species of scarab beetles. And several of these are dung beetles."

"Does that mean what I think it means?" asked John. He glanced around as he realized that someone had turned on the computer.

Mrs. Coeur de Lapin laughed her squeaky-toy laugh. "Yes," she said. "They collect dung from the sheep or the camels, form it into a ball the size of a tennis ball, and then roll it to their underground homes where the female lays her eggs on the ball. And when the larvae hatch, they eat the dung."

"Get out of here," exclaimed John. Seeing Mrs. Coeur de Lapin look uncomprehending he added by way of translation, "You're kidding."

"No," laughed Mrs. Coeur de Lapin. "I'm not kidding." She went over to the computer and switched it off. "Did you turn this on?" she asked him.

John was too busy being shocked about the dung beetle to answer this question.

"They eat camel dung?" he said. "I can't see what's remotely sacred about that. And it's hardly the sort of animal I'd use as the inspiration for an ornament." He smiled a rictus smile, like a dead man, and sneaked another quick look through the telescope at Nimrod's drawing room where still, nothing was happening. This assignment was proving much more difficult than he had foreseen, what with Mrs. Coeur de Lapin showing him her scarabs, tousling his hair, and always her incessant chatter.

"On the contrary," said Mrs. Coeur de Lapin. "It's a remarkable little animal. The Egyptians believed that the scarab beetle represented their sun god, Ra. Ra was the Egyptian god who rolled the sun across the sky and buried it each night. Just like the scarab beetle. These carved scarab beetles were supposed to give the owner the same characteristics as the scarab beetle."

"What?" frowned John. "You mean like eating dung?"

Mrs. Coeur de Lapin tut-tutted loudly. "John," she said, "don't be silly. No, the Egyptians admired the beetle's persistence in rolling a dung ball, as well as its ecological usefulness. It is a symbol of new life. Of resurrection, too, the way the beetle comes out of the ground."

Philippa dropped the scarab she was holding onto the carpet by Mrs. Coeur de Lapin's feet, as if she had been a little shocked by this for her action concealed a purpose. "I'm sorry," she said.

"It's quite all right," said Mrs. Coeur de Lapin, bending down to pick up her scarab. "They are very strongly made. Even now after several thousand years, they are almost impossible to break."

As Mrs. Coeur de Lapin stooped to collect the green stone scarab off the rug, Philippa grabbed the opportunity to bend over the Frenchwoman's head and take a closer look at her black-and-gold headband; as she did so, she formed the distinct impression that, for a brief moment at least, the headband swelled very slightly and then compressed again, almost as if — Philippa could think of no other explanation — it had filled itself with air. And even as Philippa began to suspect that the headband around Mrs. Coeur de Lapin's head had inhaled and then exhaled *a breath*, she remembered why the headband seemed somehow familiar to her. The headband she was looking at was almost identical to the headband Akhenaten had been wearing in the mural on the wall of the tomb. Almost identical, except that this gold-and-black snake — if indeed that was what it was — had no apparent rearing head.

John hadn't noticed anything. He was too busy taking advantage of Mrs. Coeur de Lapin's bending down to retrieve her scarab to look through the telescope again, to pay any attention to her headband. Philippa decided that there had to be a way of finding out for sure if the headband really was a living snake or not. *What do snakes eat?* she asked herself. *Small rodents? Would any self-respecting snake, even one that chose to live wrapped around the silly head of the French Ambassador's wife, be likely to pass up a free meal of, say, a mouse?* Philippa began to concentrate very hard, much harder and longer than was usual, as perhaps befitted the creation of a living creature, which was something she had never done before. Finally, when her concentration seemed complete, she uttered her focus word as loudly as she dared.

"FABULONGOSHOOMARVELISHLYWONDERPIPICAL."

"Did you say something, my dear?" asked Mrs. Coeur de Lapin.

"Um, I said, thanks and gosh for showing us such a fabulous collection," said Philippa, trying to ignore the tiny field mouse she had caused to appear in the haystack of blond hair on top of Mrs. Coeur de Lapin's head.

Philippa was not overly fond of mice but, seeing the mouse in Mrs. Coeur de Lapin's hair, she realized that the idea of a mouse was rather less appealing than the cute little animal that was already exploring its surroundings, and she hoped that her suspicions about the gold-and-black headband might be proven wrong, if only for the sake of the mouse. But even as she watched, the headband began to turn on Mrs. Coeur de Lapin's head like a top unscrewing itself from the neck of a bottle, and what had once appeared to be silk or satin was now clearly revealed as glistening snakeskin.

Philippa felt her blood run icy cold and kicked John on the back of the leg as the flat, sinister head of a very large Egyptian cobra appeared from the center of Mrs. Coeur de Lapin's curls and, flicking its tongue, stared hypnotically at the mouse. John looked around, bordering on outrage and then, catching his sister's eye, glanced up at Mrs. Coeur de Lapin's hair as, sensing its peril, the mouse peered over the edge of the snake's body, trying to judge the height of the jump required to leap from the Frenchwoman's head onto the floor. Too late! For the next second, the snake struck with the speed of a whiplash. Within a matter of seconds, the poor mouse was being swallowed whole.

CHAPTER 20

ALL BOTTLED UP

"Awesome," breathed John as the snake closed its mouth and started to squeeze the mouse down its long body.

"I don't like this," whispered Philippa. "I think we should be going."

"Maybe you're right," agreed John, pushing the barrel of the telescope away quite nonchalantly, as if he wasn't in the least bit concerned about anything to do with Mrs. Coeur de Lapin's hairdo. Smiling politely, he dismounted the ladder and edged toward the door.

"You can't leave," protested Mrs. Coeur de Lapin, seemingly oblivious of what was happening on top of her own head. "You've only just arrived." Then she gave a little jerk, as if a spring had snapped inside her. "You've only just arrived. You've only just arrived." It was as though Mrs. Coeur de Lapin was a recording that was on a loop. "You've only just arrived. You've only just arrived."

And then she went all glassy-eyed and vacant; her mouth

sagged open, some false teeth lolled out and her head rolled forward on her shoulder, as if someone had switched off the power at the back of her neck.

"Let's get out of here," said John.

"I'm trying," said Philippa, "only I don't seem able to move my legs."

"Hey! Me neither. What's happening? I'm paralyzed."

"I wish Nimrod were here."

Having swallowed the mouse, the Egyptian cobra raised its head and upper body in front of Mrs. Coeur de Lapin's face and began to uncoil its body, which seemed endless until, finally, it reached the floor. Once there, the cobra started to grow in size until its body was as thick as a man's and its head the size of a shovel.

"Don't look in its eyes," said Philippa. "It's trying to hypnotize us."

"I don't mind being hypnotized half as much as I mind being bitten," said John, who was feeling a little hypnotized already, for it seemed to him that the snake was growing arms and legs, and apparently becoming a man with a hooked nose, a smallish fair beard, and an unpleasant expression on his thin face. A second or two later, the reptile had been quite absorbed by a handsome, arrogant-looking Englishman smelling strongly of snobbery and snake.

Finding that she could not run, Philippa tried to contain her fear. "Iblis, I presume," she said coolly.

"You presume too much, you wretched little toad,"

sneered Iblis. "If there's one thing I hate more than a young djinn of the Marid, it's two young djinn of the Marid." Iblis swallowed uncomfortably and placed a hand on his stomach. "I suppose you think you're pretty clever with that mouse, eh?"

"Not so clever." Philippa trembled.

"Have you any idea how disgusting a mouse actually tastes? Ugh, I feel quite sick. And I smell like the reptile house at London Zoo." He licked the inside of his mouth several times, snorted horribly from his nose onto the back of his throat, and then spat, greenly and horribly, onto the carpet. "No, I thought not."

"Then why did you eat it?" asked Philippa.

"Because, little Miss Clever Clogs, that's what snakes do," said Iblis. "Snakes eat mice. I ate it before I had time to ask myself how a mouse came to be crawling around in Mrs. Coeur de Lapin's hair. She may be French but, contrary to popular belief, even the French wash their hair now and again."

Iblis wore a Savile Row pin-striped suit, a pair of hand-made snakeskin shoes, and carried an ornately carved walking stick with a silver knob on top. He loosened his old Etonian school tie, undid the collar button on his Turnbull & Asser shirt, and coughed unpleasantly. The cough turned into a loud retch.

"That's what comes of assuming human shape so soon after eating a mouse," said Iblis, retching more green slime onto the floor. "It's the fur that does it." He retched again.

"Sticks in your throat. Even snakes throw that bit up after they've eaten."

Iblis went over to the drinks tray, picked up a smoked-glass brandy decanter, and drained the entire contents with one enormous gulp. For a moment he looked around irritably at the computer, as if momentarily distracted. Then, with his eyes narrowed, he stared hatefully at the twins. "Of course, I wouldn't have had to take on human shape again quite so suddenly if you hadn't dipped your grubby little fingers into my lamp oil."

He shook his head impatiently and smiled sarcastically. "But no. You couldn't resist, could you? That is so typical of you Marid. Always interfering. There was I, disposed to be merciful to you on account of your youth, and you had to throw that bloody mouse at me." Iblis retched horribly again and this time, he managed to vomit the mouse onto the floor.

"Well, get ready to be sorry, kids," snarled Iblis.

Soaked with brandy, the mouse lay still for a moment and then sat up for, incredibly, it was still alive. It rubbed its whiskers for a second and then ran toward the door. Philippa gave a silent little cheer that the mouse had survived its terrible ordeal.

"See that mouse?" said Iblis, and inches before the mouse reached the door and freedom, Iblis blasted the poor creature to a cinder with one hard stare from his cruel eyes. "When I've finished with you two," he continued, "you're going to think that mouse was luckier than the man who fell out of a plane without a parachute and landed in a mattress factory. The only reason you're not dead already is because I haven't decided if I'm going to eat you or throw your useless little bodies into the world's deepest cesspit, which, in case you wondered, is in a hotel in St. Petersburg, Russia. Believe me, you have not tasted real suffering until you have stayed in a Russian hotel. As for the cesspits, they are like something from Dante."

Even as Iblis spoke, John sensed that Philippa was trying to gather her willpower for the moment when together they might break free of the djinn force that held them rooted to the spot, and tried to do the same.

"Don't even think of trying to use your power against me," sneered Iblis, adjusting the impeccable cuffs on his beautiful handmade shirt. "Young djinn like you don't stand a snowball's chance in hell against a djinn with my experience and malevolence. I'd eat you like a really thin, tasteless Scottish cracker with my morning coffee. Besides" Iblis held up a few strands of hair in his fingers — "I have your hair. Which makes binding you both a piece of cake."

"So that's why you were always running your hands through our hair," said John. "I knew there was something weird about that."

"And I have known there was something weird about you. Ever since I took control of this woman in order to keep an eye on Nimrod. I've been onto you both since that picnic.

No human kids would ever have eaten caviar and *foie gras* any more than they would eat a mouse." Fastidiously, Iblis picked a last piece of fur from his lips.

"We've done nothing to you," John said defiantly.

"You're forgetting the mouse, surely."

"Apart from the mouse."

"You want to beg for your lives?" Iblis sat down on the uncomfortable modern chair and grinned. "Go ahead. After eating a mouse, I could use a good laugh."

"No, really. Why do you want to kill us?" insisted John.

"Oh, I can see that dear Uncle Nimrod's been falling down on the job if he hasn't told you that much," said Iblis. "We're on different sides in this war, sonny. That's why. You might as well ask why mice don't get along with snakes. I deal in bad luck, and your tribe deals in good luck. Except that in your case, good luck would seem to be in rather short supply."

"It doesn't have to be like this, surely," argued Philippa.

Iblis laughed as if genuinely amused by Philippa's remark. "Such touching naïveté," he said. "The famous Marid conscience, I suppose." Iblis's face turned very nasty as, standing up quickly, he brought it closer to John's, close enough for John to smell the mouse on his breath. "What is it with your tribe? This desire to spoil the fun for other djinn. As young djinn, you especially must understand how much more fun it is to inflict bad luck on people than try to create a bit of good. And what an uphill struggle that is."

Iblis frowned and then caught his breath as he saw some doubt in John's face.

"Or didn't Nimrod tell you? I can see he hasn't. The truth is, we all start out the same way. Marid, Ifrit, Jann, Ghul. We all like a joke. Pulling a chair away from under a fat lady. Tossing a banana peel in front of a stupid police officer. Don't we, John? Haven't you ever wanted to deepen a puddle of water in front of a blind man crossing the road? Or make a fountain pen leak on a bridegroom's white tuxedo? I can see you have." Iblis smiled and straightened up.

"When he was young, as young as yourselves, there was nothing Nimrod liked better than to hand out a bit of bad luck himself. Oh, yes. He hasn't always been a good boy. It's just that as he got older, like the rest of your tribe, he got all pompous and boring. The Marid conscience. The homeostasis. Rubbish. There is no homeostasis. The truth is that there is always going to be more bad luck around than good and that your tribe is fighting a losing battle." Iblis looked closely at John again. "I can see that's something you think yourself, isn't it, John?"

"No," said John. "I hate you and all you stand for."

"Very principled, aren't we?" Iblis laughed again. "You're as pompous as your uncle. Not that it matters. The Ifrit have always hated the Marid and vice versa. Always have. I would say 'always will' except for the fact that, as a tribe, your days are numbered. Just as soon as I get my hands on the lost djinn of Akhenaten."

Iblis wiggled the brandy decanter he was still holding in his hand.

"But as it happens, I'm not going to kill you. That would be a waste. I'm going to bottle you up and keep you in my fridge until the day comes when you're ready to call me 'master.'"

"That day will never come," said Philippa.

"We'll never call you 'master,'" said John.

"Brave words, young djinn, but you haven't read *The Baghdad Rules*. You have no choice in the matter. You are obliged to give three wishes to whomever frees you. Me included."

"Never," said Philippa.

"Not that the Rules really matter. You see, you can rest assured that you'll feel very different after a year or two stopped up inside this bottle," Iblis said, wiggling the decanter in his fingers. "Being imprisoned in a bottle or a lamp concentrates the mind wonderfully. Take my word for it. There's nothing you won't do, no evil deed you'll refuse to perform after you've had a chance to cool your heels in here."

He dropped the last few drops of brandy onto his greenish tongue and then placed the decanter carefully on the table among Mrs. Coeur de Lapin's scarabs.

"Any last requests for mercy? Words of defiance? No? Pity."

"Drop dead," said John.

Iblis laughed. "You'd better hope I don't, sonny djinn," he said. "Think about it. If I drop dead, then who will know you're doing time in this crystal decanter? You might very easily end up like that idiot Rakshasas. Agoraphobic. Bats. Out to lunch. Old Rakshasas was stoppered up in a dirty milk bottle for fifty years. Think of it, children. Fifty years. Apparently, the smell of sour milk, cheese, and then mold, of course, drove him quite crazy. Really, it's amazing that he manages to function at all in normal djinn society. Think about that when you're doing a long stretch in this brandy decanter, eh?"

Thick smoke began to appear underneath the feet of the twins so that for a second they thought that the carpet might have caught on fire. But gradually, it enveloped their bodies until they could no longer see Iblis or, indeed, the room they were in.

"And just be grateful I'm not using a double bind. And I'm stopping you up inside a decent-sized bottle," said Iblis, "instead of something much smaller. I might just as easily have confined you to the inside of my fountain pen or the hollow poison chamber inside my walking stick. At least you'll be comfortable."

Iblis's voice seemed to be rising above them, and it was a moment or two before the twins realized that this was because they were dissolving and changing into the smoke. For a minute or so they felt themselves floating away, before being gathered together again, slowly at first, and then more quickly as the smoke began to enter the bottle, which it continued to do for a while, by a slow and equal motion, and in a smooth and exact way, until nothing of them was left outside and a loud chiming sound far above their heads and a sudden silence announced that the decanter had been stoppered.

Now the process seemed to reverse itself, and what was smoke began to solidify and take on human shape, and the strong sensation of floating gave way to a feeling of being grounded again, followed swiftly by a palpable appreciation of enclosure. When the last wisp of smoke had disappeared into their shoes and socks, the twins found themselves in what appeared to be an enormous glass room and, immediately overcome with claustrophobia and brandy fumes, it was several minutes before either twin felt able to address their new situation.

Philippa let out a profound sigh and, sitting down on the smooth glass floor, muttered, "So much for Nimrod's plan." Stifling an inclination to cry, she added, "What are we going to do now?"

"It could be worse," offered John. "We could be dead."

"Yes, I suppose so." Philippa bit her lip. "I'm afraid, John," she confessed.

"So am I," said John. "I guess this is it, then." Running his trembling hand along the smooth shiny wall, he added, "Home sweet home. Until someone rescues us."

"I can't imagine choosing to travel around the world like this," said Philippa. She tried to take a deep breath but seemed to find there was a limit to how much air she could draw into her lungs. "I wish there was more air in here."

Seeing his sister's labored breathing seemed to affect John, and he tried himself to take a deep breath to control a growing sense of panic. "You don't think we're going to run out of air in here, do you?"

"Didn't you hear what Iblis said? That Mr. Rakshasas was inside a bottle for fifty years."

"Don't remind me." John shook his head. "How did he breathe, I wonder?"

"It's that smell. It probably makes you think there's not enough air. What is that smell, do you think? It's kind of intoxicating."

"Brandy fumes, I suppose," John said as he sniffed the wall, laughing uncomfortably.

"I don't see what's funny," said Philippa.

"I was just thinking. Djinn in a brandy bottle."

Philippa smiled a sarcastic sort of smile.

"I'm just trying to look on the bright side of things," said John.

"There's a bright side to this?" Philippa took out her handkerchief and dabbed at the corner of her eye. "Tell me more."

"We've got each other," said John. Sitting down beside her, he put his arm around her shoulders. "I'd hate to be in here on my own."

"Me, too," said Philippa.

"I mean, I'd rather you weren't here, if you know what I mean. But now that you are, well, I'm glad, that's all."

After a while, Philippa threw off his arm and walked all around the inside of the brandy decanter, which took several minutes. "Curious," she said. "How much larger it seems on the inside."

"We're outside of three-dimensional space, that's why," said John.

"I wonder if that means we're outside of time as well.

That's what Einstein said, isn't it? That time is relative. It depends on the space."

"Meaning?"

Philippa shrugged. "I dunno. Just, maybe, that time goes at a different speed inside this bottle."

"Oh, that's a comforting thought," said John. "I was trying to get used to the idea of spending fifty years stuck in here, and now you're suggesting that fifty years might actually seem a lot slower than that."

Philippa swallowed nauseously. "You're right." And then: "On the other hand, maybe time goes more quickly in here. So fifty years will seem like five minutes. Either way, I wish I had some of mother's charcoal pills."

"Why not give it a shot?" said John. "Didn't Nimrod say something about using djinn power inside a bottle, to furnish the place, make food and drink? Some charcoal tablets shouldn't be too difficult."

Hardly hesitating, Philippa muttered her focus word, and two pills appeared on the palm of her hand.

"Neat," said John and swallowed the pill she offered him.

"What do you say to a rug?" said Philippa. "This floor is a little hard and slippery."

"What color?"

"Pink," said Philippa. "I like pink."

"Pink?" John made a face. "Why not black? I like black. Black is cool. And besides, wouldn't a TV be better?"

"You want to watch TV now?"

John shrugged. "What else is there to do?"

After several attempts, which looked more like modern sculpture than a television set, John succeeded in making himself a TV and, as soon as he made an armchair, he sat down and switched the set on.

"Typical," said Philippa. "We're stuck in here, and all you can think about is television."

But as the picture appeared, John let out a groan. "Great," he said. "Egyptian TV."

"What do you expect? We're in Egypt." Philippa shrugged. "Maybe you can learn Arabic."

John hurled the remote control at the TV screen, let out a yell of rage, and buried his face in his hands. "We're never going to get out of here," he sighed.

CHAPTER 21

THE SEKHEM SCEPTER

Inside the bottle, minutes turned into hours, and the hours turned into days, and the twins diverted themselves with trying to decorate and furnish Mrs. Coeur de Lapin's brandy decanter to their mutual satisfaction. This proved to be impossible, however, and after a week, they agreed to divide the floor space into two by means of a screen, and to choose completely separate design styles: John created for himself a very high-tech living space in gray and black, complete with a large leather reclining armchair, a huge refrigerator, a PlayStation, and a wide-screen television with a DVD player so he always had something to watch, provided it was an old film, as it proved impossible for him to create a DVD that he hadn't seen before. Philippa's living space was altogether more pink and fluffy, with a large bed, lots of soft toys, a radio (playing only Egyptian music, which she almost learned to like), a library full of books about the pharaohs, and a well-equipped kitchen where she taught herself to cook. One day, she decided to cook a meal for John and invited him over to her half of the bottle. They had just sat down to eat when a loud chiming sound high above their heads heralded the decanter being unstoppered again.

Philippa gulped quite audibly as she began to disintegrate once more.

"Perhaps Iblis decided to kill us after all," said John, as the bottle began to refill with smoke.

"Whatever happened to looking on the bright side?" asked Philippa.

"Just as long as it's quick, I don't care," said John. "I'm going crazy stuck in here."

"What makes you think that Iblis is the kind of djinn to give anyone a quick death?" she asked and let out a cry of alarm as she felt herself carried up through the neck of the bottle and into the outside world again.

When the smoke cleared, the twins found themselves returned to Mrs. Coeur de Lapin's library. The Frenchwoman was lying on a chaise lounge with her eyes closed, snoring loudly, but there was no sign of Iblis, or even a cobra, and instead the twins were delighted to see Nimrod sitting in the uncomfortable modern chair smoking a large cigar and looking very pleased with himself.

"What happened?" asked John.

"Where's Iblis?" asked Philippa.

"Iblis?" Nimrod waved the little antique scent bottle that the twins had presented to Mrs. Coeur de Lapin. "Oh, he's safely in here," he said. "He'll not trouble us again."

"You captured him?" exclaimed Philippa. "How?"

"I couldn't have done it without you two, really I couldn't. You see, I'm afraid I sent you over here on false pretenses. Ever since that picnic, I've had my suspicions about Mrs. Coeur de Lapin. I was rather counting on you both suspecting Mrs. Coeur de Lapin. Especially since you were to spend a whole day with her. Iblis has been controlling that poor woman since we arrived in Cairo."

"So all that stuff about the casket, and keeping an eye on it with the telescope was complete baloney," said John.

"You used us as bait," said Philippa. "Like a goat for a tiger."

"Oh, I say, I think that's a little strong," said Nimrod. "You were never in any real danger."

"We could have been killed," insisted Philippa

"Oh, no," said Nimrod, puffing his cigar happily. "Iblis would never have wasted two perfectly good djinn such as yourselves. Especially being as young as you are. Two more to do his bidding? I should think not. He's not stupid. All that stuff about eating you and burying you in a cesspit was just to soften you up."

"You heard him say that? How?" asked John.

"You don't think I'd have let you come here on your own, do you? I was inside an inanimate object. Well, almost inanimate."

"What, you mean you were here all along?" said Philippa.

"Of course. I was inside the computer on the desk. Mind

you, there was a moment back there when I thought he was onto me. I inadvertently turned myself on for a moment."

"I remember that," said John. "I thought it was a bit strange at the time."

"Yes, well, so did Iblis. He's a cunning devil, that Iblis, I'll say that much for him. Anyway, I knew he'd bottle you up. And that was the moment I was waiting for. You see, a djinn is at his weakest when he's using his powers on another djinn. And even weaker than that when he's obliged to use his power on *two* djinn. And if those two djinn also happen to be *twins* — well, you get the idea. The minute he put you in that brandy decanter, I made my move. I can assure you there was no other way to tackle as formidable a djinn as Iblis."

"So where have you been all this time?" demanded Philippa. "We've been in that bottle for weeks."

Nimrod shook his head. "It just seemed like weeks. In actual fact you've been in there for, let's see now," — Nimrod checked his watch — "about fifteen minutes."

"Fifteen minutes?" said John. "Is that all? Are you sure?"

Nimrod winced. "Yes, I'm rather sorry about that. It's what I was telling you about the inside of a djinn bottle being outside three-dimensional space. I'm afraid I didn't have time to tell you about the proper way for a djinn to transubstantiate and enter a bottle. In the Northern Hemisphere you have to remember to go in anticlockwise, against the normal Northern hemispheric screw, or time goes slow, and vice versa in the Southern Hemisphere. It's the same principle as water going down a drain in a bath. Well, sort of. Granted, it's more diffi-cult to remember that sort of thing when it's someone else who puts you in the bottle. But if you get it right, it can save you a lot of time. For example, a flight from London to Australia, which normally takes about twenty-four hours, can seem like only twenty-four minutes. Get it wrong and it might easily seem like twenty-four weeks. Time is relative to space. These days, I thought they taught you stuff like that in the first grade.

"Everything's worked out splendidly. And you were quite magnificent. I'd never have thought of making that mouse appear in Mrs. Coeur de Lapin's hair like that. That was in-spired. You drew him out perfectly, Philippa."

But the twins were still looking a little peeved with their uncle.

"I'm sorry to have deceived you both," said Nimrod, "but honestly, there was no other way. You wouldn't have come here at all if you'd thought you were being kept out of the real action. And I couldn't tell you that you were part of my djinn trap, not without the risk of you giving the whole game away. Please say that you'll forgive me."

"Oh, all right," they said.

"Shouldn't we grant you three wishes?" said John. "Ac-cording to *The Baghdad Rules*."

"No need. Section 18. Consanguinity. We're related, so there's no need."

Nimrod puffed his cigar happily and blew a smoke ring shaped like a rearing cobra.

"But how did you know that Iblis was controlling Mrs. Coeur de Lapin?" asked Philippa.

"The headband, of course. It's the same as the one Akhenaten is wearing on the mural in the tomb. Well, that was one reason."

"And the other?"

"Something you yourself told me, Philippa."

"What was that?"

"The word of truth you heard when the scorpion that Iblis used to bind me to Akhenaten's tomb was consumed by the fire."

"Rabat?"

"That's right. Except that the word you heard wasn't Rabat at all, but something very like it. Rabbit, to be precise."

"Rabbit!" exclaimed John. "Of course. *Lapin* is the French word for rabbit."

"Exactly," said Nimrod. "For all his cleverness, Iblis is a lazy sort of djinn. I hoped he might give Hussein Hussaout a word of binding that would give me a clue as to where he was and what he was up to. Even so, it took me a while to connect rabbit with *lapin*."

"But what about the rest of the Ifrit?" asked John. "Palis, the foot-licker. And the others."

"Oh, they won't dare try anything now. Not with their tribal leader, Iblis, out of the way. They're much too cowardly." Nimrod leaned back on his heels and blew an enormous column of smoke up to the ceiling, which took on the shape of a Churchillian V for victory. "I can't tell you what a wonderful thing we've done. We may not have found the lost djinn of Akhenaten, but we've done the next best thing. We've stopped the Ifrit from finding them."

"As a matter of fact," said Philippa, "I've got a theory where we might look for them. The lost djinn of Akhenaten."

The ash fell off Nimrod's cigar as he regarded Philippa with some surprise. "You have?"

"Yes." Philippa knelt down beside the uncomfortable modern chair and, picking up the book about Akhenaten that Mrs. Coeur de Lapin had been reading, she removed a torn page that was being used as a bookmark, and handed it to Nimrod.

Nimrod and John looked at the page on which appeared four color pictures, each of the same strange-looking object. The object was about two feet tall and shaped a little like a walking stick, with a large lozenge-style top that was three or four inches thick and six or seven inches long.

"These are Sekhem scepters," she said. "Royal scepters used by Egyptian kings and high officials as a mark of authority, and waved over offerings at tombs to give power to the Ka of the person who was dead." She shrugged. "I've been doing a lot of reading for the past fifteen minutes."

Nimrod smiled kindly at Philippa. "But I don't see how these could help us to find the lost djinn."

"Someone has circled the picture of another royal scepter in this book," said Philippa. "Assuming for a moment that it was Iblis who circled the scepter, or Mrs. Coeur de Lapin under his direction, then that would seem to indicate that Iblis is interested in royal scepters."

"Go on," said Nimrod.

"First," said Philippa, "there's this. In the newspaper report of the break-in at the Cairo Museum, it said that several royal scepters had been broken."

"Yes, it did," Nimrod said thoughtfully. "But there were also some canopic jars that had been opened, too. Egyptian storage jars."

"Suppose those were just a red herring, for the newspapers, designed to throw us off the scent. Suppose it really was just the scepters they were after."

"All right," said Nimrod. "Suppose it was. Why would anyone want to break a Sekhem scepter?"

"When we were in Akhenaten's tomb," said Philippa, "the picture on the wall — the mural — showed the pharaoh holding the royal scepter high above the heads of the seventy djinn. You remember the way the rays of the sun seemed to emanate from the top part of the scepter — that fat part — and touch each one of the djinn?"

"Yes, I do," said Nimrod.

"Well then, here's the third part of my theory. It was something Iblis said when he was imprisoning us inside that brandy decanter. He said we were lucky that it wasn't his fountain pen or the hollow poison chamber inside his walking stick. And that set me thinking. Suppose the thick part of the scepter was hollow, too. Wouldn't that be a good place to keep the seventy djinn from whom your power was derived?

Not in some jar or bottle, but in your scepter, in the very symbol of your authority. I've only been inside a brandy decanter. But it strikes me that you could easily fit seventy djinn inside that. And if in that, then why not inside the top part of the scepter, where all the hieroglyphs are located?"

"The Sekhem scepter is connected with Osiris," said Nimrod. "Osiris was sometimes called Great Sekhem. Sekhem means 'power' or 'might.' But you're right, Phil. With the djinn being the source of Akhenaten's power and might, it would be the perfect place to keep the seventy djinn." Nimrod looked at the picture of the scepters more closely. "I don't see why there wouldn't be room for them all in there, if the top was hollow, like you said. It might even conceal a secret bottle. Yes, by my lamp, it's a brilliant theory."

"But how did Akhenaten gain power over so many djinn in the first place?" asked Philippa. "We still don't know that."

"I think we do," said John. "Now that we've seen how Iblis held power over Mrs. Coeur de Lapin. I'll bet you anything that four thousand years ago, the Ifrit were holding power over Akhenaten in the same way as Iblis kept Mrs. Coeur de Lapin in his power. That one of them had taken the shape of a real snake in the king's headdress."

"Yes," said Nimrod. "That's not bad at all, John." He went over to the table and picked up the telephone.

"Who are you calling?" asked John.

"The police," said Nimrod. "I want to ask them a question about the break-in at the museum."

Nimrod spoke in Arabic for several minutes and when he replaced the receiver, he looked very excited. "The scepters were not snapped in two," he said. "It was the top part with the cartouche that was damaged. Smashed, in fact, as if someone might have been trying to find out if they were hollow."

He walked quickly to the door.

"Where are you going?" asked Philippa.

"Home. We have to tell Mr. Rakshasas about this. Immediately."

"What about her?" said Philippa, pointing to Mrs. Coeur de Lapin, who was still sleeping on the sofa. "Will she be all right?"

"She'll be fine after she's slept for a while," said Nimrod. "I don't suppose she'll remember much about it when she wakes. Probably just as well, really. Anyway, she's French. When she wakes she'll probably think she had too much wine for breakfast."

Back at Nimrod's house, Groanin brought the bronze lamp containing Mr. Rakshasas into the library and rubbed it vigorously to summon the elderly djinn. Mr. Rakshasas listened patiently to what Nimrod told him and then nodded. "I can see no other possible explanation," he agreed. "Your niece is to be commended for her ingenuity."

"Isn't it marvelous?" said Nimrod. "Now we know what we're looking for even if we don't yet know where."

"It is true," said Mr. Rakshasas, "there are lots of royal scepters in museums all over the world." He nodded at the twins. "I believe there is one in New York's Metropolitan Museum. But I know of only one Sekhem scepter from the Eighteenth Dynasty that exists outside of Cairo. And that is in the British Museum in London."

Nimrod sighed. "Isn't it just the thing? Thirty years I've been looking for these lost djinn, and it turns out they might have been right under my nose all along."

"Does this mean we're going back to England?" asked John.

"Yes, I'm afraid it does," confirmed Nimrod. "Mr. Groanin. You had better call British Airways and get us all on the next flight to London."

"Thank goodness for that," said Groanin, walking smartly to the door. "I say, thank goodness for that. I can't take much more of this heat."

"It's a great shame," said Nimrod, ignoring his butler. "And just as you were discovering your djinn powers. Away from the heat of the desert these may be greatly diminished."

"Can't be helped." John shrugged.

"This is something much more important," agreed Philippa.

"We can always come back to Egypt another time," said John. "Can't we?"

"Of course," said Nimrod. "The next time you have a vacation from school."

"You were right, you know," John told Nimrod. "What you said about Cairo. I never expected to like it so much. It may be dirty, it may be smelly, it may be overcrowded, but there's nowhere on Earth that's quite like it."

"Did I say that?" said Nimrod. "Well, it is marvelous, of course. But wait until you see Alexandria. And Jerusalem. And Delhi. And Istanbul. Not to mention the Sahara Desert. Even Berlin, which as you know, is where the Blue Djinn of Babylon now resides. Only right now, none of them are as important as London and the British Museum. What we find there could affect the whole future of not just the djinn, but of the mundane world, too."

CHAPTER 22

ROOM 65

As usual, Londoners were not enjoying London's summer very much. The days were too hot or too cool. There was too much rain or there was not enough rain. And it seemed that there was always someone to complain about the weather, whatever the weather. Almost the only Londoner who never complained about the London summer was Groanin.

"It's the variety of weather I like best," he explained as they arrived back at the house in Kensington. "No two days are ever the same. Now today it's hot, very hot for London. So tomorrow, it'll probably be raining, and the day after that, it might well be windy. Just try to watch a four-day game of cricket if you don't believe me. You get all sorts of weather during a cricket match."

John, who found that cricket was hard enough to watch for four minutes, let alone four days, told Groanin that he would have to take his word for it.

The very next morning, at exactly ten o'clock, Nimrod took the twins to Bloomsbury and the giant building that was the British Museum or, as Nimrod preferred to call it, the "BM."

The BM is an imposing building that looks a little like a large Greek temple and, in particular, the large Greek temple that was sacred to the goddess Athena Parthenos on the Acropolis, in Athens. But mounting the front steps that faced Great Russell Street, Nimrod and the twins found merely a whole busload of tourists who had come to London to worship Hermes, the Greek god of travel, commerce, and ludicrously expensive handbags.

Nimrod led the twins through the entrance hall, into a covered courtyard called the Great Court, and past the old Reading Room, which was an enormous round building in the Great Court's center. He waved them toward the western side of the Great Court, and they passed into the Egyptian galleries where the cream of the BM's Egyptian antiquities was displayed. Ignoring most of the larger exhibits, he led them north, up the west stairs, and into rooms 60 to 66. In a glass case, among the many mummified corpses of Egyptian royalty — some of them five thousand years old — and assorted funerary archaeology, Nimrod found what they were looking for. But, putting on a pair of glasses to more closely inspect the scepter, which was mounted on a small granite plinth, he frowned and shook his head.

"Oh, dear," he said. "It says here, royal scepter, Seventeenth Dynasty. That's too early for Akhenaten. I do hope Mr. Rakshasas hasn't made a mistake."

Philippa inspected the exhibit and shrugged. "So the BM doesn't know everything," she said and looked again. "Perhaps *they* made a mistake."

Nimrod grunted as if he didn't think that was at all likely.

"Although I have to admit," said Philippa. "It does look kind of ordinary. It doesn't look as if it might contain seventy djinn."

"True," sighed Nimrod.

"Can't you tell if this is the right one?" she asked. "I mean, doesn't it give off some kind of vibration or something?"

"I'm not a dowsing rod," Nimrod said, "or a medium. Anyway, if it did give off vibrations, as you say, don't you think that after several decades I, or another djinn, would have noticed by now?"

"I suppose so," said Philippa.

His nose pressed up against the display case, and taking as close a look at the Sekhem scepter as the glass permitted, John was almost inclined to agree with his sister when he noticed something strange.

"Wait a minute," he said. "Haven't you noticed something?" He took several steps back and pointed. "It's only a hairline, but there's a crack in the glass."

Nimrod and Philippa retreated from the display case as John added, "And guess what? It looks just like the one on my bedroom wall."

"You're absolutely right, John," said Nimrod. "Well done. I must get some different glasses. These are hopeless."

"Yes, but what does it mean?" asked Philippa.

"It's a message, of course," said John. "And this time I think I know who it's from."

"Who?" asked Philippa.

"The lost djinn of Akhenaten, of course," said John. "That's who."

"My God, yes," breathed Nimrod. "You're right, John. That has to be the explanation."

"It's a sign so we'd know that this was the right scepter," said John.

And for a moment or two they just stood there and looked at the scepter.

"Is it gold?" asked Philippa. "It doesn't look like gold."

"If it were gold it would have been too heavy to carry," said Nimrod. "A scepter's no good if it's too heavy to carry. No, it's wood, covered with gold leaf."

"Are we going to steal it now?" asked John.

"Good grief, no," said Nimrod. "We are doing what is known in the criminal underworld as 'casing the joint.' Establishing the lay of the land, so to speak. In short, having a good look around the place before devising a plan that will enable us to get our hands on the scepter."

"Why not just make the protective glass disappear and then grab it?" asked John. "Shouldn't be too difficult with that crack in the glass."

Nimrod looked at John and then nodded at the security camera located in a top corner of the room.

"Make that disappear, too," said John.

"My dear young nephew," said Nimrod. "Have I not advised you to use your djinn power sparingly? Did I not warn you of the price to be paid for the profligate working of your will? Wherever and whenever it is possible, we try to do things the mundane way. Besides, in this particular situation, using djinn power might actually be dangerous."

"Dangerous? How?"

"Now that we know this Sekhem scepter really does contain the lost djinn of Akhenaten, using djinn power so near to it might prove hazardous to those contained inside it. Or, indeed, to us. And so, while we may enter the BM itself using djinn power, to break into this display case, I think it better that we should use more conventional methods of B and E." He smiled. "Breaking and entering."

"Such as?" asked Philippa.

Nimrod tapped the glass experimentally. "A blowtorch," he said. "This glass is actually plastic. Which means that while it might not break very easily, it will melt like butter."

"Great," said Philippa. "Can we wear black roll-neck sweaters? Just like they do in the movies when they knock over a place?"

Nimrod winced. "We are not, as you put it, intending to knock over the BM."

"But we are planning to make an illegal entry," said John.

Nimrod glanced uncomfortably at some tourists who were giggling as they set about photographing one another while sitting next to one of the mummies, and turned away from the Sekhem scepter. "Can you speak up a little?" he hissed at

John. "I don't think those tourists quite heard you." Nimrod glanced around Room 65 as if searching for something.

John followed his eyes. "What are you looking for?" he asked.

"A good place to hide when we come back here later on," said Nimrod.

"Won't the camera see us?"

"No, because we will be inside some sort of container."

John nodded as one of the tourists produced a bottle of Coca-Cola from his backpack and began to drink it. "Such as a Coke bottle, perhaps," he said.

"Yes," agreed Nimrod. "No one would notice one of those."

John walked across the room and bent down as if to view one of the mummies, only his eyes were on the gap between the bottom of the case and the carpeted floor. "Mr. Groanin could put a Coke bottle containing us underneath one of these mummy displays," he said.

"Yes," Nimrod said thoughtfully. "That might be possible." He drew his forefinger along the edge of the display case and inspected the grime it had accumulated. "From the filth in here, I should hazard a guess that it might be several days before one of the cleaners found it."

Nimrod stood up and rubbed his chin thoughtfully as he considered John's plan. "Yes," he said. "We'll come back here, inside a bottle, just before five o'clock, when the BM closes. Mr. Groanin will place the bottle under this poor fellow and, later on, after dark, we will transubstantiate and set to work."

John was reading the exhibit notes on the case. "An

unknown Egyptian of high rank, Nineteenth Dynasty." He shook his head. "Seems kind of weird to end up like this. In a glass case in a museum. I don't think I'd like it to happen to me. The poor guy doesn't even have a name. Nor does this one next to him. Kind of sad, really."

"I think it's gross," said Philippa. "All these people had lives. Friends, parents, children. They were just like us, probably. Well, not exactly like us, but you know what I mean. There ought to be a law against this kind of thing."

"I expect there will be one day, if there isn't already," observed Nimrod. "There seems to be a law against everything in Britain except being ignorant or stupid. But right now, I'm rather more concerned with the lost djinn than the human rights of this old bag of bones. Besides, after five thousand years I don't think you're too particular about where you end up. Myself, I've always rather fancied being buried at sea and being eaten by fishes. Seems only fair, considering the amount of fish I've enjoyed eating myself. Which reminds me. It's lunchtime."

After a lunch of dressed Cornish crab and Dover sole at The Ivy, a restaurant where Nimrod was well known, he bought himself a blowtorch at a local hardware shop in Seven Dials and tested it out on a window in his conservatory at the side of the house. Apart from making an awful smell of burning plastic, the experiment went well and it took Nimrod less then fifteen minutes to melt a hole the size of a dinner plate in one of the panes.

"I hope the security people don't have a good sense of smell," said Philippa. "It stinks."

At around three o'clock, John drank a bottle of Coca-Cola that Groanin then washed scrupulously. When the twins were dressed in a way they considered as suitable for carrying out a burglary (with roll-neck sweaters, blackened faces, and haversacks), Nimrod, whose only concession to the nefariousness of their enterprise was to wear a darker suit and a black wide-brimmed hat, transubstantiated the three of them into the empty bottle.

"Here," he said, handing them each a charcoal pill. "Best take one of these. We might be here for several hours." He smiled. "Relatively speaking, of course."

"This is the part of being a djinn I like least of all," admitted Philippa, walking impatiently around the circumference of the bottle's interior.

"You'll get used to it," said Nimrod. "And have you traveled on a plane in economy class lately? Or on the London Underground? If you ask me, the inside of a Coke bottle is much more congenial. Anyway, I haven't finished making us comfortable yet. We need some seats."

Nimrod used his powers to create three enormous leather reclining chairs with seat belts. "I always use this design," he said. "These are the same seats that they have in First class on British Airways. Very useful for traveling." Feeling the bottle begin to move, he added, "Incidentally, you'd better buckle up. In my experience, Mr. Groanin can be a little rough when he's handling the djinn bottle. It comes from his never having been inside one himself, of course."

John and Philippa yelled out loud as suddenly the bottle started to swing like a bell.

"He's walking to the car," chuckled Nimrod. "That's the trouble with having one arm. He will keep swinging it."

"I think you should give him a taste of what it's like in here," said John. "If only to make him a little more considerate in the future."

"Oh, no, that's quite impossible," said Nimrod. "Mundanes are just not up to the experience. You wouldn't have noticed it yourselves, but a djinn doesn't need to breathe very much when he or she is inside a bottle or a lamp. When a djinn is in this immaterial state we can survive for long periods on virtually no air at all. It's a little like suspended animation. But mundanes, you see, die not just from the necessity of their breathing in, but of the equal necessity of their breathing out. It's the carbon dioxide that kills them, not the lack of oxygen. So don't ever be tempted to put one in a bottle. That's why we turn the ones who annoy us into animals, you see. So they can breathe."

"By the way," said Philippa. "What happened to the bottle containing Iblis?"

"He's in my freezer," said Nimrod. "Back at the house in Cairo. It's for his own good. Djinn are a little like lizards, you see. They slow down in the cold."

"In the freezer?" said Philippa. "Isn't that kind of cruel?"

"Aren't you forgetting something?" said John. "He was ready to do the same to us. Possibly worse."

"Your brother is right, Philippa," said Nimrod. "Don't feel too sorry for Iblis. He is a very nasty piece of work. Keeping Iblis semi-frozen will stop him from getting angry, so that if anyone did accidentally open that decanter, then he wouldn't immediately start to destroy things. The Ifrit are notoriously short-tempered, even at the best of times. You've heard of the Great Fire of San Francisco in 1906, which was caused by an earthquake? That was Iblis. Mind you that was nothing compared to what Iblis's father, Iblis senior, did in 1883. He destroyed a whole island near Indonesia. A place called Krakatau. The explosion was so loud it was heard three thousand miles away; ash fell on Singapore, more than five hundred miles to the north of Krakatau, and the explosion caused a giant wave, a tsunami, more than a hundred feet tall, which devastated everything in its path. At least thirty-six thousand people were killed." Nimrod shook his head. "No, indeed. You do not want to be around an Ifrit when they've escaped from a long period of confinement."

Twenty minutes later, Groanin parked the Rolls in Montagu Place and, carrying the Coke bottle in his coat pocket, he entered the BM through the less spectacular back door. Even at the best of times he disliked coming to the BM, for the place only served to remind him of how he had come to lose his arm, more than ten years before. He could never go in the Montagu Street door, or for that matter, the Great

Russell Street entrance of the BM without reliving the events of that terrible day. How the tigers had run amok in the Reading Room, roaring loudly, before leaping over the issues desk and mauling the terrified library staff.

The library had been moved now, to a hideous brick-built warehouse in St. Pancras, which Nimrod said had all the charm of a public lavatory, but the Reading Room was much as Groanin remembered it, minus the wild beasts. And so it was, with the memory of the tigers' terrible roars still ringing in his ears, that Groanin went up to the first floor, heading toward Room 65.

In the Mummy Room, he wandered around nonchalantly, like any other tourist, before kneeling down and, in between pretending to tie up his shoelaces, placing the Coke bottle under the display case containing the anonymous mummy, and tapping it three times.

Inside the bottle, Groanin's taps sounded like a large gong being struck forcefully. Nimrod and the twins checked their watches. It was a quarter to five and darkness was still several hours away. "You're in position, right where you told me," he said. "I'm off."

"Thank you, Groanin," said Nimrod. "We'll see you tomorrow."

Then Groanin walked out, although not before taking a look at the Sekhem scepter and deciding it looked more like a paddle or an oar than a scepter, and that it was difficult to imagine seventy ants, let alone seventy djinn, confined to such a queer-looking object.

"Spot of afternoon tea, anyone?" said Nimrod, making a tea table laden with tea things appear in their midst. On a starched white damask tablecloth were sandwiches, scones, cakes, jam, a variety of teas, and some Coca-Cola for the twins.

"I'm not really hungry," confessed John.

"Tea has nothing to do with being hungry," said Nimrod. "For Englishmen, it is like a canonical hour. And almost as much of an important ritual as the tea ceremony in Japan. Except for one thing. With tea, in Japan, recognition is given that every human encounter is a singular occasion which can, and will, never recur again exactly. Thus every aspect of tea must be savored for what it gives the participants. But in England, the significance occurs in the fact that tea is always the same, and will always recur again and again, exactly. For how else is the endurance of a great civilization to be measured?"

"I'm not really hungry, either," said Philippa. She was trying to read the book that Groanin had given her: the *New Oxford Book of English Verse*.

Nimrod made a grumpy sort of noise, as if disapproving strongly of the lack of interest John and Philippa seemed to attach to taking tea. "More for me then," he said, greedily heaping his plate with some cucumber sandwiches.

"I don't know how you can eat," said Philippa.

"It's easy," said Nimrod. "I just put the food in my mouth and chew it for a while until I'm ready to swallow." He glanced around at the greenish-colored glass walls. "Of course this is not what I'm used to. A Coke bottle. I usually travel in a rather attractive bottle made of Venetian glass that I've fitted

CHILDREN OF THE LAMP

out rather handsomely. There's a gymnasium, a small cinema, a kitchen, of course, and a rather magnificent bed. I call it the Grotti Palace. Bit of a joke. Don't suppose you'll get it, but there we are. Remind me to show it to you sometime."

John opened a bottle of Coca-Cola and drank it before realizing how odd it was to be drinking Coke inside a bottle of Coke. "I bet that's not been done before," he told himself.

"I don't know how you can be so calm," Philippa told Nimrod. "We're planning to rob the British Museum and you're talking about tea. Doesn't what we're going to do make you just a little bit nervous?"

"Oh, my dear, that's a little strong, don't you think?" protested Nimrod. "We're not exactly criminals."

"I feel like a criminal," said Philippa.

"I daresay that's because you insisted on looking like one," remarked Nimrod, pouring himself some more tea. "Blackened faces, roll-neck sweaters, leather gloves, sneakers? If I were to dress like that I would call the police and have myself arrested immediately. The two of you appear positively desperate." Nimrod produced a pillbox from his pants pocket. "Here. Have another charcoal pill."

The time passed very quickly and before they knew it, it was nine o'clock and Nimrod was reminding the twins of the advantages of an anticlockwise transubstantiation in the Northern Hemisphere, and saying that it was now safe to re-materialize from the Coke bottle into Room 65. "I expect the cleaners will have gone by now," he said. "If they came at all. Things at the BM are not what they once were."

"What about the security cameras?" asked John.

Nimrod dipped his hand into his pocket and took out a small electronic device, no bigger than a computer mouse.

"A little unit I designed myself," he said. "I call it my 'Idiot Filter.' It interferes with radio and television signals. I use it on people with cell phones on trains, to stop their chattering. I made it in order to overcome my previous inclination, which was to make such people mute for a couple of hours. But it works perfectly well on almost any broadcast signal, such as the CCTV." Nimrod pointed west. "Philippa, I want you to go to that doorway over there and keep watch, in case anyone comes up the stairs to see what's wrong with the camera. Not that there's much in here worth stealing. There's not really a big market for five-thousand-year-old corpses."

"Please don't mention them," said Philippa. "I'm freaked out enough as it is."

"John, you can help me to unpack our gear."

Nimrod set his equipment down on one side of the gallery, in front of the glass display case containing the scepters. In the middle was another glass case containing a selection of sarcophagi, and on the other side of the gallery, in a third glass case, were dozens of mummies, including several human mummies — shrunken dead bodies wrapped in gray bandages, stacked one on top of the other like so many cigars in one of Nimrod's humidors. There was something much more sinister about the Egyptian galleries at night than during the day. Shadows seemed to alter their positions, while the silent reflections on the glass cases played strange tricks on the imagination so that there were several times when both John and Philippa had to look at some exhibit twice to check that it had not moved. But it was not just the light or lack of it that preyed on the minds of the twins but also the sense of an ancient desecration.

Philippa wrapped her arms around herself like a shawl. "This place gives me the creeps," she said.

"I suppose there *is* a bit of an atmosphere in here," admitted Nimrod, taking out his cigarette lighter. "You know, one of these old sarcophagi, the gold one I think, has the reputation of having once contained the mummy that was on the *Titanic*. With the concomitant curse of course."

"There was a mummy on the *Titanic*?" said John, handing Nimrod the blowtorch. "I never knew that."

"That's right," said Nimrod, lighting the blowtorch. "The Princess Amen-Ra. The *Titanic* sank, causing the deaths of fifteen hundred people, and at the time, 1912, there were lots of people who ascribed the blame to the princess's mummy. Hardly surprising really, given the number of people who had already met a strange death through their acquaintance with Princess Amen-Ra. Apparently, before the mummy left this room, bought by an American collector, the night watchmen and cleaners wouldn't dare go near her sarcophagus. They actually claimed they could hear hammering and sobbing from inside the casket." Nimrod laughed scornfully. "It's just a story, of course. And I wouldn't worry about her. As I said, her mummy is at the bottom of the Atlantic

Ocean with all the other *Titanic* passengers who didn't get off the ship. So she won't bother us."

"That's very comforting," said Philippa.

"There used to be many more human mummies in here, of course," said Nimrod. "The few displayed now are only a very small selection of the many dozens possessed by the BM. The bulk of them are stored in the basement vaults, I believe. Hidden away so as not to offend people. I can't see why they would be offensive, myself. After all, when you're dead, you're dead." Nimrod laughed. "Not that it's just human mummies they have in there," he said. "I think they have quite a few animal mummies, too." He shook his head. "I'm surprised that the animal rights people haven't complained about it."

While Nimrod applied the blue flame of the blowtorch to the plastic glass in front of the Sekhem scepter, John looked again. It was true: there were mummified cats, baboons, dogs, crocodiles, falcons, cobras — there was even a mummified eel. John shook his head impatiently. "Why on earth would anyone want to mummify an eel?" he muttered, and tried, unsuccessfully, to put death and mummies out of his mind. What with his terror of the mummies, the smell of burning plastic, and Nimrod's creepy conversation, he was beginning to feel a little sick.

"Of course," continued Nimrod, "everything the Egyptians believed about resurrection, they got from us djinn, you know. Not that there's any truth in that stuff, even for us djinn."

But John was hardly listening to his uncle, for it seemed to him that one of the mummies had moved very slightly. Or had he imagined it? Another moment or two passed and he told himself that he *must* have imagined it, that the fumes from the burning plastic had made him a little light-headed, and that five-thousand-year-old mummies didn't move except in creepy old horror movies. He told himself that he was in London, in the twenty-first century, and that it wasn't possible for dead things to come back to life. Those night watchmen Nimrod had talked about, surely they had been mistaken. It was impossible for Princess Amen-Ra to have stayed alive for five thousand years.

He bit his lip in an attempt to control the trembling that affected his jaw. That was strange, too. It was as if his body already recognized what his mind refused to admit. And then, something in the display case moved again. John blinked, rubbed his eyes, and, looking once more, he realized that it wasn't one of the mummies that had moved, but something from inside the mummy that had the shape of a human being, but which somehow he could see through, as if it wasn't quite there at all. For a moment, he thought it was the reflection of the blowtorch on the glass in front of the mummy case before he realized that Nimrod had already turned off the torch and was now inspecting the hole in the display case that housed the scepters, quite oblivious of what was happening in one of the other glass cases behind him.

The shape stood up from the horizontal mummy and stepped out of the glass case. Taller than he had supposed.

And quite obvious to the nose now, as if the emanation brought with it a foul, decaying smell from an ancient grave, like a very old book that had gotten damp and had mildewed and perhaps smelled of something worse.

"Uncle Nimrod," he said more loudly, hardly daring to take his terrified eyes off the tallish, near transparent figure inside the glass case housing the mummies, although he didn't dare to look at the face. The first time had been one time too many. "Do you think it's possible that ghosts exist?"

"Oh, yes. There are ghosts all right."

"Then I think you'd better take a look at this."

CHAPTER 23

AKHENATEN'S RETURN

Keeping watch on the west stairs in the doorway of the Mummy Room, and eager to perform her appointed task properly, Philippa paid little attention to what was happening behind her back in Room 65. Hearing the blowtorch turned off, she assumed that the job was nearly completed and called out to Nimrod for a progress report. There was, however, no reply and when Philippa turned to go back, she found the way into the Mummy Room blocked by the electric-bluish outline of a very large and very fierce-looking male baboon that came walking toward her on its knuckles.

"Whoa," she gulped. "What is that?"

Philippa had never seen a ghost before, let alone the ghost of a baboon, for that was what it was, but she kept her head and did not, as was her first inclination, yell with fright because she did not want to alert the security guards. So she and the ghostly baboon circled around each other warily for a moment before, barking loudly now, its fangs bared aggressively, the baboon began to advance on Philippa. Trying to control her fear, she backed into Room 65; but the baboon stayed where it was, as if guarding the doorway.

"Nimrod," she said. "There's a ghost out here. At least I think it's a ghost. Of a baboon, I think."

"Yes," said Nimrod, in a quiet, even sort of voice, as if he was hardly surprised by this news. "That would be a *chaeropithecus*. It's from one of the mummies in here, I suspect. Just try to stay calm, my dear."

"That's easy for you to say," said Philippa.

The baboon was joined by a similarly ghostly looking crocodile. And then a cobra.

"There are more of them now," she wailed. "A crocodile and a cobra. And they don't look too friendly. Come and see."

"I'm afraid I can't, Philippa," Nimrod said calmly. "You see there's a ghost in here, too."

Philippa backed away from the ghostly animals, around a glass case, and then looked over her shoulder to see Nimrod and John standing perfectly still, as if frozen to the floor of Room 65. On first glance, she thought they were looking at some sort of statue made of a reflective bluish stone and it was only when the figure moved that she realized with horror that the figure was nearly transparent, and made of the same insubstantial stuff as the animals. At the same time, she let out a gasp and her hair seemed to stand on end as she recognized the ghostly figure. For there was no mistaking the ghost's long sinister face, cruel almond-shaped eyes, thick lips, drooping jaw, corrupt pot belly, and enormous thighs.

This was the ghost of an Egyptian king. It was the ghost of the Heretic Pharaoh, Akhenaten himself. John shuddered. Perhaps because it was a ghost, Akhenaten looked much more terrifying than Iblis.

"Get behind me, John," said Nimrod. "You, too, Philippa." The twins obeyed without hesitation. "There's nothing to worry about, but don't do anything unless I tell you." With the twins now behind him, Nimrod straightened his back and stared coolly into the face of the king's ghost.

"How on earth did you get here?" Nimrod asked the ghost.

The spectral voice that answered started out as a whispered, deathly moan, like soft rock crushed to ash on a wooden floor, but which gradually grew more menacing as it became stronger.

"You brought me here, djinn," said Akhenaten's ghost. "Your own djinn power summoned me and my mine. For almost two centuries I have lain here in this unholy place, robbed of my name and all my treasures, asleep and as anonymous as the sands in the desert. But one day I knew that a djinn, like yourself, would come to this place in search of that."

Akhenaten's ghost pointed across the gallery at the Sekhem scepter still standing in the display case in which Nimrod had torched a hole.

"My royal scepter and the hidden power it contains." The thick fleshy lips parted to reveal a hideous smile. "And when you did, I used your own djinn power against you, to return."

"You've been here all this time and no one knew who you were?" said Nimrod, backing himself and the children away as the baboon and the crocodile advanced on him.

"That's right," said the ghost. "When you conjured yourselves out of that bottle, you were right underneath Akhenaten's mummified body. And there was more than enough of your djinn power left over to help bring back my spirit from eternity. Me and several of my creatures."

"But how could you come back?" asked Nimrod. "Djinn don't become ghosts. Unless —" Nimrod paused. "— Unless it's a djinn spirit that possesses Akhenaten's human ghost."

"At last, you understand," said Akhenaten's ghost.

"I begin to," said Nimrod. "It wasn't Princess Amen Ra those night watchmen were frightened by. It was you. But that was in 1910. Why so silent for all these years?"

"There was a séance here. In 1910. Another djinn came here in secret."

"Of course. Harry Houdini."

"He sensed something was wrong and stopped before I could make myself manifest. But you brought two other djinn. More than enough to bring about my return."

"Well, it's been fascinating," said Nimrod. "And I'm sorry to do this to you after all these years. But it's time you were going." Nimrod waved his hands in the air and then uttered his focus word, more loudly than the twins had ever heard before.

"QWERTYUIOP!"

Akhenaten laughed. "After five thousand years, it would

take more than one djinn to bind me, Marid," hissed the ghost. "And there are many more ways of binding a djinn, ancient ways, than are even dreamed of in your philosophy." Akhenaten glanced down at the ghostly baboon. "Babi!" he growled.

Nimrod yelled with pain as suddenly the baboon sprang forward and sank its fangs into his leg. He cried out again as the baboon followed him across the room and bit his leg again. In a flash, the baboon came to his evil master's side and, upon command, allowed a drop of Nimrod's blood to drop from its sharp fangs onto a piece of material covered in hieroglyphs that Akhenaten held in his hand.

"Now all I need is your ancient name." Akhenaten's ghost smiled. "Your Gemetrian name, it is called today."

Staggering toward the door and away from the twins, Nimrod shouted to the twins, "John, Philippa, run for your lives!"

But before they could move, Akhenaten had grabbed the twins. "Tell me your ancient name, or I will tell Babi to tear out their throats," said Akhenaten.

"Don't tell him, Uncle," yelled Philippa, which made the baboon bark furiously at her.

Nimrod did not hesitate and told Akhenaten his secret name.

Akhenaten smiled and released the two children from his ghostly grip. Then he took a large canopic jar from a plinth and proceeded to remove the baboon-headed lid before tucking it under his arm.

"Run, children, run!" said Nimrod and, attacked by the crocodile and the snake, he struggled to lead Akhenaten away from the twins. "You don't have enough power to fight him."

Akhenaten's ghost stared malevolently at John and Philippa. "I'll be back for you two, when I've finished bottling him," he said and walked, without haste, in pursuit of Nimrod.

The twins looked at each other desperately.

"What are we going to do?" said John. "We can't leave him."

In the doorway, Nimrod screamed with pain as the ghostly baboon bit him for a third time. He looked around to see Akhenaten's ghost bearing down on him, holding the canopic jar open meaningfully. He tried to fight back but he knew it was hopeless. An evil djinn animating a human ghost was formidable enough, but Akhenaten seemed to have the strength of several djinn. Thousands of years in the tomb had done nothing to weaken him, and what was suddenly, painfully clear to Nimrod was that he was dealing with something much more powerful than Akhenaten on his own Akhenaten and the nameless Ifrit who had once controlled him must have met their deaths at the same time, for their spirits were now entwined.

Akhenaten laid the canopic jar by Nimrod's head. "You will be my slave," he said. "For all eternity."

"Run," Nimrod yelled out one last time to the twins — a yell that became a sustained scream as the baboon's ghostly jaws took hold of his upper arm.

But still, John and Philippa remained in the Mummy

Room, afraid to stay, yet also afraid to abandon Nimrod to a terrible fate.

"Didn't Akhenaten say that it would take more than one djinn to bind him?" said John and, reaching through the hole Nimrod's blowtorch had melted in the plastic glass, he took hold of the Sekhem scepter, turned it lengthwise, and pulled it out. "Well, there are seventy djinn in this scepter. Surely that's more than enough to take on Akhenaten."

"But how do we know they'll help us?" said Philippa. "After all, these were the djinn that once did Akhenaten's bidding."

"A djinn must keep the promise it makes upon being released," said John. "That's the rule." He started to examine the upper, thicker part of the scepter very carefully in the beam from Philippa's flashlight. "But how do we open it?"

A voice from within the scepter answered him and for a moment John almost dropped the ancient object on the floor. "You must bring seventy to life," said the voice. "Look to the writing. Let the writing help you."

"I'm looking!" yelled John. "But I don't see how that helps."

"The hieroglyphs," said Philippa. "He means the hieroglyphs. Look, that circle thing is called a cartouche and contains just one symbol: the ankh, which is the sign of life. And I think each one of these symbols that looks like the letter *N* underneath that cartouche is a number ten."

"You're right," said John. "There are seven of them.

Seven times ten equals seventy. That must be the answer. But how do we bring those seven symbols to the ankh?"

John's fingers started to press the hieroglyphs. Suddenly, he felt one of the *N*s, meaning a ten, shift. "It's like a puzzle," he said. "The hieroglyphs move around." He pushed one of the tens up into a cartouche beside the ankh. "It's working!" he yelled.

"Wait," said Philippa. "We haven't yet extracted a promise from the djinn inside the scepter."

And speaking to the voice inside the scepter, John said. "Listen djinn, I will release you all if you swear to destroy Akhenaten and work only for Good."

Without hesitation the voice replied, "For three thousand years we have awaited your coming, young djinn. We await your command."

John's fingers were already sliding the seven tens into the cartouche containing the ankh of life. Immediately, he felt something happening. "I think it worked," he said, and instinctively let go of the scepter.

The scepter remained standing on its own and, for a moment, it was quite as still as a petrified reed. Then, like a large golden flower, the upper part of the scepter opened and a cloud of dank greenish smoke began to pour out of the ancient object, much more than when Nimrod and the twins had escaped from the Coke bottle. John thought it smelled like mildew, and Philippa thought it smelled like the inside of Akhenaten's tomb in Egypt. The three-thousand-year-old smoke quickly filled the room, setting off the smoke alarm, and was soon so thick that it was almost impossible for the twins to see each other. John grabbed his sister's hand.

After what seemed like an age, Room 65 suddenly cleared of smoke to reveal the gallery full of the djinn they had released from inside the Sekhem scepter — dozens of small, bald-headed, shadowy-eyed men dressed in the white robes of Egyptian priests, who looked exactly like the figures from the wall relief in Akhenaten's tomb near Cairo. Each man put his heavily ringed hands together, bowed gracefully, and muttered an obeisance to John and Philippa before joining a circle around Akhenaten and his ghostly animals. Then, chanting in a language the twins did not recognize, the seventy djinn began to collectively will Akhenaten's defeat.

"Stop!" yelled Akhenaten's ghost. "I command you!"

But the chanting of the djinn continued, louder now, a chilling sound, and although John and Philippa understood none of what was spoken, it was plain from the hysterical barking of the ghost baboon and the curses of Akhenaten himself that some powerful force was being invoked. It was at this point that a terrible wind seemed to blow through the Egyptian galleries, heading straight for the center of the circle as if intent on gathering up Akhenaten and carrying him off to some nameless oblivion. The crocodile roared and the baboon barked hysterically, as the chanting and the wind seemed to combine in one unholy crescendo.

"No," screamed Akhenaten's ghost. "No!"

It was such a forlorn, plaintive cry that Philippa almost felt sorry for him.

When at last the wind stilled and Akhenaten and the animals had been silenced, the twins jostled their way toward the doorway where last they had seen Nimrod, in the hope of finding him safe and sound, moving through the strong-smelling bodies of these ancient beings who, at least until John and Philippa had bound them to their will, had held the balance of power between Good and Evil. The djinn bowed again as the twins came through their midst.

"Nimrod," called John. "Are you all right? Where are you?"

The limestone canopic jar with the baboon's head lay on the floor at the foot of one djinn priest who appeared to be the leader. He picked up the jar, touched it with his forehead and, bowing deeply, presented the jar to John, with one word. "Akhenaten," he said.

"He's in here?"

The djinn priest nodded.

Philippa glanced around the room. "But where's Nimrod? Where's our friend?"

Momentarily, the djinn priest's eyes fell upon the canopic jar.

"You're not telling us he's in there, too?" said Philippa.

The djinn priest nodded again.

John took the jar and made as if to remove the lid but the djinn priest stopped his hand, and shook his head. "Akhenaten," he said. "Akhenaten."

"He's right," said Philippa. "We can't release Nimrod without also releasing Akhenaten."

John lifted the jar up to his head and shouted, "Nimrod? Can you hear us? Are you okay?"

A voice, very faint, for the jar was very thick, replied as if from a great distance but neither John nor Philippa could hear what was said.

"What are we going to do?" asked John.

Already they could hear the shouts of security guards coming up the western stairs.

"We can't just leave the jar here," said Philippa. "Someone else might open it and let Akhenaten out accidentally."

"Good point," said John.

The djinn priests began to sit down on the floor of Room 65 as if awaiting their capture.

"Come on," said John. "I've got an idea." He grabbed the Idiot Filter and started to walk in the opposite direction from the west stairs. "There's no time to lose."

It was true. Already there were security guards coming up the mosaic-lined stairs, and their astonishment at finding what looked like seventy men wearing ancient Egyptian costumes was audible.

"Blimey," said one. "Where did this lot come from?"

"What do you think you're up to, Mustapha?" demanded a second. "Is this some kind of sit-in? Or performance art?"

"Call the police," said a third. "Call the Home Office. Call Immigration. I think these blokes are from out of town."

"It might be a flash mob," said another. "I've read about these things in the paper."

With so many bald-headed men blocking the doorway to Room 65, the guards did not notice the twins fleeing the Mummy Room in the direction of the Greek and Roman collection.

John led Philippa into a room that was home to some smaller Roman and Etruscan vases of minor interest. It was a warm night, quite humid in the BM and, thanks to the close proximity of his twin sister, John felt his djinn power was unaffected by the English climate. He concentrated very hard on the glass for a moment and then said, "ABECEDARIAN!"

A neat-looking door appeared in the display case and, opening it, John began to rearrange the exhibits.

"What are you doing?"

"You'll see. Bring the jar."

Philippa handed her brother the jar containing Akhenaten's ghost and Nimrod, and John placed it very carefully at the back of the display on a wooden plinth he had cleared that was labeled APULIAN VASE.

"They won't ever know the difference," he insisted, relegating the real Apulian vase to the opposite side of the display case. When he was satisfied with his rearrangements, he closed the door.

"Wouldn't it have been better to have put the jar in one of the Egyptian galleries?" objected Philippa.

"Maybe," said John. "But the Egyptian galleries are

probably crawling with guards by now. What's more, they might spend days checking the displays to see what's been stolen. Perhaps they'll even close the gallery for a while. Whereas this room looks quite undisturbed."

"That's all very well," said Philippa. "But where are we going to hide?"

"I've thought of that, too," said John and pointed to a cobalt-blue vase that occupied a glass case on its own. He was already using his djinn power to create a small hole in the top of the case through which they might transubstantiate themselves.

"But we've never done a transubstantiation before," said Philippa. "Not by ourselves. And certainly not in a cool climate."

"We've got no choice," insisted John. "It's that or we get caught by the guards. And if we get caught we'll be sent home probably and then Nimrod will be stuck in here for ages. Besides it's a nice-looking vase. And in case you hadn't noticed, it's a nice hot night. I feel strong. I think we can do this." John took Philippa's hand. "We'll zap ourselves into this vase and then, tomorrow, when the fuss has died down and the coast is clear, we'll come out, grab the canopic jar containing Nimrod, and then go home."

"Why don't we just go home now?" she asked.

"Because with Akhenaten's ghost inside it, we can't risk using djinn power on the canopic jar," said John. "We'll have to wait until the museum reopens tomorrow morning at ten o'clock, and then try to sneak it out the main door in my haversack."

Approving of John's plan, for she could think of no other herself, Philippa nodded. Standing in front of the vase, they held hands and tried to compose themselves. Philippa started to concentrate on the vase they were planning to enter.

"This is the Portland Vase," she said. "Made around the beginning of the first millennium. The vase was smashed into more than two hundred pieces by a young Irishman in 1845, but is best known today as the subject of a famous poem by John Keats entitled 'Ode on a Grecian Urn.' Oh, that's in my book of poetry," she said, nodding back at her haversack. "The one that Mr. Groanin gave me."

"Have you finished?" John asked impatiently. Outside the room he could hear the sound of police dogs barking.

"Yes," said Philippa. "I was just trying to concentrate on the vase, that's all."

"On three?"

"On three."

"No wait. We have to remember to go in anticlockwise." John looked at her blankly. "Northern Hemisphere. Remember? Space, time. In order to make the time inside the vase seem to go more quickly."

John nodded. "On three, then."

Philippa nodded back. "On three."

"One — two — three —."

"FABULONGOSHOO —"

"ABECEDARIAN!"

"MARVELISHLYWONDERPIPICAL!"

CHAPTER 24

IN THE PORTLAND

For John, it looked like it would be a long night inside the Portland Vase, made even longer for him by his sister. As soon as she was seated comfortably on a pink chair of her own design, she took out the *New Oxford Book of English Verse* from her burglar's haversack, and started to read.

"How can you read at a time like this?" demanded John, pacing up and down the interior of the vase. "After what happened to Nimrod."

"I'm trying not to think about what happened to Nimrod," said Philippa. "If I do think about him, I'll cry. Which would you prefer?"

"You're right," agreed John. "Go ahead and read. I could use a little distraction myself."

Philippa read aloud the first verse of the poem written by Keats that had been inspired by the Portland Vase:

"Thou still unravish'd bride of quietness,
Thou foster-child of silence and slow time,
Sylvan historian, who canst thus express
A flowery tale more sweetly than our rhyme:
What leaf-fring'd legend haunts about thy shape
Of deities or mortals, or of both,
In Tempe or the dales of Arcady?
What men or gods are these? What maidens loth?
What mad pursuit? What struggle to escape?
What pipes and timbrels? What wild ecstasy?"

"You wouldn't think anyone would want to write a poem about a stupid old vase," declared John. "Keats. He might have felt very differently about a Grecian urn if he'd had to spend the night in one."

"I don't know that we'll have to spend the night in here," said Philippa. "Relatively speaking, at least." John regarded her blankly. "We went in anticlockwise, right?" John nodded. "In which case we can assume that time outside the jar will pass more quickly than time inside it."

"Of course," said John. "We only have to stay in here for ten or fifteen minutes and it should be tomorrow morning." He looked at his watch. "Any minute now, we should get ourselves out of here."

"I hope we see Mr. Groanin," said Philippa. "He'll worry if he can't get back into the Mummy Room to look for that Coke bottle."

"Not as much as he'll worry if he does get in, takes the bottle home, and then finds out we're not inside it."

Pressing their ears to the glass, for that is what the Portland Vase is made of, they listened very carefully to the sound of the room beyond, to find out if anyone was there.

"Sounds quiet enough," said John.

"Sssh, keep listening," said Philippa. "People are always quiet in a museum. If they went around making noise they'd be asked to leave probably."

Another minute passed and still they heard nothing.

"I think we should risk it," said John. He took hold of his sister's hand. "Ready?"

"Ready."

The Portland Vase is only ten inches tall. The deep blue glass of the main body of the vase is overlaid with several human figures made of white glass. These human figures are mythological: Poseidon, Aphrodite, and, possibly, Paris, the great Trojan warrior. Because of these figures the vase has a somewhat magical air, as if the snake held by Aphrodite might suddenly grow large and consume the flying Cupid that hovers over Aphrodite's head. Or so the art student sketching the case for his classwork thought.

At first, he wondered if the smoke billowing out of the vase was an optical illusion, or that he might have been imagining it for, without a doubt, he had been putting in several late nights finishing a portrait for a customer. It was said that van Gogh had gone out of his mind through overwork, and the art student told himself that if he, too, were going crazy then at least he was in some illustrious company.

He put down his pencil and his pad, took off his glasses, and rubbed his eyes, by which time the smoke had descended to the floor and in a way that seemed to be hardly like smoke at all, more like ectoplasm, which is what some people believe ghosts are made of. Instinctively, the student took several steps back from where he imagined the vase to be, for the smoke was quite thick now. He was just on the verge of running out of the room to raise the alarm when the smoke cleared with unusual rapidity to reveal two children, about twelve years old and both dressed in black with boot-blackened faces, like two small burglars.

"Distract him while I go grab the canopic jar," muttered John out of the side of his mouth.

Philippa smiled nicely at the student, and picking up his sketch pad surveyed his drawing with interest. "Not bad," she pronounced amiably. "I imagine that this is rather hard to draw."

The student took his sketch pad from Philippa and shook his head. "I'm not talented. If I were talented, everything would be different. I so wish I were talented."

"Oooh, I feel a little weird," she said, sitting down on the floor. But she knew what the feeling was. It was the same feeling she had felt back in New York when Mrs. Trump had wished she could win the lottery. "It is rather cool in here."

"Are you all right?" asked the student. "Can I get you a glass of water?"

"No," said Philippa. "I'll be all right."

John came over and helped her to her feet. His haversack looked heavy with the weight of the canopic jar. Philippa shot him a questioning sort of look and John nodded back.

"I'm okay," she said, smiling kindly at the student. "Mr. — ?"

"Finger," said the student. "Frederick Finger."

Philippa touched his sketch pad and looked at the drawing again, recognizing the inherent truth of what he himself had said. The drawing was by an artist with little or no talent at all. But that would be different now. She was certain of it.

"Well, we must be going," she said. "And Mr. Finger? You're wrong. You do have talent. Lots of talent. You just haven't found it yet. Take my advice and look for it again tomorrow. I think you'll be surprised at just what a difference a day makes."

"Come on," hissed John. "Let's get out of here."

"Did you grant him a wish?" asked John when they were on the stairs.

"You said I should distract him," said Philippa. "That's exactly what I was doing."

"Bit of a loony, if you ask me," said John. "Why would anyone want to draw an old vase?"

"He's an artist. That's what artists do."

A few minutes later they were outside the BM, standing in front of a newsstand, looking for a cab. Which was when they saw the headline on a copy of *The Daily Telegraph*: 70 EGYPTIANS

326

BREAK INTO BRITISH MUSEUM, and a picture of several of the djinn priests climbing into a police van. Philippa bought a copy of the newspaper and read the story aloud.

"As many as seventy men dressed as ancient Egyptian priests were arrested on Tuesday night when police were called to the British Museum following reports of a break-in at the Mummy Room of the ancient Egyptian galleries. It is uncertain if the men, who were all shaven-headed, and dressed as priests of ancient Egypt, and could speak very little English, had gathered to protest the exhibition of mummified corpses, some of them several thousand years old, that were removed from their original places of rest toward the beginning of the last century. A British Museum spokesman confirmed that several smaller artifacts were damaged or missing. A lawyer for the men, all of whom seem to come from the Middle East, although so far none of them has been positively identified, told the *Telegraph* that the men would be seeking asylum in the U.K. On Wednesday, the Prime Minister told the House of Commons that if it transpired that all the men had entered the country illegally they would be sent back home. In recent years, there have been several calls from campaigners that the mummies in the British Museum should now be given a decent burial. Mrs. Deirdre Frickin-Humphrey-Muncaster of the pressure group Mums for Mummies said, 'This incident highlights a scandal that has existed for decades at the British Museum. Everyone has the right to a decent burial, no matter how long they have been dead.'"

"I agree with that," said Philippa. "It's time we learned to respect other cultures a little more."

John groaned loudly. "Don't mention time to me," he said, grabbing the newspaper out of Philippa's hands. "Look." He pointed to the masthead on the front page. "This is Thursday's newspaper describing the events of Tuesday night. We must have been in that jar for about thirty-six hours!"

"Oh, no," sighed Philippa. "Groanin is going to be so worried."

They hailed a cab and drove back to Kensington where they found Groanin and Mr. Rakshasas waiting anxiously for them.

"By heck you had us worried," said Groanin. "I couldn't even get near those Egyptian galleries yesterday, what with the police crawling all over them. And first thing this morning when I went there, I found nothing. Not even the Coke bottle." Groanin frowned. "Where's Nimrod?"

"It's a long story," said John and told them what had happened. How Nimrod was now stuck inside the canopic jar with the djinn that possessed the ghost of Akhenaten and that they were hoping that Mr. Rakshasas would know what to do next. The old djinn listened carefully to the problem, examined the canopic jar that contained both Nimrod and Akhenaten's ghost, and then shook his head sadly.

"Whatever we do," said Mr. Rakshasas, "we can't take the lid off this jar, otherwise we'll let Akhenaten out again." He sighed resignedly. "Poor Nimrod."

"But Nimrod will be able to make himself quite comfortable in there, won't he?" asked John.

"Oh, he won't dare use his power very much," said Mr. Rakshasas. "For fear that it might help to strengthen Akhenaten."

"Then what are we going to do?" asked Philippa.

"This is most perplexing," he admitted. "To be sure, it's hard to know how to eat the egg without cracking the shell. I am reminded of the Twelve Labors that Eurystheus sets Hercules to perform. Or, for that matter, the riddle of the Sphinx. Aye, indeed, it is a conundrum."

"That much we already know," said John patiently. "How are we going to solve it?"

"I don't know," admitted Mr. Rakshasas. "I honestly never encountered such a problem before. Not in all my djinn years."

"There must be a way," insisted John. "Hercules performed the twelve labors set for him, and Oedipus solved the riddle of the Sphinx. Surely we can solve this problem if we all put our minds to it."

Mr. Rakshasas nodded benignly. "Your young minds are so much more agile than mine," he said. "An old pipe gives the sweetest smoke, but a new one burns more quickly. It may be that you can think of something. But I confess that, for the moment at least, I cannot."

"I'll make some coffee," said Groanin who disliked thinking very hard when there was cricket on television.

Philippa tapped the side of her head with the knuckle of a forefinger as if, somehow, she might dislodge some useful thought from the least-used parts of her brain.

Which seemed to work.

"When we were in the Coke bottle," she said eventually, for the thought took some time to reach her mouth. "There was something Nimrod said about Iblis. Something about djinn being like lizards. How their hot blood slows down in the cold."

"I remember," said John.

"How he put the bottle containing Iblis into the freezer back in Cairo, to slow him down. I was thinking, suppose we took the canopic jar somewhere really cold and let Nimrod and Akhenaten cool down in the same way. Then, when they were both quite torpid, that's to say when the cold had slowed them down a lot, we could open the jar, pop inside ourselves and help Nimrod out; and then close the jar again before Akhenaten could escape."

"But," objected Mr. Rakshasas, "once in the jar, you would get cold yourselves; and being cold, your own powers would be greatly diminished."

"We could wear space suits," said John, liking Philippa's plan. "In space, the temperature is absolute zero, but in a space suit you can stay nice and warm. That way we might enter the jar and remain unaffected by the cold."

"Excellent idea," said Philippa. "But where is cold enough?"

"How about the North Pole?" said John. "That way, if Akhenaten did manage to escape there would be less chance of anyone being injured. And of him damaging anything."

"I always wanted to see the North Pole," said Philippa.

"Me, too," said John. "Let's hope that Nimrod can last for however long it takes us to get there."

CHAPTER 25

THE COOLEST PLACE ON EARTH

With Groanin and the lamp containing Mr. Rakshasas, the twins flew to Moscow, on the first leg of their journey to the North Pole. As soon as they had landed, a stone-faced Russian customs official asked the twins to open their backpacks and, inspecting the canopic jar containing Nimrod and Akhenaten's ghost, asked them to open that, too.

"That's torn it," said Groanin, turning away from the scene as if he could hardly bear to look.

Philippa muttered her focus word as quickly as its length permitted; she didn't dare use djinn power on the canopic jar itself, but she thought it was probably okay to use it on the customs official.

"Open please," repeated the official.

Philippa took a step backward and pointed to the official's peaked cap with obvious distaste. Frowning irritably, the official snatched off his hat to find that, like many things at Moscow's Sheremetyevo Airport, it was crawling with large cockroaches. He yelled with disgust and dropped the hat on the floor. Taking advantage of the official's obvious distraction, Philippa uttered her focus word again, this time creating a perfect facsimile of the canopic jar containing Nimrod and Akhenaten's ghost, while at the same time placing the original jar back in her backpack. And as soon as the official had composed himself, she whipped the baboon-headed lid off the top of the second canopic jar to reveal a second, smaller identical canopic jar; and taking the baboon-headed lid off that one, another; and then another; and then another, until the official's table was covered with the tops and bottoms of more than a dozen canopic jars, just like a Russian Matrushka doll. Tiring of this inquiry and finding yet another cockroach crawling on the nape of his neck, the official waved them on impatiently.

"Blimey," said Groanin, when Philippa had closed her backpack again. "I thought the game was up for a moment back there. I said, I thought the game was up. That all of us were headed for a labor camp in Siberia."

"That was quick thinking, Phil," said John. "Well done. The roaches were inspired. Wherever did you get the idea?"

"Roaches?" Philippa pointed at the counter of a nearby coffee bar where several cockroaches were making their way lazily across a piece of uneaten cake. "The place is crawling with them. I didn't think a few more would look out of place on that guy's hat."

With a couple of hours to wait at Sheremetyevo Airport,

the discovery of a plague of roaches hardly encouraged them to eat at any of the restaurants before boarding their next flight, to Norilsk.

From Norilsk, which is one of the biggest cities inside the Arctic Circle, they flew to Khatanga, on the Taimyr Peninsula. From Khatanga, they flew north again, across Cape Chelyuskin, which is the northernmost point of Eurasia, to Srednij Island, where they spent the night. Srednij was home to a small military detachment, a few glacier scientists, a lot of seals, and almost as many polar bears. The bears were a nuisance, said one of the scientists; at night they came to steal the garbage and they were also extremely dangerous.

From Srednij Island, they flew by helicopter to the Ice Base — an airfield situated on drifting ice that was fewer than seventy miles from the North Pole. Here the days were twenty-four hours long and the temperatures always well below zero. There was nothing to see except the snow under their feet, which seemed only marginally different from the blue-gray sky, the brightly colored tents in which they would spend their second night in Russia, and an old military helicopter that had seen better days, and which would carry them to the North Pole the next day.

"I don't know what I'm doing here," complained Groanin that night, when the three of them sat shivering inside their storm tent. "Really, I don't. How I allowed myself to be drawn into coming to this godforsaken place, I'll never know. This is the last place on Earth I want to be right now. I thought Egypt was bad, but this is much worse. It's all right for Mr.

Rakshasas. I daresay he's very snug inside his lamp. I'll bet he has all the creature comforts. But I don't mind telling you, I've had enough. A man of my age and disability. I'm not cut out for any kind of traveling in which I might end up as lunch for a flipping polar bear. I could hear them last night, snuffling around the garbage bins outside. I didn't sleep a wink. I say, I didn't sleep a wink."

Philippa handed Groanin a cup of hot coffee in the hope that it might stop him groaning.

"Look here, you two," he said, tugging on the beard he had grown since arriving in Russia. "What do you want to go traipsing all the way to the North Pole for, anyway? If you ask me where we are now is quite cold enough for your purpose. It's not going to be any colder there than it is here. It's not even as if the North Pole is a proper place. It's just a compass reading on a map, or a satellite navigation thingy. It's not like you can take a picture or anything. I tell you, if I had three wishes now —"

"Don't," said John. "Don't."

"He's got a point, though," said Philippa.

"Of course, I've got a point. Look, why don't you open the jar here? Tonight. At midnight. When everyone is asleep. With twenty-four-hour sunlight, it'll be as easy to see what we're doing then as it would be at midday."

"It is rather cold," said Philippa. "And it might be best to do this sooner than later, for Nimrod's sake."

"All right." John took the canopic jar out of Philippa's backpack and stood up purposefully.

"Where are you going now?" asked Groanin.

"To put the jar outside in the cold," explained John. "I want to make sure that Akhenaten's ghost is virtually deep-frozen when we take the lid off this thing. Meanwhile, you'd better tell Volodya that there's been a slight change of plans."

Their guide, Volodya, a small, bespectacled man with dirty glasses and a thin, straggling mustache was, understandably, bewildered when Groanin and Philippa told him that they had changed their minds and didn't actually want to travel to the actual geographical point — zero degrees latitude and longitude — that marked the North Pole.

"But your explorer's certificate," he said. "To say that you've been there. What about your certificate?"

Philippa shrugged. "It's just a bearing on a compass, isn't it? It's not like there's a flag or anything, is there?"

"I can't give refund," he said. "If that is what you mean."

"We don't want a refund," said John. "No, that's not what we mean. It's just that the adult member of our party, Mr. Groanin, he's had enough, really."

Volodya shrugged. "To come all this way and then stop just short of our intended destination. It seems a bit strange, that's all. But you have a point. This is North Pole as much as place seventy miles north of here. Seventy miles is nothing out here on the ice." He tapped his head. "North Pole is a state of mind. So maybe I give you all explorer's certificate after all, yes?"

"That's the spirit," said Groanin. "By the way, Volodya. What's for dinner?"

"Seal stew and ice cream," said Volodya, smiling his gap-toothed smile. "Good, yes?"

"Not again," said Groanin. "We had that flipping seal stew of his last night. It was like eating slices of hot rubber."

"Rubber," grinned Volodya. "Very good, yes?"

"No," said Groanin. "Haven't you got any polar bear or something?"

"Very difficult to kill polar bear," said Volodya. "But polar bear kill hunter real easy." Volodya shrugged. "Seal is best. And, of course, Russian ice cream."

"If you say so," said Groanin.

"What's the matter? Don't you like Russian ice cream? Everyone knows Russian ice cream is the best in the world."

"Who told him that?" asked Groanin, when they were back in their own tent. "I say, who told him that Russian ice cream was the best in the world? It's obvious to me he's never eaten Italian ice cream. Now that is the best in the world. Not that there's anything wrong with English ice cream, mind. Or American ice cream, for that matter. At least our ice cream has got eggs and milk and sugar in it. About the only ingredient in Russian ice cream is ice."

"What does it matter if it makes him happy to believe that?" asked Philippa.

"Yes, but it's just not true," argued Groanin.

"Yes, but what does it matter? When you're out here, and there's nothing else to eat but Russian ice cream, it probably helps to think that Russian ice cream is the best in the world."

After dinner in the big tent next to the chopper, Volodya played cards with the helicopter pilot, a gloomy woman named Anna, whose teeth were almost as bad as Volodya's, and who had an alarming habit of belching every time she lost a hand.

"If it were me," observed Groanin. "I think I might let that woman win a few hands. We'd all benefit from her having a run of good luck, I think."

"I wouldn't disagree with that," said Philippa and muttering her focus word made sure that Anna won the next four hands, which, as Groanin had predicted, improved the general atmosphere in the main tent quite noticeably.

Groanin and the twins went next door to their own tent about half an hour later, and Groanin went to sleep. John and Philippa waited up until they heard the two Russians had stopped playing cards and gone to bed, before waking Groanin and summoning Mr. Rakshasas from his lamp. With his white beard and red survival suit, there was no getting away from the fact that, in the snow, Mr. Rakshasas looked exactly like Santa Claus. While the two men waited for the twins to climb into their space suits, they stared across the frozen empty wastes and shivered. A cold breeze blew the flap of the tent and, from time to time, the ice would shift ominously beneath their feet with a loud crack.

"This is a terrible place," said Mr. Rakshasas, looking around sadly.

"I quite agree," said Groanin, hoisting the backpack containing Nimrod's survival suit onto John's back.

"Pray," asked Mr. Rakshasas, "what is that terrible smell?"

"Seal stew," said Groanin. "Believe me, however bad it smells is nothing compared to how it tastes."

"It smells very meaty," said Mr. Rakshasas, his wrinkled nose wrinkling even more with disgust. "Myself, I never eat meat. Not at my age. Meat is for young people. Not the old. It requires good teeth and a great deal of metabolic effort to digest the stuff."

"I wouldn't know about that," admitted Groanin. "But you can take my word for it. You didn't miss much. The food is lousy. And the tents are poor quality. I hate to think if that helicopter is fit for aviation. The only thing that's doing well out here is my beard."

" 'Tis often said that in winter the milk goes to the cow's horns, right enough," said Mr. Rakshasas.

When the twins had finished climbing into the NASA—surplus space suits that John had bought at Harrods, he and his twin sister stepped outside the tent and faced the biting north wind feeling as warm as toast.

"One small step for man," he joked. "One giant leap for mankind."

John collected the canopic jar from where he had left it in the snow and pointed into the distance. "Let's move away from the tents," he shouted, to make himself heard from inside his space helmet. "In case someone hears us." Communications between himself and Philippa were easier, with radio microphones inside their space helmets.

And still holding the jar in both of his orange space

suit-gloved hands he walked about a hundred yards north of the camp.

"This looks like as good a place as any," he said, looking up as something light and fluffy floated through the air and landed on the visor of his helmet. It was starting to snow — with flakes that were the size of saucers. John hoped they might complete their mission before the wind picked up and they had a blizzard, which might make things even more difficult. He put the canopic jar down on the snow and took a step back.

Mr. Rakshasas knelt down beside the jar and placed his gloved hand on the baboon-headed lid. "I'll wait until you start to transubstantiate before I remove the lid," he shouted above the strengthening wind. "If I suspect that Akhenaten is the first to try to leave the jar, I'll replace the lid immediately. Is that quite understood?"

"How will you know that?" asked Philippa.

"One beetle recognizes another beetle." Mr. Rakshasas smiled. "I'll know if it's Nimrod or not."

John and Philippa gave him the thumbs-up and then took each other by the hand.

"You must take hold of Nimrod and each other before you start to transubstantiate," continued Mr. Rakshasas. "And on no account should you transubstantiate if Akhenaten is touching you. That would be very dangerous for all three of you."

Another thumbs-up sign.

"I shall count you down," said Mr. Rakshasas. "Three — two — one —"

"FABULONGOSHOO — !"

"ABECEDARIAN!"

"MARVELISHLYWONDERPIPICAL!"

The cold air in front of their helmets turned to smoke and Mr. Rakshasas lifted the lid on the canopic jar. The last thing the twins saw before the anticlockwise smoke enveloped them and transported them into the jar was a giant polar bear trotting hungrily toward them.

Somewhere in the space between the outside of the jar and the inside of the jar, John said, "A bear. Did you see that? A huge polar bear. He must have smelled the seal stew."

"At least someone likes it," said Philippa.

"What do you think they'll do?"

"That all depends on whether Mr. Rakshasas is able to use any djinn power," said Philippa, as the smoke cleared, and they found themselves inside the semifrozen canopic jar. "More likely they'll just try to run away."

Wearing a thick fur coat, hat, mittens, and boots, Nimrod was sitting on the floor of the jar, leaning against the curving, limestone wall with his knees drawn up to his chest. His hair was as stiff as a wire brush and there was no trace of breath coming from his mouth or nostrils. At the opposite end of the floor lay what at first glance looked to the twins like a piece of modern art: a shiny, bluish, semitransparent outline of the same grotesque statue they had seen in the Cairo Museum. It was Akhenaten's ghost, similarly frozen.

The twins knelt by their uncle and peered into his frost-whitened face. Nimrod did not move a muscle nor show any visible sign that he registered the twins' presence alongside him in the canopic jar. His usually warm, twinkling brown eyes were quite still and open and, when John laid a gloved hand on him, he found his uncle's body hard to the touch, as if he was frozen solid. For a moment, both twins were silent.

"Is he dead?" whispered John.

"If he wasn't what he is, then I'd say yes," replied Philippa, biting her lip fearfully. "But since being inside a lamp or a bottle is the same as suspended animation, and outside the normal space-time continuum, which implies that while we're in here, none of us is alive in the normal sense of the word, then I don't see how he could be dead exactly."

"Say that again," said John. "No, on second thought, don't say it again. I don't think my brain could take it."

"What I mean is, he's not dead because he's not really alive in here. We have to get him out and get him warm, and then we'll have a better idea of his state of health."

Suddenly, the jar wobbled precariously and both twins looked around at Akhenaten's frozen ghost to see if he was responsible, but he had not moved. The next thing they knew, a gust of air came rushing into the jar.

"The bear," yelled John. "He's sniffing inside the jar to see if there's anything to eat."

Another gust of air flooded into the jar and Philippa's keen eyes saw the tip of a lock of Nimrod's frozen hair bend a little and then turn into a drop of moisture. "He's melting," she yelled, picking herself up off the floor of the jar and, staring into her uncle's face, it seemed to her that the pupil of one of his eyes narrowed very slightly. "He's alive. He's alive."

John checked the outside temperature gauge on his space suit. "That's because the temperature in here is rising," he said. "Look! The bear's hot breath is warming the interior of the jar."

Even as he spoke he looked nervously around at Akhenaten and saw that the pharaoh's djinn ghost was melting, too, and more quickly than Nimrod, for in truth, ghosts, even djinn ghosts from Egypt, have a greater tolerance of cold than any djinn. There was no doubt about it, Akhenaten's almond-shaped eyes were beginning to open, as if from a long, deep sleep.

"There's no time to put Nimrod into a survival suit," said John. "We have to get out of here right now, while he's still frozen, and before Akhenaten revives."

"What about the polar bear?" said Philippa. "It might attack us."

"We'll have to risk it. I don't think we can do anything else. Let's hope that the smoke from our transubstantiation will confuse him just long enough for us to think of something." John took hold of Nimrod's hand and then his sister's. "Ready?"

"Ready."

"Go!"

"FABULONGOSHOO — !"

"ABECEDARIAN!"

"MARVELISHLYWONDERPIPICAL!"

Seconds later, they were outside lying on the snow just a few yards away from the bear, which continued to push its nose greedily into the jar, apparently convinced that there was something good to eat inside. Of Mr. Rakshasas and Groanin there was no sign.

The heat of the combined djinn power of the twins and their transubstantiation was enough to revive Nimrod a little more, and he let out a loud, involuntary groan. Hearing this, the bear turned around and saw them.

"Uh-oh," said John and stood up. It was clear that the polar bear was about to attack. John had a matter of seconds to decide what to do.

The huge polar bear had never eaten a human being or even a djinn, but he was certainly willing to give the new meat a try. His coal-black nose sniffing the air between him and his prey, the bear galloped toward the three djinn, roaring loudly.

There was not much time to think. Or even to concentrate very hard. It was the very first thing John could bring to mind. He remembered the day when Nimrod had taken them into the desert to try out their focus words and the first thing he had created with his new focus word. A picnic.

"ABECEDARIAN!"

A very large picnic, complete with tartan rug and hamper appeared immediately in front of the charging polar bear. Not just any old picnic, either. This was the world heavyweight champion of picnics, for the heavyweight champion of teddy bears, with hams, roast turkeys, cold mutton, a whole poached salmon, several dozen sandwiches, two enormous trifles, a cheesecake, and four large bottles of lemonade. John didn't know if polar bears drank lemonade. Not that it seemed to matter very much because hardly believing its luck, the polar bear stopped on its enormous feet, sniffed at one of the hams, licked its chops, and sat down to eat.

"Br-br-br-bravo," croaked Nimrod.

"Phew," said Philippa. "That was too close for comfort."

"The-the-the-jar," said Nimrod, his teeth chattering violently. "P-p-p-p-put the l-l-lid on the j-jar."

With the bear eating happily and hardly even paying attention to the three djinn, John still gave the creature a wide berth lest it think he intended to share its picnic, and sprinted toward the abandoned canopic jar.

It looked as if he was just in time, for a thin, bluish smoke was slowly beginning to appear near the top of the jar, like the smoke from an almost extinguished cigarette, and John guessed that this must be Akhenaten's ghost attempting to make its own semifrozen escape. But where was the baboon-headed lid to the canopic jar? Made of white limestone, it was hardly the easiest thing to find on the snow-covered ground.

"Come on, come on," he said, urging himself to find it before Akhenaten could make his escape. He threw off his helmet in the hope that without its orange-colored visor, he might see the lid more clearly.

He was still scouring the ground when, thirty or forty

yards away, a large mound of snow moved and, for a second or two, John thought it might be a second polar bear. Then, from inside the snow that revealed itself to be a kind of igloo, emerged Mr. Rakshasas and, behind him, Groanin.

"Is this what you are looking for?" said Groanin, and tossed John the lid of the canopic jar. For anyone with a normal arm, the throw would have been a difficult one; but for Groanin's well-developed single arm it was a piece of cake, and the lid of the jar whizzed toward John's outstretched mitt like an outsized hockey puck.

Even as he caught it, John dived toward the open canopic jar. He reached the jar just in time and clamped the lid down hard on the emerging evil inside the jar. For a moment he felt a resistance underneath his gloved hands, and then all was still.

Mr. Rakshasas and Groanin helped him to his feet.

"Well held, young fellow," said Groanin. "That was a good catch. You would make quite a cricketer."

"That was quite a throw," said John.

"I used to bowl a bit when I was a lad," said Groanin.

"Congratulations," said Mr. Rakshasas. "You were just in time, I think. In another second, Akhenaten would have been free."

"What happened when the bear appeared on the scene?" asked Philippa. "We were worried about you."

"When the bear turned up?" said Mr. Rakshasas. "I used my very limited powers to create an igloo around us. To be sure, it was all I could think of at the time."

"Not a moment too soon, either," said Groanin. "But for that igloo we'd have been in that bear's belly by now."

Warily they all looked in the direction of the polar bear which, fortunately, continued to ignore them all as it started on the poached salmon. There is nothing a bear likes better than salmon. They continued to give the bear a wide berth as they followed Philippa and Nimrod back to camp.

"How are you feeling?" John asked Nimrod when they were back at the camp.

"Not too bad," said Nimrod. "Thanks to you and Phil. No uncle ever had a braver niece and nephew. You are a credit to all djinnkind."

"What shall we do with him?" said John, indicating the canopic jar he still held in his hands.

"Yes, you're right," said Nimrod. "I won't feel comfortable until this bestial spirit is safely disposed of."

An hour or so later, when Nimrod's djinn powers had recovered in the warmth of the tent, he bound the jar with a basket of titanium wire and dropped the jar into a deep hole in the ice he had bored right down into the Arctic Ocean. "There," he said. "I think that's the last we'll hear from Akhenaten's ghost."

"I hope so," said Philippa.

"And now," said Nimrod. "If you don't mind, I think it's time I was getting into your lamp, Mr. Rakshasas. I need a hot bath, a cup of tea, and then a long sleep. You've no idea how tiring it's been inside that infernal jar. Fighting off

Akhenaten's evil spirit, morning, noon, and night. I'm exhausted."

"It's all right for some," complained Groanin after Nimrod and Mr. Rakshasas had disappeared inside the bronze lamp. "I say, it's all right for some. I wish I could have a hot bath and nice cup of tea."

John and Philippa looked at each other and smiled.

"Why not?" they said.

And incredible as it would have seemed to Volodya, Groanin spent his last hour in the tent on the Ice Base, before they all flew back to Srednij Island and then home, enjoying a cup of tea and the best bath he had ever taken.

CHAPTER 26

EPILOGUE IN ZUOGUE

Back in London, the big news was that the seventy lost djinn of Akhenaten, who were now known to the newspapers as the Bloomsbury Seventy, had been deported back to Egypt. This made them all very happy for, after several thousand years, all of them had been very homesick for their own country and a sight of the pyramids. Meanwhile, a heat wave had descended on the city, much to the satisfaction of the twins. With temperatures in the nineties, London was almost as hot as Cairo, and for the short time that remained to them before they went home to New York, John and Philippa were able to take advantage of desertlike temperatures to continue their instruction as djinn under Nimrod's expert tutelage. They began to learn how to undo three wishes, how to travel outside the limits of their bodies, and how to detect other djinn. They learned more djinn history and considerably more of *The Baghdad Rules* from Mr. Rakshasas. And they also learned how to play Astaragali.

"All self-respecting djinn learn how to play Astaragali," explained Nimrod. "It's an old dice game, invented two or three millennia ago, that was designed to minimize the effect of luck. Seven hexagonal dice are rolled inside a box with a lid, concealed from view, and offered to the next player along with a claimed bid better than the previous bid. When a bid is challenged, the offerer or recipient loses a wish depending upon whether the bid was genuine or a lie. It's the skill in making the bid, be it true or false, that diminishes the effect of luck. The game is only played by djinn these days, but there was a time when even the Romans played Astaragali. However, I believe it is still enjoyed by some humans in Germany where it is called Unwahrheit Notluge, which, as I'm sure you know, is German for white lies."

The twins took to the game with enthusiasm and proved to be especially subtle in bidding strategies, so much so that Nimrod told them that they should think about entering the forthcoming United States Open Astaragali Tournament, which was to be held in Chicago, often considered to be the unluckiest city in America, later that same year.

"As entrants in the junior tournament, it will be a great opportunity for you to meet some other djinn of your own age," said Nimrod, "as well as to see the Great Blue Djinn of Babylon, who usually attends in her capacity as the Ultimate Arbiter."

"Will you be going?" asked John.

"I never miss it."

"Then we'd like that," they said.

"In which case, I advise you to practice hard," said Nimrod. "It's the only arena in which the six tribes of djinn ever meet in conditions of absolute neutrality and, for obvious reasons, the competition is fierce."

Too soon, it was time for the twins to fly home to New York on British Airways. So much had happened to them since they had been away and yet, Nimrod advised them of the need to keep most of the details from their father and mother.

"Tell them you went to Egypt and that you had lots of fun," explained Nimrod, while Groanin drove them to Heathrow Airport. "Fun is good. Parents like their children to have fun. Fun is what young people like you are supposed to have. But breaking into the BM and almost fatal adventures in the Arctic Circle are something else altogether. No parent wants to hear about his children nearly being eaten by a polar bear. Your mother will suspect much, of course. She may have forsworn her own djinn power, but it's certain she will have felt the change in the homeostasis that has been occasioned by the lost djinn of Akhenaten being claimed for Good. Thanks to you both.

"Tell them then that you've been to lots of museums. Which is true. And seen lots of interesting things, such as the pyramids. Which is also true. Mundane fathers like to hear about museums and how interesting they are. And tell them all about the books you've read. Better still buy some more books and read them. That's an order. You can never read too many books. Read newspapers, too. Start practicing the piano. This is how two young djinn should behave when they have a human for a father.

"In other words, try to be mundane. Be as mundane as possible for two young djinn to be. That means no granting people wishes, Philippa. If you hear somebody wish for something, take a deep breath, count to a hundred and while you do that, try to reflect on whether or not that person's life would really be improved by them having what they want most in the world just handed to them on a plate. I don't think I've heard anyone put it better than you, Groanin."

"Thank you, sir."

"Remind the twins what it was you said again, Groanin."

"Be careful what you wish for," said Groanin. "Not because you'll get it, but because you're doomed not to want it very much when you do."

"Don't worry," said Philippa. "We've thought of a way to make them feel more relaxed about our return to number 7 East 77th Street."

And after they told them what this was, Nimrod agreed that as well as being promising Astaragali players, they probably had careers in the diplomatic service ahead of them, too.

"I'm going to miss you two," said Nimrod, when they got to the airport.

"Not half as much as we're going to miss you," said Philippa hugging Nimrod, and wiping a tear from her eye.

"Do you promise you'll come see us soon?" said John, feeling a little tearful himself.

"Of course. I said I was coming to Chicago, didn't I? For the Astaragali Tournament?" Nimrod took out his red handkerchief and blew his nose.

On their arrival back in New York, the twins were met at the airport by their father's driver, and they went straight to their summerhouse in Quogue, on Long Island for Labor Day weekend.

Mr. and Mrs. Gaunt were very pleased to see their children again, and of course the twins were very pleased to see them, too, for it was only now that they realized just how much they had missed them and how much they loved them. Mr. Gaunt was especially delighted to see his children had grown so cultural and thoughtful, and seemed to have quite overcome his earlier fear of John and Philippa and had forgotten how it was that Mrs. Trump, his housekeeper, came to work every day in a stretch limousine and wore a Tiffany diamond necklace while washing the kitchen floor.

The two Rottweilers, Winston and Elvis, formerly known as Neil and Alan, were no less pleased to see the return of the twins and, in time, John and Philippa quite forgot that once they had plotted to murder their father. They were just two devoted family pets and would always behave as such, so long as they were dogs.

Of course their mother, Layla, sensed that a lot more had happened to the twins than they were letting on. Being one hundred percent djinn herself, she had felt a change in the balance of power between Good and Evil that had been brought about by the discovery of the lost djinn of Akhenaten; it did not require any great powers of deduction on her part to credit her own family with the discovery of these lost djinn, and their conversion to Good.

"So are you going to tell me what really happened?" she asked them on their first night at the waterfront house in Quogue.

"Uncle Nimrod told us all about how we are djinn and showed us how to do lots of stuff," said Philippa. And then, trying to deflect her mother's curiosity, Philippa sought to turn the tables on her. "But what I'd like to know is this: Are you going to tell us why you didn't clue us in yourself on who and what we are?"

"That's right," agreed John. "Instead of leaving it all to Nimrod."

"Simple," said Layla. "Because I promised your father that I'd try to bring you up as two normal children. And so long as you were just like any other children, I stuck to that promise. But everything changed when your wisdom teeth came in. From that moment on, you were djinn. And I was no longer bound by my promise to your father. He was worried for you, which is why he was also afraid of you."

"Which is why we have a suggestion to make," said Philippa. "We were thinking that, for the sake of our family, we have decided not to use that power without consulting you first."

This was the idea that they had discussed with Nimrod.

"You can't expect us to pretend that nothing has happened

or to deny what we are," added John. "But you can expect us to use that power with discretion and responsibility."

"I think that's an excellent suggestion," agreed Layla. "So if someone—it could be your best friend at school, Mrs. Trump, or even your father—were to make a wish?"

Philippa nodded. "We will take a deep breath, count to a hundred, and then reflect on whether or not their life would really be improved by having what they want most in the world just handed to them on a plate."

"And then do nothing," added John.

"I'm impressed," admitted Layla. "I can see you've learned something very important. That wishes are danger-ous. Especially when they come true. Remember that. The whole world gets turned upside down by the wish for riches and power. If wishes were horses, beggars would ride. If wishes were soldiers, then weak men would rule. And if wishes were elixirs, then all men would live forever."

"If it's appropriate," said Philippa, "we'd like to discuss one small wish with you now."

"I'm listening."

"We wish that you might be reconciled with Nimrod," said John.

"That's easy." Layla smiled. "I'll call him tonight, how's that?"

"Wonderful."

"You father is so pleased to have you home," she said.

"You think so?"

"I know so," said Layla.

"How can you tell?" asked John.

"I can tell."

And even as they spoke they heard a sound they had seldom heard before. It was their father singing in his bath.

If you would like to write to P. B. Kerr,
please visit www.pbkerr.com